EXTRAORDINARY
OCTOBER

EXTRAORDINARY OCTOBER

DIANA WAGMAN

PUBLISHING
NEW YORK, NY

Prited in the United States of America
First trade edition

Please direct inquiries to:

Ig Publishing
Box 2547
New York, NY 10163
www.igpub.com

ISBN: 978-1-63246-036-3 (hardcover)
ISBN: 978-1-63246-037-0 (paperback)

For Thea,

who is extraordinary

PROLOGUE

I was never anything but ordinary. Average in every way. Brown hair, brown eyes, not short, not tall, not fat, not thin, and your basic "B" student. I had no group I belonged to, no after school activities; I couldn't play an instrument or draw a recognizable picture. Three months before my high school graduation and people I'd been in classes with since elementary school still didn't know who I was. The only thing anyone ever remembered about me was my name. October. I was named for the month my parents met and my dad gave up drinking. People always laughed when they heard it. It didn't seem to matter that there was that beautiful actress, January Jones, and there was a girl named June in school and two girls named May. My month, my name, October Fetterhoff, always made them laugh. I even tried going by Toby, but it didn't stick.

But I should have known there were good things about being ordinary. I should have appreciated being unremarkable. I could travel under the radar, go completely unnoticed. I could think whatever I wanted, do whatever I wanted, and nobody paid any attention. Nobody was ever watching me.

And then all that changed. I was anything but ordinary and my extraordinariness was going to get me killed.

1. Four Days Until My Eighteenth Birthday

It all started with an itch. A bad itch. A terrible, bone deep, muscle shuddering itch. Out of control. I had to scratch. Had to. Immediately.

The itch started on the bottom of my right foot my shoe. I yelped loudly in class, couldn't help it, and Mr. Fleming turned around from the board.

"There's something in my shoe." I couldn't get it off fast enough. I was wearing my tall, lace-up boots—my favorites—and I was cursing how long it took to get my foot free.

"How could there be something in there?" Jacob the jock asked. "She never takes them off."

The class snickered. Okay, so I wore those boots a lot. Every day in fact, and for a moment I was kind of flattered he'd noticed, but the itch had taken over. I knew something hadn't actually bitten me. This was deeper than that. It came from way inside my foot, somewhere close to the bone. I peeled off my striped sock and attacked the bottom of my foot with both hands.

"Put it back on!" Jacob pretended to gasp from the smell.

"Pee-ew," his sidekick, Lance, echoed and held his nose.

Juveniles. I was too absorbed in the itch to make a snappy comeback. If I could have thought of one. The problem was the scratching wasn't helping. It made it worse, made the itch stronger. I was feeling it behind my knees, all the way up in my stomach, a jittery, weird sensation. I couldn't help it; I started scratching all over. My arms, my legs, the part of my back I could reach. The class was laughing. I was practically crying. Scratching was useless. Finally, I sat on my hands and tried to will it to stop. I was starting to sweat and I could feel my hair frizzing from the heat.

Mr. Fleming frowned. "All right now, Miss October?"

The class laughed at me again and Mr. Fleming shrugged his apology. When people tack on the "Miss" in front of my name it makes me sound like a Playboy centerfold. Years of teachers doing it by accident and it still got a laugh. Ha ha ha.

"I think I need to go to the nurse," I said to Fleming. What I really needed was to get outside, take off my clothes and roll on the ground so I could scratch all over.

"Go ahead," Mr. Fleming nodded. "Be sure to get the homework from someone."

I knew I looked ridiculous hobbling out of class in one shoe, clutching my books, boot, sock, and backpack. As I shut the door behind me I looked back, but my fellow students had already forgotten me and turned back to the board. I was even less interesting than the Dual Alliance of 1879. Typical.

Out in the hall, I stopped to scratch the bottom of my bare foot against the laces on my other boot. That felt pretty good, better than anything else so far, and I closed my eyes and leaned against the wall. Then my neck started itching and my scalp. I wondered if I had some dread disease, like leprosy or skin-eating bacteria. An itch ran up my spine and I rubbed my back against the rough cinderblock wall, back and forth and up and down.

"Like a little bear." A guy's voice startled me.

I stopped scratching and looked into the bluest eyes I had ever seen. Beautiful, startling, turquoise, no, a brilliant sky blue. And the eyes were surrounded by a face that was just as attractive. I blushed and the itching intensified. Even embarrassed as I was, my foot could not stop scratching itself.

"What are you doing out of class?"

Surprise, surprise, Principal Hernandez was there too, but I hadn't noticed him beside Blue-Eyes.

"On my way to the nurse," I said. "Something bit me."

"Then go!"

"Need any help?"

The handsome young man was talking to me. Yes, I wanted to say, scratch. Put your hands on my body and scratch. Everywhere. But I just blushed again, shook my head and limped away. I knew he wasn't a new student; school would be out in just three months and anyway, he looked too mature, too put together to be a high schooler. On the other hand, he didn't look old enough to be a teacher. I sighed. Whoever he was, he thought I looked like a bear. Terrific. I lifted a hand to scratch my chin and dropped my boot. Bending over to get it, I dropped my books; then my backpack swung around and hit me in the face.

So far it had not been a very good day.

The skinny nurse, Ms. Raynor, looked frazzled when I came in. I could hear a kid puking in the little bathroom, creating a new definition for the word 'retch.' A girl from my English class, Luisa, was lying on the only cot holding her stomach and groaning. Luisa was definitely faking—she stopped suffering long enough to wink at me—but Ms. Raynor listened to the kid vomiting, looked at me, then looked at Luisa and said, "I'll call your parents."

"No, my sister," Luisa said. "She's the only one around. My folks are at work."

I didn't think Luisa had a sister.

"Fine." Ms. Raynor picked up the phone.

"I can use my cell," Luisa smiled, weakly. "You're so busy."

"Thank you."

Luisa immediately started texting. Grinning instead of groaning. As Raynor turned to me, Luisa gave me a secret thumbs up.

The nurse frowned at my one bare foot. "What's wrong with you?"

I noticed the hem coming out of her uniform and her hair falling out of her bun. Her eyes were red and dripping. As if everything about her was unraveling.

"Something bit me," I said. "Or maybe a bee sting?"

"You're not supposed to be barefoot in school."

"I wasn't. I mean it crawled inside my boot I guess. I itch all over."

Raynor took my foot into her lap and peered at the bottom. I was glad I'd cut my toenails.

"I don't see anything," she said. "You say you itch?"

"Like crazy. Everywhere."

Her breath on the bottom of my foot was agony. My leg was twitching in her lap and I was scratching my arms so hard I was leaving red welts.

"Could be body lice," she said.

Body lice? I'd had head lice in first grade. Now there was body lice?

"Or mange."

Wasn't that what stray dogs got? "Wait a minute," I said.

She inspected my arms, then lifted my T-shirt and peeked at my stomach. "No rash," she concluded. "Could be viral. Or an iron deficiency. Still, I think you should go home."

"Really," I said. "None of those sound very good."

She leaned toward me and whispered, "Are you pregnant?"

"No!" I practically shouted. Unless you could get pregnant from a fantasy life.

The puker came out of the bathroom wiping his mouth.

Poor little guy, probably a 7th Grader. He tried to smile at me and his teeth were bright white in his truly green face. I smiled back. I felt bad for him but the throw-up smell was overpowering.

"I'll go wait out front," I said.

Raynor sighed. "I'll call your parents. Fetterhoff, right?"

"Right." I was surprised she remembered.

"I know your dad," she said. "Say hi to him from me."

Outside, Luisa was sitting on the front steps waiting for her 'sister' and spinning a Frisbee on one finger. She was beautiful and ultra fem, and for some reason she always had a Frisbee. She was also kind of a friend of mine. She seemed to turn up wherever I was and more than once had steered me out of trouble. Last winter I'd been coming home late and I got off the bus in the dark and I was sure someone was following me. Someone big. Someone creepy, although I never saw him (or her). Out of nowhere Luisa had driven by and picked me up. And over spring break I'd gone to the "party of the century" at someone's house and these older kids had crashed. I don't drink—thanks to my dad being an alcoholic—and this guy kept trying to get me to have a beer. Just a sip. Come on. Just one. It got harder and harder to say no and then Luisa arrived, put her arm around me and told the guy to crawl back under his rock. That's exactly what she said, "Crawl back under the rock where you came from, troll." And he did go away. She and Jed, her boyfriend forever, gave me a ride home that night too.

I sat down beside her on the steps. She smiled at me, tossed her shiny dark hair over one shoulder and crossed her long smooth legs. I heard the rumble of dual headers and Jed's cherry red, souped-up classic Charger turned up the driveway.

"Your sister sure has changed," I said.

Luisa laughed. "I know, right?" She tossed Jed the Frisbee

through the open window and scampered into the car. They zoomed away.

A cool wind blew. People say you can't tell which season it is in Los Angeles, but I knew it was definitely spring. There was a freshness in the air, the promise of warmer days to come. Daffodils in the grocery store and even a few in people's yards. I liked sunshine. I liked being able to be outside and go barefoot year round. I took my other boot off. I turned my face up to the sun. I wasn't wearing a sweater and the breeze soothed my scratched, red skin. And then I realized I didn't itch anymore. Not at all. Not my foot, my back, or my arms. It had stopped as suddenly as it began.

I was contemplating going back to class when my dad drove up. His car was not cherry red nor was it classic, it was just old and needed a wash. Which it would never get unless my mom or I did the washing. Plus I couldn't help but notice it was crooked, definitely tilting lower on the driver's side. I guess I'd never really looked at it coming toward me before. It made me sad to see the car like that. It hit me again everything that was wrong with my dad. He was fat. Truthfully, he was obese. Way over 300 pounds. He met my mom and he gave up drinking and then they had me, and in the early pics he looks pretty good. But he was just substituting sugar for alcohol and now, eighteen years later, it had caught up with him. He couldn't walk more than ten feet— worse than that he could hardly breathe. He couldn't fit in a seat on an airplane or in a movie theater. He had to stop working and our family finances had seriously suffered. My mom wanted him to get the lap band, but he promised he'd do it himself. He told us over and over he got sober by himself, he could go on a diet. He could do it. He could give up sweets. And then what, I wondered, take up heroin?

"Hey Pumpkin." He hollered out the window.

I hated his nickname for me—another October reference. I waved and gathered my stuff, trudged down the steps and into the car. "Hi," I said. "Thanks for coming."

He backed down the school's long driveway because it was too uncomfortable for him to crank the wheel enough to turn around. Through the windshield I saw the mystery guy with the blue eyes come out the front door with Principal Hernandez. They shook hands and seemed to be agreeing about something. My dad screeched to a stop to avoid a car behind us, and Blue-Eyes looked up. I cringed, hoping he didn't see me, but it looked like he did because he turned away from Hernandez and watched me until we went around the corner. Great. Just great.

"So Birthday Girl, what's wrong?"

My eighteenth birthday was four days away, but my dad had been calling me Birthday Girl for two weeks. It was a way bigger deal to him than it was to me. He kept reminding me that soon I'd be able to vote, buy cigarettes, and join the armed services. So what. At that particular moment in my life, I have to admit I wasn't very excited about it. Another milestone I'd be celebrating with just my parents.

"I'm okay," I said. "I think something bit me."

"An itch, huh?" It seemed to interest him. "Bad?" I nodded. "Really bad?" I nodded again. "Where did it start?"

"My foot. Then everywhere."

"Your back?"

"Everywhere, Dad. I mean everywhere."

He nodded, even smiled. "Fascinating."

"To you, maybe."

"Have you had lunch?" he asked.

"It's 10:00 in the morning."

"If your stomach's not upset, we can stop by Village Bakery. Maybe that will make you feel better."

A big old cheese Danish sounded like just what the doctor ordered, but I had agreed with Mom we would not be enablers. "No, thanks," I said. "I just want to go home."

Actually home was the last place I wanted to go. Mom would be at work. Dad would be tinkering in his workshop, building another flipping birdhouse. He'd want me to come hold a stick or something. Still I could look up Body Lice and Mange online, although if I had those things why would the itch just go away the minute I got outside? Maybe I was allergic to school.

2.

Our neighborhood was a "planned community" on the very eastern edge of Los Angeles. Every house was one of three designs in one of three color combinations. Every driveway led to the same two-car garage. The wide sidewalks, the appropriate landscaping, even the mailboxes were unexciting and humdrum on purpose, so that no one and nothing would stand out. Only we were different. Our house was Model Number Three, just the same as every other third house, but our yard was unusual. Unfortunately it wasn't because of the flowers or a vegetable garden. It was the 24 birdhouses, all different shapes and sizes and colors, strategically placed on poles. Our front lawn was like a forest, except the trees had no bark, no branches and no leaves, and they were painted colors to match the birdhouses on top. It was my job to mow the lawn through that obstacle course, and I have to admit I had sort of given up. We weren't supposed to water the grass because of the drought so it was mostly dead anyway. Dad didn't care. He loved birds. Interestingly, so did I. I don't know why I found the little feathered things so amazing, maybe it was our name Fetterhoff which is German for Feather-House, but my Dad and I used to trek deep into the woods with our binoculars and spend hours looking up. Of course, that was before he got too fat to trek. Now he built birdhouses and stared out the window and his cheeks were so plump, his blue eyes were barely visible.

Maybe that was why I didn't like the birdhouses—aside from the fact they looked ridiculous all over our lawn—they just reminded me of the guy my dad used to be.

"Sure you feel okay?" Dad asked as we pulled into the garage. "Betty, uh, the nurse, said maybe you have a virus."

It didn't even register that he was on a first name basis with the nurse. "I'm fine," I said as I got out of the car. "It seems to have passed." I was half hoping he'd take me back to school, otherwise the day stretched ahead of me long and empty. Nothing to look forward to until the good TV started that night. Of course I had plenty of homework. Tons in fact. Second semester seniors should not have to write long papers about World War I or do pages of Trigonometry problems. School was so over for me.

I watched him struggle with the one step up from the garage into the house.

"Damn knees," he panted.

"Dad," I began.

"Don't." He held up a hand. His fingers were so fat he couldn't wear his wedding ring anymore. "I talked to your mom this morning. I'm going to see someone."

"A doctor? A nutritionist?"

"Hypnotist," he said. "The best in the country. Helena Gold. People swear by her."

I couldn't help but sigh. Sounded like baloney to me.

"Not Overeaters Anonymous?" I asked for the umpteenth time. "A.A. worked for the drinking."

"I don't need more meetings, just a jumpstart."

He needed to eat less and get up off his ass and move around, but he was waiting for a magic wand. I knew he'd never find it, I knew there was no such thing as magic. Hypnotism? Whatever. At least he was trying something new.

"Okay, great." I acquiesced. "Will the hypnotist make you walk like a chicken?"

He laughed with me. "Your mom wants her to make me lose some weight and fall in love with housework."

"Everybody's happy."

"It's a win-win." He waddled off toward the den: birdhouse central. He used to work in the garage, but standing up at his workbench got too difficult. Now he sat behind a card table with an old shower curtain spread over the floor. It was only bad when he started painting. The enamel really smelled. "Come see the latest," he said. "It's an open-fronted nest box for the robins." He paused. "And I'd like to talk more about that itch of yours."

"It's gone."

"Already? Really? I mean, good, but still—"

I knew he wanted company. "Let me put my stuff away."

I took the stairs up to my room two at a time. It was odd how good I felt after feeling so terrible. Better than fine, better than not itching, I felt lighter, springier. I closed my door and turned to the full-length mirror on the back. I usually avoided my reflection, but I took a deep breath and studied my face. Same brown eyes. Same few freckles across my cheeks. Hair brown as always, but looking good at the moment, shiny, smooth. Perfect, I thought, when I'm home alone so no one can appreciate it. I didn't see any sign of illness. I pulled up my shirt and examined my stomach for little creepy-crawly things or rashes or anything weird, but everything looked normal. Same as always.

I wasn't ugly. My parents always told me I was beautiful, but I knew I wasn't. I was absolutely ordinarily kind of pretty. Everything fit together on my face and sometimes, with make up and when I was really happy, I had a little glow. I was 5'5", average height and weight. Some days I wanted to lose five pounds, but living with my dad kept my own sweet tooth under control.

Mom said we were both healthier because of his condition. She's a stick woman, really skinny. My dad said when he and my mom walked down the street together they looked like the number 10. Ha ha ha.

I could hear Dad down in the kitchen at that moment, rummaging for something to eat. I shuddered remembering the night of my tenth birthday party. I couldn't sleep, so I came downstairs and saw my dad eating my leftover birthday cake right out of the big bakery box. I hid behind the door and watched him read the newspaper and eat bite after bite. He ate the whole thing and it was a lot. I was shocked. He was overweight then, but he wasn't enormous. I know it's a sickness and he can't control himself so we just don't have the stuff in the house anymore. I never wanted another birthday cake.

My cell phone rang. That was a surprise; almost no one ever called me. I had to dig it out of my backpack, way down in the bottom under the papers, old lunch bags, pencils, and crap. Had to be a grown up. Maybe Mom. Anyone else would text me.

"Hello?"

"October Fetterhoff?"

"Yes."

"My name is Walker Smith. We saw each other at school today—in the hallway."

I almost choked on my own saliva. Blue-eyes? He was calling me?

"Oh yeah," I managed. "I was scratching."

Stupid! I kicked the side of my bed. As if he needed reminding.

"Yes. Are you okay?"

"Perfect. Thanks. Right as rain." Ugh. Now I was sounding like some fake British girl out of a Disney movie.

"Great. Well. I'm a psychology major at Hayden College

and I'm going to be doing an experiment at your school and I wondered if you'd like to participate."

"Really?"

"It won't take much of your time."

He wanted me! But would I have to wear a hospital gown, or be filmed sleeping? I didn't want him to see me drooling. "What kind of experiment?" I asked.

"It's about the effects of college placement on the late adolescent."

"I haven't been placed yet." My applications were all in, but I wouldn't hear for a month.

"Exactly. I have a list of questions about your thoughts about the process, your hopes and aspirations and any fears you might have. Honestly, you're the first I've tried this on. You'll be my guinea pig."

Great, first I was a bear, then a pig. "When would this start?"

"We could start today," he said and when I didn't answer right away, he continued, "You'll be glad you did. Trust me."

"Today. Okay. That'd be like, way cool." I groaned again. Seemed I could not speak like a normal person. "I guess I shouldn't meet you at school since I went home sick."

He laughed a deep, warm, manly chuckle. My toes curled against the rug. Those eyes. That laugh. I hoped the experiment would take forever.

"How about Henderson Park?" he asked.

"Sure." We agreed on a time and a particular bench by the swing set. I hung up. I wasn't itching, but I had a weird, jittery feeling. A good one. The thought that I was going to sit and answer questions for Blue-Eyes, Walker, was—well, the most exciting thing that had happened to me in a long, long time. Pathetic, but true.

The big question was what to wear. My new jeans were in

the laundry. I didn't think I could get them washed and dried in time. I forced myself to look in the mirror again. Old favorite jeans: check. I'd worn them a day or two, but they weren't too baggy. Gray 80's band T-shirt: sort of check. It was okay, not great. I held up my new summer blouse, an early birthday gift to myself, that I hadn't worn yet. It was pretty, kind of revealing, but if I changed it might appear as if I was trying to impress him, or worse, seduce him. Not that I knew how. I looked outside. It was getting cloudy. I decided to put on my favorite sweater, a soft, black V-neck. A girl wasn't supposed to freeze to death for a psych experiment, was she? I looked good—for me. But what to tell my dad? It would have to be the truth—minus Walker being the most beautiful man I'd ever met. I needed the car if I was going to Henderson Park.

The doorbell rang. I started down the stairs to answer it and was surprised to see my dad had beaten me there. He opened the door to a young red-haired woman who had to be six feet tall. She was incredible looking. Her face almost didn't look real, or as if she'd had plastic surgery to look like a Disney princess. Her skin was flawless and a creamy coffee color with a faint blush on her high cheekbones, her green eyes very large and framed in long dark lashes, her eyebrows a perfect arc and her lips shaped like Cupid's bow. I thought she might hypnotize my dad just by her perfection. Oddly for someone in her twenties, she wore a long dress with wide, flapping sleeves plus layers and layers of scarves and flowing material—all in shades of rust and orange. She floated in the door.

"Hello, Neal," she said warmly.

She took my father's two hands in hers and looked at him for a long, long moment. He stared back at her without moving, his mouth hanging open. Yup. It was just as I feared. A gorgeous woman had never looked at him that way and he was stunned.

Finally I'd had enough and I cleared my throat.

My dad shook his head. "Hey, Pumpkin." He looked kind of embarrassed. As well he should have.

I walked over to the two of them. It was my turn for her eagle eye; she stared at me like she was trying to see through my skin to my bones. It wasn't comfortable. I stepped out of her line of sight and half behind my dad.

"This is my daughter," Dad began and for the first time ever in my life, he blushed as he continued, "October."

"What a beautiful name," she said and turned to me. "Pleased to meet you." She tried to grab my hand in hers, but I moved back and sort of waved. For some reason, I didn't want her to touch me.

Dad said, "This is Madame Helena Gold."

"You're the hypnotist?" I said. "You make house calls?"

"I go wherever I am needed." Madame Gold gave a little flutter and her sleeves and dress swirled around her. "How are you feeling, October?"

Did I imagine it or was she asking as if she knew something? "I feel great," I said.

"I hope we can be good friends."

She tried to look me in the eye and I avoided her. Maybe she was only twenty-five or six, but I still didn't want to be her friend. I turned to Dad. He was staring at her. "Dad." I snapped my fingers by his ear. "Yo, Dad. Can I take the car?"

"Please stay," Madame Gold said before he could answer. "I would love to get to know you better."

"Don't you have a lot of hypnotizing to do?"

"My method includes the entire family," she said. "We all have many influences, the surrounding energies are so important."

"Well. I wish I could stick around and watch you work," I said. "Too bad I've got to get to the library." Adults always backed down for homework. "Big research paper due."

But she knew I was lying, I could see it on her face that she could see it on my face. Her green eyes narrowed. "Neal?" she turned to my dad.

"You should stay awhile," he said to me. "You can go to the library later."

She had already hooked him. He was enthralled, captivated, under her spell, and she hadn't even made him count backwards from 100 or anything.

"Okay," I said. "Fine. But I'm meeting…someone at two o'clock."

"What for?" Dad asked.

" I can't be late. He's a college psych student. I'm part of an experiment."

I could swear Madame Gold gave a little gasp.

An hour later—a long, long, long hour later—I had to admit whatever Madame Gold was doing was working on my dad. He was mesmerized. I sat with the two of them as long as I could stand it while she talked about the wind and the clouds and the primal forces and that some people are lambs and some people are wolves and some people are raccoons. I'd never heard such a load in my life, but when I brought out tea and the secret stash of cookies my mom kept just for an occasion like this, my dad didn't eat one. He didn't even look at the bag; he barely drank his tea. He just sat in his chair listening to her. On the other hand, I was starving and managed to devour at least half the plate. Of course by this time it was one o'clock and I hadn't eaten anything since some yogurt for breakfast.

It was rude, but finally I asked, "How much is this gonna cost? I mean you've been here for forever."

"How sweet of you to be concerned." I could tell she didn't think it was sweet at all. "Your father and I have it all worked out."

I nodded and helped myself to another cookie. Maybe my

dad would lose 100 pounds and I'd gain fifty. I was beginning to feel sick and kind of dizzy. First the itch. Then I felt so good. Now, all of a sudden, I felt lousy. My head hurt and my palms—just my palms—were red and itchy. I was hot in my black sweater. I wanted to look good for Blue-Eyes, but I was beginning to wonder if I was well enough to go at all. Madame Gold just kept talking. Something about how obviously my father was a bird, a small beautiful bird. No wonder he built all those birdhouses. I looked over at her and she wavered and undulated as if she were underwater. I knew I had a fever. I was coming down with something bad. Maybe my flesh-eating disease was taking its next step. Hadn't Nurse Raynor said it could be viral?

"Excuse me." I stood up and the room was spinning.

"Let me help you," said Madame Gold.

"No." I backed away from her, for some reason desperate that she shouldn't touch me. I turned and rushed upstairs. I hoped I'd make it to the bathroom before hell broke loose.

I slammed the door behind me and sort of collapsed on the floor. The white tiles were cool through my jeans. I swallowed hard, ready to puke, but I didn't feel sick anymore. I could smell my mother's perfume. Mom, I thought. Mom. Somehow thinking of her made me feel better. I got up and opened the little window behind the shower and stood in the tub taking big, deep gulps of fresh air. Something about me was not right. I was sick, but with what? The symptoms were all over the place. I concentrated on breathing in and out and my head began to clear. The sky was a strange putty color, like the file cabinet in the school office. The clouds looked like overcooked cauliflower. The beautiful morning sun had vanished.

Then I saw something lying in the grass below me. A stuffed animal? I looked closer. It was a cat. The sweet little black and white cat that belonged to our neighbors. I waited for it to move.

We had too many birds around for the cat to be in our yard. "Scat!" I hissed out the window. But nothing. It was lying on its side not moving. I watched for a moment and I knew it wasn't sleeping. The cat was dead. I swallowed. My father hated cats. He always had and since the birdhouses he hated them even more, but this was—had been—a nice cat. A big black crow flew down and landed beside the body. I turned away as it began to peck at the poor cat's eyes.

It was after one. I had to go. I absolutely had to get out of the house. I splashed some water on my face and looked at myself in the mirror. I was a little pale, but not green like that kid in the nurse's office. And I realized I felt fine. My palms were fine. Once again, whatever it was had passed. I ran my brush over my hair, pleased that it was still looking good. As I turned to go, I caught a glimpse of my neck. There was an inch long raised red mark, like a burn. I must have scratched myself running upstairs.

Dad was standing at the bottom of the stairs as I came down. "You okay?" he asked.

"Fine. Funny. It's been a weird day." I looked around. "Did she leave?"

He nodded. "Isn't she something?"

"I don't know. I'm not crazy about her."

"Let's give her a chance."

"Okay." I gave him a hug. Big as he was, he was still a great hugger. "You're a bird, huh? That explains so much." We laughed. "I wonder what I am."

"She said you were a bear."

"Second time I've heard that today." And I didn't think it was a good thing. I grabbed the car keys off the end table. "Gotta run. I'll be home for dinner."

"Have fun." He headed back to his birdhouses and I headed out the door.

3.

It's embarrassing, but I was four days from turning eighteen and had never had a boyfriend. Yes, I was still a virgin. Oh boy, was I. Far from having sex, I had never been kissed—unless you counted that time in 6th Grade playing that stupid Truth or Dare game. I had to kiss Jacob the Jock, but I didn't want to and neither did he so it was more like a peck. Afterwards he pretended to throw up.

It wasn't that I was afraid or frigid or wanted to wait until I was 30. I just hadn't met the right person. I'd read books. I'd seen plenty of movies. I just wanted someone like that—someone who made my toes curl, my breath come faster, my stomach flip. As I drove to Henderson Park thinking about Blue-Eyes was definitely making me sweat. Maybe it was the itch, maybe it was the color of his eyes—the opposite of my own—but for the first time ever I felt my heart thumping and jumping in my chest. I knew it was nuts and of course unrequited, he was older and way out of my league, but I tapped my fingers on the steering wheel, I rolled up the window so my hair wouldn't get messy, and I kept checking my reflection in the rear view mirror.

I saw the car behind me, a Ferrari, low and black and expensive. It was odd that I, the car lover, hadn't noticed it before. The woman driving looked a lot like Madame Gold. Oh no, I thought. It was Madame Gold. Was she following me? No, she had left my house way before I did. The neighborhood surrounding Henderson Park was much more upscale than ours. I figured she lived nearby. Who would have thought hypnotists made so much money? Begrudgingly I admitted she had nice taste in cars.

The weather had taken a turn for the worse. I could feel the wind pushing on my old car and it rattled the windows. Leaves and sticks and trash skittered across the street. An empty rubber trashcan blew right in front of me and I jammed on my brakes just in time. Madame Gold's tires squealed behind me as she swerved and zipped past. She lifted one hand in a wave—obviously she had recognized me too—before she peeled around the next corner and disappeared. I was breathing hard. The trashcan continued rolling out of the way and I drove on.

Walker Smith was sitting alone on a bench as I walked across the playground from the parking lot. He was texting someone furiously and I got a quick pang of jealousy.

Stop it, I told myself. He's a college student. You're in high school. This is just an experiment.

I knew what kind of experiment I wanted it to be.

"Hey," I called to him.

He looked up, saw me and grinned. His face opened like the sun coming through the gray clouds. I stopped. I wanted to spend a moment just bathing in that smile, letting it warm me. Driving over I'd been so nervous, but seeing him my stomach calmed, my shoulders relaxed. The only way to describe it is that he seemed familiar, comfortable, as if we were members of the same tribe. Which, I told myself, we couldn't be. He was from the College of Incredibly Handsome and I was from Camp Ordinary.

"Sit with me," he said.

I sat beside him on the cement bench. Some brainchild juvenile delinquent had written "ass" on the edge of the seat in black marker, not even on the part where your ass actually went.

I wanted to add an arrow. I looked at Walker. He didn't have a laptop with him, or a notebook, only his phone that he had put away. What about the experiment? I waited for him to say something. Instead, he took my hand. I felt the touch of his fingers all the way up my arm, into my chest. He closed his eyes and put two fingers to my wrist, taking my pulse.

"Your heart is racing," he said.

"Is this part of the experiment?"

He laughed and opened his eyes. "You're a worrier."

"I'm thoughtful," I countered. "There's a lot in this world to think about."

"Not for long," he said.

I didn't know what he meant. "I don't think the world's problems are going away any time soon."

"Other things will become more important."

"Like what?" I wondered if this was part of the experiment. I wondered if holding my hand was part of the experiment. Was the point to totally throw me off balance and then ask weird questions?

He played with my fingers. "Still itching?"

"Not at all."

"Right as rain," he nodded. "Isn't that what you said?"

I blushed, mortified that he chose to remember that of all things.

"Don't be embarrassed. It's perfect." He looked up at the darkening sky. "Rain is always exactly right."

I didn't want him to let go of my hand, but everything he said was a little confusing. He had blond, curly hair that was casually messy and I wondered if he worked hard to make it look that way. His jeans were expensive, if well worn, and he wore nice sneakers and a gray sweater that looked like cashmere. A blue T-shirt exactly the color of his eyes was just visible around the neck of the sweater. That T-shirt was definitely on purpose. He knew how good-looking he was and in my experience— okay, in books I'd read—guys like that were not to be trusted. I didn't know anything about him, I'd never even heard of Hayden College, and more importantly, no one knew where I was.

"When is this experiment thing going to start?" I forced my voice not to quaver.

"Soon." He saw my discomfort and apologized. "I'm just curious, so curious."

"About what?"

"You." He did seem to be studying me. He smiled. "How did the itch begin?"

I groaned. I really didn't want to talk to him about that. "It went away." I hoped that was enough, but he was persistent.

"Did it come on slowly? Gradually? Like a little tickle first, then a little more?"

Maybe if I told him we could move on to a more interesting subject. "It started out of nowhere," I said. "In the middle of History class. The bottom of my foot. Bang. Like that. Like an explosion on my foot, followed by a fire everywhere."

"Bang," he almost whispered it. "You're lucky."

"I am?"

"A strong itch means a strong reaction."

"To what?"

"To turning eighteen."

Birthdays didn't cause itching, did they? And how did he know I was about to turn eighteen? I supposed Principal Hernandez could have told him I was almost eighteen. I was a senior. The experiment was about applying for college. It wasn't so far fetched.

"I'm nervous," I said. "About graduating. Moving away from home. Were you nervous when you went to college?"

"You'll be fine. I think you're made for this."

"Made for what?" Okay, now he was creeping me out.

"Do you like the outdoors?"

I wasn't going to tell him. It was time to go home, past time. Lots of serial killers are attractive; I remembered that from the psycho-murderer show on PBS.

"I have to go," I said. "I told my dad I wouldn't be long." I tossed my hair back and Walker's grip tightened.

"What's that on your neck?"

With my free hand, I touched the red mark I had seen in the mirror. It was raised, bumpy, and kind of hot to the touch. "I don't know. I must've scratched myself."

"Was there someone at your house today?"

"My dad."

"Anyone else?"

"This kooky woman."

He frowned and waited for me to go on, but I didn't want to tell him about my dad and Madame Gold.

"I must've bumped into something." I stood up, pulled my hand from his and immediately shivered as if an ice cube had dripped down my spine. I wanted his warm hand back, but I turned away. "Thank you. Maybe we can try this at school one day."

"I'm not here long." He paused. "Four days. Tops."

I shrugged and stepped back toward the parking lot.

"Yoo hoo!" A girl's voice rang out across the park. "Walker! October!"

It was Luisa and Jed, her tall, skinny boyfriend. They tossed the Frisbee back and forth as they walked toward us.

"What is she doing here?"

"She's part of the experiment," Walker said.

I sighed. Next to Luisa's shiny dark hair and lovely long legs,

I faded away.

"You didn't think you'd be the only one, did you?" Walker asked. "What kind of experiment would that be?"

Across the park I saw the puking kid from the nurse's office riding his bike in our direction. "Him too?"

"Chris Lee. Yes."

"You just took everybody who went to the nurse."

"Pretty much." He smiled at me and stood up. "I need you all to have something in common."

"Luisa wasn't even really sick. And I just had an itch. And this kid is too young for college. Plus he's going to give us all the stomach flu."

"Trust me," Walker said.

I took a step away from him and crossed my arms in front of my chest, but he moved closer.

"Don't worry," he whispered. "You are why we're here."

"What does that mean?"

"October."

"Yes?"

"Answer a question?"

"Is this finally part of the experiment?"

He nodded, but I was not prepared for the question. He looked into my eyes and asked, "When you have your first kiss, what should it be like?"

I blushed to my toes. Was it so flipping obvious that I'd never been kissed? How did he know? The itch was tingling, threatening to erupt again.

"Tell me," he said. "What do you want it to be?"

His blue eyes had darkened into pools of inviting water. I could fall into them. I could fall in and never come up.

"I don't want much." I shrugged, tried to laugh, tried to be so much cooler and experienced than I was. "When someone kisses me, I expect the earth to move."

"The earth to move," he repeated. "Not much at all." He didn't smile.

"Hey. Let's get this party started." It was Jeb.

The connection between us broke and he turned to the others. I hoped no one noticed my red, embarrassed face. And then, worse, my stomach growled. I was flustered and suddenly I was starving and to top it off I had to pee. His experiment didn't make any sense. What did first kisses have to do with going to college? I waved at Luisa and motioned I was going to the bathroom. Walker didn't seem to notice as I walked away. He was busy shaking hands with Jed and little Chris, or Green, as I would forever think of him. I was cold and hurried over to the stucco park building. A gust of wind whipped my hair into my eyes blinding me.

I stumbled over a rock and somehow startled two crows. They flapped up in front of me, squawking. "Hey!" I cried as they circled my head and landed right in front of the door to the women's room. "Scram!" I waved my arms.

They just cawed back at me and in my imagination I heard them teasing me, "we're gonna get you." Why would a crow want to get me? I thought of the crow in my yard, pecking at the dead cat. Crows are my least favorite bird, and one of the most common. They are everywhere in the United States. Corvus brachyrhynchos, a fancy Latin name for a flying rat. So black, so big, and they make that horrible noise. I know they steal the eggs from other birds and sometimes even kill and eat the young chicks. That makes them cannibals. Disgusting. But I was never afraid of a crow until the two in front of the bathroom. They stared at me, turning their heads this way and that to see me from each beady black eye. I stamped my feet. They didn't move. I really had to go to the bathroom. They were just a couple of birds. I stepped toward them reaching for the door handle and they attacked. They flew at me, wings beating the air. One of them landed on my shoulder and then hopped up and got its talons caught in my hair. The other one clawed up my leg and pecked at my thigh. I spun and slapped at them, but they attacked my hands. All the while I could have sworn I heard them speaking to each other, cheering each other on.

Then Walker was there, swinging at them with a tree branch. The birds backed off, but they didn't leave. They circled me until Green and Jed ran forward shouting with big sticks and they and Walker chased the two crows across the park. Green took a straw out of his back pocket and blew something, a rock or a bead, at one of them. He hit it, the crow gave a little squeal, "that hurt!" and fled, the other one following, and Jed and Green high-fived each other.

I put my head between my knees. I had imagined I could understand them. Not that it was difficult to figure out what a crow would say, but between that and the attack, the scratches and peck marks, I was dizzy.

"Has that ever happened before?" Walker ran up to me.

"Yeah, of course. Crows attack me all the time."

"You should have asked me to go with you."

"To the bathroom?"

"Or take Luisa."

"Good idea," I scoffed. " Luisa, who seems to have disappeared. Bet she's hiding under a picnic table."

"Here I am." Luisa came out of the bathroom with her ever-present Frisbee. "All clear," she said to Walker.

And then I screamed as she let her Frisbee fly. I ducked, turned and saw her Frisbee smack into a final crow coming my way. The crow squealed—as much as a crow can—and flew away fast. An impressive, perfect shot. I'd never seen a Frisbee used as a weapon before. Then again, I'd never been attacked by crows before either.

Luisa trotted over to get her Frisbee. I looked from her to Walker to Green and Jed and back around again. They were all staring at me. Green cocked his head like a puppy, as if something about me was puzzling. He turned to Walker.

"That was interesting."

Luisa said, "Your dad makes birdhouses, doesn't he?"

"He does. And I like birds too. Really." On cue, two small birds tweeted above me. I looked up. "Cactus wrens, campylorhynchus brunneicapillus."

"Huh?" asked Jed.

"My one skill. For some reason I remember all the Latin names."

The little birds were pretty with speckled bellies and darker stripes of brown on their wings. They looked at me one way and then the other.

"We won't let them hurt her," said one.

"Hate those crows," said the other.

"Me too. Me too. Me too."

I was sure I was losing my mind. "I have to go home."

"But we only just got here," Green said.

"You can't go now," Jeb echoed.

"Don't worry. I won't let anything happen to you." Walker said. He gestured at the others. "We won't."

I wanted to believe him. I wanted to believe he and they could really truly take care of me. Mostly, I wanted to curl myself against his soft gray sweater and into his arms. My want was tangible; I felt it like the breeze on my skin, or my hunger, or my need to pee. I didn't like the feeling. I blinked my eyes to stop the tears.

"Turning eighteen wasn't such a big deal for me," Luisa said to Walker.

"She's very strong. We don't know what's going to happen."

I turned to him. "I thought you had questions for me about college."

Luisa looked incredulous. "You still want to go to college?"

"I want to be a veterinarian, maybe a zoologist. Or an ornithologist. You know, study birds. I love animals."

Walker shook his head. "You don't have to go to school to do that."

"That's like me saying you don't have to go to school to study people. Isn't that what psychology is? The study of people's behaviors and feelings?" I started for my car. "You need to take a few more classes."

Walker came with me. "I'll follow you."

"I'm fine."

"I'm following you home."

I didn't argue. He could do what he wanted. I couldn't wait to be back in my own room, alone and inside, away from birds and people, reading a book and listening to music. Walker walked beside me, but he didn't say anything. I felt the warmth radiating from him. I looked up searching for crows and saw those two little brown cactus wrens hopping along branch-to-branch above us. Nuts. This day had been plain nuts.

I opened the door of my dad's beat-up car and Walker continued over to a lovely silver Porsche. Some college student, I thought.

"Listen," I said. "I don't want to be part of your experiment."

He nodded. I had expected a fight, but he gave up right away. "Okay," he said. "Maybe that wasn't the best idea. I'm sorry."

Him being nice was worse than when he was a jerk. He was so incredibly cute. Then I caught a glimpse of my reflection. There was a big scrape down my forehead and flecks of blood on my cheek. I looked terrible. Quickly, I jumped into my car and shut the door.

He followed me all the way home, and waited in front of the house until I parked and went in my front door. By the time I looked out the window, he had gone.

4. Three Days Until My Birthday

I woke up the next morning itching again, this time centered on the top of my right foot. I itched so badly I could almost ignore the embarrassment and pain I felt when I thought about Walker. I'd been an idiot the day before, scared of a couple crows and then going home like a sullen baby. I hoped I'd see him at school so I could apologize. There were lots of other senior girls going to college and I tried not to think about him sitting on a bench with one of them.

I gritted my teeth, from the itch or the image or both. I poked my foot out from under the covers and saw I had scratched it practically raw. There were long red scrapes and a bizarre, almost flower-shaped bruise on my ankle. It would have almost been pretty if it didn't itch so badly. I hobbled to the shower, stopping to check the cut on my forehead in the mirror. It was an inch and a half long and scabbed over. Gross. And just as suddenly as the day before, the itch stopped. Gone. Vanished. Poof. If only the cut on my face could have disappeared as easily.

I dressed for school—and a possible Walker sighting— carefully. I wore my new jeans and my purple T-shirt that fit perfectly and my second hand, but cool black leather jacket. In case the itch returned, I left my big boots at home and wore a little pair of flats I'd bought myself. My mom hated them. I don't know why, but she was partial to my big old boots. Go figure. In the flats my feet felt light and nimble—not usual for me. In fact, as I walked up the steps into school my whole body seemed to be floating into the air. Maybe I had been wearing those boots too much.

But at school it seemed every kid had heard about my itch. Total strangers asked me about it in the hall. "How's that itch?" and "Scratch much?" One girl offered me a bottle of lotion. I thought she was being nice until all her friends cracked up. The handwritten label read Miss October's Centerfold Itch Cream. I did my best to ignore everyone. I ducked into English class just after the bell and was relieved Luisa wasn't there.

Half way through class—which was actually kind of interesting for a change—the door opened and Principal Hernandez entered with a new kid. A guy. He looked around the class and then at me. Right at me. Immediately I felt a little twinge in my gut, as if there was a string attached to my belly button and he was tugging on it.

"Class, attention." Hernandez bounced up and down. He always sort of stood on his tippy-toes. We all knew it was a sign of sexual frustration. He continued bouncing as he said, "This is Trevor Rockman. He's going to finish his senior year with us."

Hernandez handed some paperwork to Ms. Campbell, the English teacher, while Trevor kind of smiled at all of us but mostly me. Dark, shaggy hair and high cheekbones, dark olive skin, full lips, and eyes like smoldering coals. Okay, I'd read that in a romance novel and it wasn't his eyes—I was the one smoldering. Something had definitely revved up my pheromones; I was hot and bothered, first for Walker and now this guy. I blushed and looked down. Ms. Campbell offered him the empty seat behind me and to my right. He walked down the aisle and stopped at my desk. I looked up.

"What happened to your forehead?"

"Killer crow attack." It sounded ridiculous. I don't know why I didn't lie and say something awesome, like motorcycle accident.

"Not going for a Harry Potter look?"

I laughed. "Definitely not."

He laughed with me. "It's kind of cute." And continued to his seat.

Forget whatever Ms. Campbell said after that, he was all I could think about. Right behind me. I heard every move. Every exhale. I heard his pen scratching in his notebook. When class was over, I was disappointed he rushed out of the room, but then I found him leaning against the opposite wall. He was waiting for me.

"What's your name?"

"October. Really." I added that before he could ask.

"Very nice," he said. "Really."

English class was right before lunch and I found myself walking with him toward the cafeteria. He wasn't very tall, and he wasn't drop dead gorgeous or anything, kind of thick with big feet and hands to tell the truth, but he had my motor racing. As we went down the hall, the other kids looked him over, but seemed only as interested as they would be in anyone new. I was the only one having trouble breathing.

"Hungry?" he asked.

"Not very."

He took my arm and pulled me outside to the breezeway. It stretched between the classroom building and the gym and was where kids used to hang out to smoke back when smoking was allowed. Now it was just a place to gather, smoking forbidden of course, and all the little cliques had their areas. The fountain was for the popular girls so they could sit down together and the sunlight could show off their salon highlights. The corner by the gym was of course for the jocks. The stoners sort of drifted on the steps down to the parking lot. Trevor and I stopped by an empty pillar.

"Tell me all the school secrets," he said. "Who are these people?"

"Your companions for the next three months of your life." I dropped my voice as I nodded at various kids. " She's most likely to end up in jail. He's most likely to fail 11th grade—again. That one? Most likely to be pregnant before graduation. Probably just like the kids at your last school. Why did you transfer so late in the year?"

"Usual. My dad's job."

"You've moved a lot."

He nodded. He looked kind of sad and I wanted to say something comforting. It had to be hard to come into a school so late.

"Stick with me," I said. "I belong to no cliques and no clubs. I can't introduce you to anyone because I don't know their names."

"Snob," he said, but he was smiling.

"That's me."

"Thank you for allowing me to be your entourage of one."

"I may forget who you are tomorrow."

He gave a funny, shy, sideways look at me and said quietly, "I hope not."

My heart thumped. How sweet was that? I was trying to think of a great reply—I might still be trying to come up with that great reply—when Jacob the jock pushed through the double doors and saw me.

"Hey Miss October," he jeered. "How's that itch?" He snickered and gestured at his crotch. "I got something you can scratch."

He was such a jerk I wasn't even embarrassed. "You should see a doctor about that," I said. "I think it comes from too much masturbation."

"Ouch." Trevor laughed.

Jacob was pissed, but after a look at Trevor, he didn't say anything else. He walked over to his buddies in the jock corner, whispered something to them and they all snickered.

"Want me to beat him up for you?" Trevor held up his fists like a boxer. He was kidding, of course, and it was funny, but then he said, "What is this itch everybody's talking about?"

I was not going to share it with him. Absolutely not. "I've gotta get to the library," I said. "I'll see you later."

He frowned. I sort of hoped he'd offer to come with me, but then he shrugged. "Okay."

I fled. Damn Jacob. He had teased me since 3rd Grade and been rude and disgusting since 9th, but this year he had basically ignored me—thank God—until the itch. Please, I thought, don't let the itch be my defining moment. I could see the yearbook and underneath my photo: "Girl Most Likely To Scratch."

I turned the corner to the library and literally collided with Walker Smith. He dropped the book he was holding and we both bent to pick it up and bumped our heads. Just like a comedy routine, only it was more of a tragedy. Every time I saw him I did or said something stupid.

"You okay?"

"Going to the library."

"Your forehead."

"It's fine."

I didn't want to look up into those blue eyes. I tried to think about the new guy, about Trevor, but once again Walker radiated safety and warmth, and I felt myself relaxing, slowing down, turning into pudding beside him.

"Sorry about yesterday," I said.

"No, no. I'm sorry. I came to check on you, make sure you're all right. Crows carry terrible diseases."

"Like what?"

Before he could answer he looked over my shoulder and gave a little hiss. I turned around. Trevor came toward us. His muscles bulged in his tight T-shirt and he walked with a fluid motion like a dancer or a gymnast. I smiled at him. He smiled back.

"Hey," I said.

"Thought you were going to the library." He stuck out his hand for Walker to shake. "Trevor Rockman," he said. "You October's uncle or something?"

I almost choked.

Walker's eyes narrowed and his chin went up. "October is helping me with a project."

"No, I'm not."

"Yes, you are."

"I don't think so."

"Guess she's not," Trevor said and offered me his arm. "We're going to the library."

"Wait," Walker said.

Trevor and I walked away. When we got into the library I laughed out loud. "Thank you."

Trevor grinned. "That guy is a little strange, huh?"

"You're telling me."

We laughed and the librarian shushed us—naturally—so Trevor led me down to the far wall, way back in the stacks. I love the smell of old books and for some reason that and the dust and even the gray piece of chewing gum stuck on the wall were like an aphrodisiac. I had goose bumps. Trevor looked up at the fluorescent light. It was buzzing, and then it flickered and went out, leaving us in the shadows.

"Perfect," said Trevor.

I was trembling. Was he going to kiss me? Was this going to be my first official kiss? I'd just met him. I didn't want him to think I was a slut, but then I decided I would worry about that later.

He whispered. "What do you say we skip the rest of the day and find a place to go swimming?"

"It's cold out."

"I'll keep you warm."

I had never skipped school. I'd never had a reason before. He leaned toward me. I liked that he wasn't too tall. He smelled good, like dark, clean dirt. I know that sounds not so appealing, but on him it was delicious. I nodded yes. I was ready to go wherever with him. I looked into his big, dark eyes, started to close mine as our heads tilted…

"Hey, October."

I jumped. It was Green, standing there with about twelve books stacked up in his pudgy little arms.

"Oh are you kidding me?" I said.

"How're you feeling?" he asked. Then he looked at Trevor. "You're the new kid. Hi. I'm Chris Lee."

Not very nicely I said, "I call him Green because yesterday he was green and puking his guts out."

"I feel much better." He spoke seriously. "October, your forehead looks bad."

I couldn't believe this pipsqueak had ruined my moment. And then the bell rang.

"You going to Chemistry?" Green asked me. "I'm walking that way."

How did he know where I was going? So much for skipping the rest of the afternoon. As we all walked toward the library doors, Trevor took my hand. I got a shock, like when you touch metal.

"Oh!"

"Sorry," he said. "The carpet I guess."

I rubbed the spot on my hand. "It's nothing." It hurt a lot.

Chris went ahead of us and Trevor stopped me in the doorway. "Can I see you? Tonight?"

It was Thursday. I didn't know what I'd tell my parents. Plus wasn't I supposed to play hard to get? "Yes," I said. So much for hard to get—he'd obviously gotten me.

"Meet me at the Stop N Shop by your house at seven."

"How do you know where I live?"

He shrugged and grinned. He was so damn attractive.

"Okay," I said. "I'll be there."

"I'll buy you an ice cream cone."

He jogged off toward his next class and I turned toward mine. Green was standing in front of me.

"What're you looking at?" I asked.

"Your forehead's bleeding," he said. "And that thing on your neck is growing."

I groaned. So attractive. Maybe Trevor hadn't noticed. Yeah, right.

I ducked into the closest restroom.

5.

School bathrooms are universes unto themselves. It doesn't matter what school you're in, public or private, anywhere in the country, they all have the same smells, sounds, and accoutrements. There is the scent of pee mixed with industrial-strength disinfectant. The toilet paper, if there is any, pulls down in a little square so thin you could read a textbook through it. It takes thirty to make a reasonable wipe. A sadist must have invented the paper towels because they're like sandpaper, impossible to use for fixing make up, dabbing tears, or blowing your nose. Good news is you exfoliate every time you dry your hands. The tile walls make everything loud and there's always hair in the sink and at least two toilets haven't been flushed and in the girls' room the sanitary products wastebaskets are always overflowing.

The cut on my head was bubbling up with blood that was beginning to drip into my eyebrows. I found a stall with toilet paper, took about fifty squares and tried to staunch the flow. It wasn't helping. The mark on my neck looked bumpier and bigger and redder than it had that morning. I was falling apart. The bathroom door opened.

"Hey. Need some help?"

Luisa. Of course.

"That crow really did a number," she said. "I have some tissues, real tissues, in my bag."

"I can do it." The blood was saturating the toilet paper. "Yuk." I tossed the wad into the trashcan and grabbed a paper towel. I winced as I tried to wipe up the blood with the stiff, rough paper. "I don't know why it started bleeding now."

"I saw you talking to that new guy." Luisa wet one of her tissues under the tap. "He looks kind of interesting."

"You think so?"

"Yeah. Here, let me." She pressed the tissue to my cut. The cool water was a relief. "Lean your head back," she said.

It made it difficult to talk, but it didn't stop me. "I feel bad for him, you know? Having to transfer right before the end of school. I've been here forever and it's hard enough for me. I don't have any real friends—I mean." I stopped. "Well, you know what I mean."

I hoped I hadn't offended her. Here she was with her hand on my head, missing class, but she wasn't really a friend. Even if time after time she turned up just when I needed her. That was luck, not friendship.

"I think Trevor's okay looking," I went on as I stared at the ceiling. "In a rugged, you know, casual kind of way."

"Not as handsome as Walker," she said.

I straightened and looked her in the eye. "Walker is weird."

"I think he likes you."

"You do?"

"I love this color on you." She changed the subject. "You look great in purple."

I sneaked a peak into the mirror. My skin—the part that wasn't bloody—looked kind of golden and my hair was shiny with red highlights I never noticed before.

"Must be the light." I waited a minute before continuing. "So, Luisa?"

"Yes?"

"Where do you go when you don't come to school?" I asked. I was thinking about Trevor. "Do you go to the mall?"

"Ugh, no." Luisa laughed. "I go down to the L.A. River. "

"What do you do down there?"

"Hang out, watch the herons and the turtles. Enjoy the nature. This city has too much cement."

"Isn't it dangerous? Homeless people and gangs?"

"Never had a problem." She turned me to face the mirror. "Look at yourself. You're hot. And you're smart. That's why Walker likes you. You should give him another chance. Trust him."

"Once was enough." I took the wad of bloody tissues from her. "And this is what I got for it." I threw it away. "Thank you for helping me."

"That's what I'm here for."

I cocked my head at her.

"You know, I'm your basic caregiver type," she said.

"Well, thank you Nurse Flores." I had stopped bleeding. In fact the cut looked much better. The scab was even gone. "You're good at what you do." The spot on my neck had faded as well. It was almost gone. "My neck—"

"If you ever want to talk," she interrupted.

"About Walker?"

"Or Trevor."

We both started laughing at that, not for any real reason, but just because. Laughing and laughing like girlfriends. Like good friends. The door to the bathroom swung open hard and Ms. Tannenbaum, the P.E. teacher, stomped in. She was not your typical P.E. teacher, she was petite and blonde and wore a ton of jewelry, but she was scary nonetheless, like a Chihuahua on steroids.

"What are you girls doing in here? You should be in class!"

"I was bleeding," I said. "Luisa was helping me." I pointed to my forehead, but the pale, pink mark did not look convincing.

"Look," Luisa said, and pointed to the trashcan and the bloody tissue.

Tough little Tannenbaum raised her eyebrows. "Out," she said.

"It's the truth," I tried.

"Uh huh." She didn't believe us. "Detention. Both of you. Today."

Luisa shook her head. "I have to work, Mrs. Tannenbaum. My job. Really. Can I stay after tomorrow?"

Tannenbaum had a soft spot for the pretty girls. Luisa's eyes were like melted chocolate.

"Okay, Luisa," Tannenbaum grumbled. "Okay. Tomorrow."

Luisa skipped out the door. "Thank you!"

Tannenbaum turned to me. "You. Today. No ifs, ands, or buts about it."

I nodded.

"Now get to class!"

I scurried past her, down the hall and into Chemistry. Detention! What would Trevor think? But then I didn't see Trevor anywhere the rest of the day, not even a glimpse of his shaggy black hair. I didn't itch and I didn't see Walker. It was just a boring regular day—with my first ever detention at the end.

After school I went into the library and sat down at the table with the other three losers. And they were losers. One of them must've been at that school for at least eight years. No lie, he had a few gray hairs. The other two were junior delinquents, well on their way to being full-fledged criminals. I took out my homework and Mrs. Tannenbaum, the detention Nazi, banged the desk.

"No homework! Detention is time to sit and reflect." She looked at the older guy. "And stay awake!"

It was agony. She kept us exactly two hours while she sat

at the desk in front reading. She even ate a candy bar. I tapped my feet—couldn't stop--and stared out the window. Looked like rain. I expected to be drenched on the way home, but I didn't care; I kept thinking about my date that night with Trevor. When she finally dismissed us, I jumped up and grabbed my backpack. The old guy asked if I wanted a ride.

"No thanks," I said. If he was too stupid to graduate after a zillion years, I didn't want him driving me anywhere.

But then I had to wait for the city bus for more than half an hour with the clouds getting blacker and bigger and the wind swirling around. I could have called my dad to pick me up, but frankly, I just didn't want to hear about how detention could go on my permanent record and colleges take those things into consideration and blah blah blah. College. It was all anybody in my house had talked about since last summer. Enough already. All my applications were in and I was just waiting to hear. Even so, every day my mom or dad had some college tidbit to pester me about. Too late, I kept saying. It's over. What will be will be.

When the bus finally came, it was almost six o'clock. Once I got home, I'd have to rush inside and immediately give the folks a story about why I wanted to go right back out to the Stop N Shop. I could always say I needed something for school, but what? What did Stop N Shop have for school? Beef jerky?

"Tampons!" I actually said it out loud.

The old man across the aisle frowned at me. I turned to the window. It was almost dark and the buildings, the cars, the sidewalks, everything was the color of lead. Even the few pedestrians huddled in their jackets were gray like the background of an old black and white movie. My dad thought this was the loneliest time of day, waiting for my mom to get home and the evening to begin. Usually I thought it was the most beautiful, in between light and dark, night and day, on the edge. Today it seemed as if there was no edge, the day would melt into the night and no one would notice the difference. My feet tapped the floor of the bus. I couldn't stop them. They seemed to have a mind of their own. I thought of the library and the way Trevor had almost kissed me. I had really, really wanted to kiss him. My pg-13 rated musings must've shown on my face because the old man across the aisle cleared his throat loudly and glared at me. I turned all the way to the window.

And then, in the empty lot by the grocery store, I saw a bright twinkle. I blinked and looked again. Another and another, more twinkles, hundreds of them. Really? What were they? Fireflies. The field was filled with fireflies flashing brightly in the gloom. Fireflies don't live in Los Angeles. I had only seen them on television. At first I thought my eyes were playing tricks on me, or that it was just broken beer bottles glittering under the streetlamps, but no, they were really fireflies. Incredible, magical, wonderful creatures. Everything about me began to twitch, to move. I wanted to dance. I had to get up. I had to see them up close.

I pulled the cord and got off the bus. Despite my full backpack, I skipped and leapt as I hurried back to the fireflies. I twirled among them. One landed on my hand and blinked before it flew off. I imagined I heard them singing to me, welcoming me and asking me to stay and dance with them. I imagined they had bright, high voices, soft but crystal clear. "You're beautiful," I said out loud. "I love you." I stayed until it began to rain, not a few drops, but a real rainstorm—also so unusual in LA—until I was wet and the fireflies were gone. Then I ran all the way home. I could have sworn my feet left the pavement for longer than humanly possible.

I bounded up the front steps and into my house. "Mom!" I shouted like a ten-year-old, "I'm home! Guess what? Guess what?"

My tiny, skinny Mom came out of the kitchen with a big fat smile on her face and a big fat envelope in her hands.

"What is that?"

"It's from Colorado," she said. "It feels pretty heavy."

Dad came out of the birdhouse room. "Go on," he said. "We've been waiting."

I ripped it open and read aloud, "Dear October: We are pleased to inform you—" I threw my arms around my mom. "I'm in!"

It was fantastic. Colorado was one of my first choices, a great school for animal sciences and far, but not too far, from home. My mother actually had tears in her eyes.

"I fixed your favorite dinner," she said. "I knew we'd be celebrating."

I was happy, happy, happy, but then I remembered Trevor. I couldn't stand him up. I'd have to take the car, run to the Stop N Shop, and explain to him why I couldn't stay. He'd understand. I wondered if he'd heard from any colleges yet. I turned to Dad to give him a hug too.

He seemed different somehow. I went in for the congratulatory embrace, and he just patted me on the back mechanically. There was something subdued about him. He was usually the most boisterous of all of us, the "Jolly Fat Man" as he called himself. But he looked down at the floor and his shoulders sagged.

"Don't worry, Dad," I said. "I'll be home for Christmas and summers."

He looked up and I saw he wasn't sad about me leaving—it was something else in his eyes. Or nothing. A blankness. He forced a smile. "Such good news," he said. "I am so happy for you."

He sounded so straight and formal, not like him at all, but I didn't have time to wonder too much about it. I looked at the clock over the mantle and said, "I have to run to the store."

"Now?" Mom asked.

"Emergency. You know." I leaned over and whispered in her ear the magic word, "Tampons."

"Take my car," she said. "Dinner will be ready in fifteen."

"Back in a flash."

As I grabbed her keys, I noticed my dad hadn't moved. He was still staring at the floor. The rug wasn't that interesting.

"You okay?" I asked.

"Fine, thank you," he replied.

He didn't look fine to me, but I was late. I'd talk to him when I got home. I ran out the front door.

The rain had stopped but the streets were wet and shiny. I drove at a speed definitely ticketable, but I couldn't help it. I was excited both with my news and to see Trevor. Would I have my first kiss along with everything else—like the cherry on top of a dish of fireflies and college? When I pulled up, Trevor was waiting for me out front of the Stop N Shop. I started to get out, but he came and got in the passenger seat.

"Hi," I said. "I can't stay, I—"

"I've missed you." He interrupted.

"Really?" It had only been a few hours.

"I keep thinking about you."

"You do?"

"For real." He turned to face me.

The neon light from the Stop N Shop sign turned his face icy blue. I had never seen such perfectly smooth skin, as if he were a marble statue. He looked down and his long black eyelashes brushed his cheeks.

"Why?" I whispered. "Why me?"

"I want to know," he began, smiling impishly. "Do you like to play in the leaves? Have you ever been swimming in a river?

Have you climbed up a mountain to see the view?"

Each thing he said conjured up images so real I could smell the dusty leaves, taste the river water on my tongue, and feel the breeze from the top of a mountain.

"Have you ever played Hide And Seek in a forest?" He kept going, "Danced on moss? Watched a mother fox with her babies?"

I laughed. I had to. He looked like such a city boy. "Sure," I said. "Some of those things. With my dad."

"Would you like to—with me?"

"I think so."

He put out his hand as if would lead me to the woods right then and there. In the shadowy car, his hand looked huge, almost inhuman. His nails were too long and dirty. Involuntarily, I leaned back.

"Let's go right now," he said.

I could see my reflection in his eyes and my face was stretched and distorted like in a funhouse mirror. He bent toward me. His breath smelled like green plants and very faintly of rot. I frowned, but for some reason I wanted to kiss him so badly I didn't care what he tasted like. He smoothed my hair off my face and blinked and my reflection was gone. I leaned toward him—

Crunch! The car jerked forward at the same time I heard metal meet metal. We'd been hit. "What the?" My mom's car was a lot nicer than my dad's. I looked at Trevor. He was furious and in his anger his chin looked pointier, his eyes larger. Then he shook all over like a dog waking up and shrugged at me.

"What a drag," he said.

"No kidding."

I got out of the car. Jed's fancy red Charger was somehow connected to my bumper.

"Oh wow," Jed said. "It's you. Wow, man, I'm sorry."

"What were you doing? Are you wasted?"

"Absolutely not. I dropped my phone. I just looked down for a minute."

"Oh my God. You are such an idiot."

When I glanced back in the car for Trevor, he was gone, and the passenger door was wide open. I was disappointed in him, running off at the first sign of trouble. What did I know about him? Nothing much. For a second I saw again his odd angry face and I could smell something dead. I shivered.

Jed jumped up on his bumper and rocked his car up and down. The two bumpers disconnected. "No problem-o," he said.

"What? Look at my car!" But surprisingly, the bump hadn't done any damage.

"Those plastic bumpers you got are awesome," he said. Then he looked around. "Where'd your friend go?"

"I don't know."

"Lock your doors on the way home, okay? This isn't such a safe neighborhood anymore."

"That's funny coming from you."

"There are worse things than a fender bender."

"Bye, Jed."

Another perfect opportunity with Trevor—ruined. Angrily I got into my car and started it up. Jed watched as I backed around him and drove away.

6.

The computer screen was the only light in my room. Sometimes I think the Internet was invented for insomniacs. I have never been a good sleeper, but the web—the perfect name for the way it catches you and won't let you go—makes the middle of the night much more pleasant. There is a whole world out there that is never asleep.

I carried my laptop into my bed and rested it on my knees. I had that WWI paper to write, due next Monday, and I hadn't even started. But instead of Gallipoli or the Treaty of Versailles, I Googled Walker Smith. Nothing—and I mean nothing—came up. Then I tried Hayden College. Turned out Hayden College was one of those for profit schools where you took classes only online. It didn't even offer a Psychology major, only dental hygienist and computer tech. I thought of how warm his hand had been, how blue his eyes. And then there was Trevor. I looked for Trevor Rockman and he came up on the school's page. He had joined the football team. What the hell? There were only three months of school left and nobody was playing football. Maybe they meant baseball.

My cell phone pinged, a text. I got out of bed and found my phone.

"This is Jeb. Have you seen Luisa?"

I texted back. "It's almost midnight."

"Look out your window. See her?"

I looked, but there was no one outside and no strange cars

in front of the house. It was the night before trash pick up and all up and down the street people had put their big rubber containers out at the curb. I thought I saw movement behind one. What would she be doing out there? I looked closer. Nothing. Just a branch moving.

There was something white in the middle of the street. It looked like a paper plate that had fallen out of someone's recycling. On closer look, it wasn't a paper plate. It was a Frisbee.

"Frisbee in the middle of the street." I texted.

He texted right back. "On my way."

I pulled on my jeans, conveniently lying right there on the floor. I took off the T-shirt I slept in—one of my dad's and enormous—and put on an old hoodie. I tiptoed downstairs carrying my shoes. I looked toward the den. The door was closed and I could hear my parents in there fighting, but in low voices as if I wouldn't know. I always knew when they were arguing and lately it had been more often. My mom was gone a lot to conferences and mycology meetings. She said it was important, but I think Dad thought it was just to get away from him. He was worried she might leave him so he was desperate to lose weight, but they were in there fighting about Madame Gold. It had been an uncomfortable evening despite celebrating my college acceptance. Mom had made all my favorite foods: fettuccini, garlic bread, asparagus, and my dad had refused to eat any of it. That's when the fight began. Usually Mom was telling him not to eat so much. That night it was because he wasn't eating at all.

"You'll get sick," she had said. "That hypnotist girl didn't mean for you to stop eating completely."

"I'm sorry, Ruth. I'm just not the least bit hungry."

He kept speaking with that unusual formality. As Mom got frustrated and started shouting, he stayed calm, also unusual for him. He was adamant about not eating. Finally he went into the den and shut the door. Mom looked furious.

"I guess the hypnosis is working."

"I don't want to talk about it," Mom said firmly. "It's not right." She sniffed the air. "I can smell it. I can smell her."

My mom has a hypersensitive nose, better than anybody. She likes people—or doesn't—often by their odor. As soon as dinner was over she followed Dad into the den. They'd been in there ever since.

I opened the front door silently. Jeb was standing outside.

"You got here fast. Where's your car?"

"Too noisy." He already had the Frisbee in his hand.

"Is it hers?"

He nodded. "She's been taken."

"What?" I knew she came from a kind of messed up family. I knew her mom worked all the time and her dad lived somewhere far away. "You mean her dad? Have you been to her house?"

He shook his head. "She would never leave this behind." He meant the Frisbee. "Unless she had to."

"Why was it in front of my house?"

He looked down the street. "I gotta go."

"I'll come with you."

"Go inside. Lock the door."

He had never been much of a talker. Now he was driving me crazy. "But what is happening?" Jeb didn't answer. He reached out as if to touch me, but then turned and ran off. He was quick and he melted instantly into the dark. "Jeb?" I whispered. "Jeb?"

Other than the circle of light from the single streetlamp it was pitch black. I thought I heard the bushes rustling. One of the trashcans thumped softly as if someone had bumped it. My mom's car keys were still in the pocket of my jeans. I hurried to the car, got in and locked the doors. Jeb couldn't say I hadn't done what he asked—I was inside with the door locked. I let out the parking brake, put the car in neutral, and coasted down the street. When I got a few houses away from home I started it up.

I'd been outside of Luisa's house only once—when she and Jeb took me home from that party and Jeb had dropped her off first. I hoped I could find it again. She didn't live near by. My particular housing development wasn't big, but East Los Angeles with all the neighborhoods that fed into my high school was huge. I wound this way and that, made some wrong turns and had to turn around. The streets were empty. There were fewer houses, more businesses. They say no one walks in LA. but it's a big city, you usually see someone around. That night I didn't see another soul, not outside a bar or in the all night market. When I finally pulled up in front of her house, it was after midnight. The house was set back from the street with a white picket fence all around. It had a front porch and looked about the same as other houses in the neighborhood. Drooping over the porch rail was a dirty pink sweater that had obviously been there a long time.

I turned the car off and sat. Was I really going to knock on the door in the middle of the night? What would I say? I woke you up because Luisa left her Frisbee in front of my house? But Luisa had come to my aid so many times. She was the closest thing I had to a friend. Beautiful, sweet Luisa. And Jeb had really been worried.

I got out of the car and crept up the front walk. I peeked in the front window, but the curtains were closed. I'm not sure what I was looking for or what I hoped to see. It had been chilly earlier, but it had gotten strangely warm. The moon and stars were hidden behind heavy black clouds. I unzipped my hoodie for some air. Along with the odd warmth, it was perfectly still, not a breeze, not a sound. Where was the wind?

I tiptoed off the porch and around to the back of the house.

It was darker in the back. I looked through a window and saw a coffee mug on the kitchen table, signs of life. I stumbled and bumped into a metal chair. It clanged loudly and I froze. I waited, but no lights came on. I was more careful as I walked down to the next window. It was raised about three inches. I peered through the glass. I made out a Brodie Smith Ultimate Frisbee poster on the wall. Had to be Luisa's room. And then I saw a bed with someone sleeping in it.

I pushed up the window. "Luisa! It's me."

The body moved, turned over, sat up.

"Are you okay?" I asked. "Jeb is worried about you."

The body stepped over to the window and I nearly jumped out of my skin. "Oh oh! Sorry!"

"October, is that you?"

It was Luisa's mom. "Hi, Mrs. Flores," I said.

"Come to the back door."

She met me there. She had been crying. She looked horrible and I knew Luisa really was gone. I started crying and she opened her arms and I fell into them.

"What happened?" I managed. "Where is she?"

She pushed me back, held onto my shoulders with both hands and looked into my eyes. She was a pretty woman usually, but her face was as pale as the nightgown she wore and everything was sagging, her eyes, her mouth, her shoulders.

"We don't know," she said. Then she actually shook me. "Unless you know something. October, do you know where she is?"

"No, no, I don't." I pulled myself out of her grasp. "Jeb came by my house. He found, we found, her Frisbee."

She sat down at the kitchen table. She rested her head in her hands. "I knew this would happen one day."

"You mean her dad coming to get her?"

"One day," she said it almost to herself. "What could we do?" She looked up at me and her eyes were hard and squinty—as if she was angry with me. "It was a mistake coming here. I should have said no, but Luisa wanted it so badly."

"They'll find her," I said. "The police are good at finding deadbeat dads. Even if he took her back to Mexico."

"You have no idea," she said. "Oh October." She gave me a small, bitter smile. "You are really clueless, aren't you?" She looked me up and down. "And why? For what?" Then she put her head down on the table and cried.

I didn't know what she was talking about. I had the creeps as I walked back through the yard to my car. A breeze rattled the palm fronds and I jumped.

"This is all your fault." A woman's voice, as clear as my own, whispered in my ear. I spun. There was no one behind me. There was no one anywhere. I was all alone standing by my car. It wasn't Luisa's mom's voice. It wasn't mine. It had to be my imagination. It had to be.

7. Two Days Until My Birthday

I was exhausted the next morning. I'd been frightened driving home and then running up my front walk and even inside my house. I checked under my bed and, after arming myself with my ancient red Elmo flashlight, looked inside the closet. I thought I was too old to be afraid of the dark, but that night all the terrors of my childhood came flooding back. Monsters, witches, vampires, and psycho murderers. I put a chair in front of the closet door and I kept the flashlight in bed beside me. Where was Luisa, my brain went round and round, where could she be and how could it be my fault? It wasn't. It wasn't. That voice was just my imagination saying the worst thing possible. The same too big imagination that pretended I could understand crows and cactus wrens and fireflies. I finally fell asleep just as the sun was coming up, a solid, heavy sleep without dreams. My alarm went off an hour later and I woke up stiff, my eyes puffy and my mouth dry. I wasn't itching, but the bruise on my ankle had blossomed into a stylized kind of flower. I must have been scratching in my sleep because the red lines were dark blue like bruises and radiated from the flower shape, circling my calf. I definitely needed to wear my jeans to cover it up. Not that I ever wore skirts.

When I plodded into the kitchen, Dad was making his favorite banana pancakes. It seemed he was back to his old, chipper self.

"Morning. You look like you could use another couple of hours."

"Don't worry," I said. "I can nap in English."

"Don't get cocky, Miss College Co-ed. English is still important. If you're going to sleep, do it in Biology."

He laughed, of course, but for once I didn't, and he looked at me with concern.

"What's up, Pumpkin? Bad dreams?"

"Luisa's missing." I blurted it out. "Even Jed doesn't know where she is."

My dad swayed as if someone had hit him. He held onto the counter.

"What? Are you okay?"

He turned to me, and his smile was big and fake. "They'll find her. Not your problem. Don't worry."

But his eyes were saying something different. He looked worried. And scared.

"What's going on with you?" I asked.

He put a pancake on a plate and handed it to me. He sounded like himself when he laughed. "You know what they say: Breakfast is the most important meal of the day." He looked at me and waited.

"All day," I responded. It was our standard joke—something I had said when I was a little kid and tried to justify eating banana pancakes at every meal—but again I didn't laugh. I wasn't even hungry. "Where's Mom?"

"She left early. Said she had another conference."

"What? She has to get back in time for my birthday."

"Two more days." Dad studied me for a moment. "How are you feeling?"

"Fine. Fine. Just tired."

"Sit down. Eat your breakfast. I'll drive you to school."

"Okay, thanks." Getting a ride sounded great.

The syrup and butter were on the table, but I liked my

pancakes plain. I picked it up with my fingers. That was another thing that would usually drive my dad crazy: I liked to eat pancakes with my hands. That morning he didn't seem to notice. I watched him cooking. Usually it was one pancake for me and three for him. One for Mom and two more for him. He had one sitting on a plate on the counter beside the stove, but he hadn't touched it.

"Delicious, Dad. Have you had one?"

"Got one right here." He gestured to the uneaten pancake. "Yummy."

I watched him until it was time to leave and he never ate one bite. Something was definitely different about him. I wondered if hypnotism could make a person starve to death. I wondered if a fat person could live longer without food than a skinny person? Mr. Snyder, the bio teacher, loved it when we came in with practical questions. I would ask him, I thought—if I was awake. Ha ha ha.

Dad tried to cheer me up the whole way to school. He told a string of terrible jokes continuing right up to when he dropped me off. "Hope you remembered your lunch," he said. "You know what's the worst thing in the school cafeteria?"

"What?"

"The food!" He was howling with laughter as he drove away.

I was glad I'd told him I'd take the bus home. I couldn't take his cheerfulness. Not that morning, not that day. It didn't seem fair that it was an absolutely beautiful spring day. The sun was warm, the air was soft, the grass in front of the school looked incredibly, shockingly green. How could it be so beautiful out when Luisa was missing and I was hearing voices, possibly losing my mind. Where were the clouds, the ominous sky? It wasn't right to see kids laughing and taking off their jackets and chasing each other around like kindergarteners. I sat on a bench with my head down, waiting for the bell to ring. Someone sat down beside me. I smelled flowers and sure enough, when I looked up, it was Walker.

"What are you doing here?" I asked. "Didn't you hear? Luisa is missing."

He reached for my hand, but I slid away from him. "Two days until you're eighteen."

"So what? Tell me about Hayden College. What's the campus like? Who's your favorite teacher?"

"Well…" he began and stopped.

"Do you even actually go to college?"

"I'm here because…" He stopped again. "Listen. You can't worry about Luisa."

I picked up my backpack and stood to go into school, but he took my hand and just like the first time, I felt it all the way up my spine. My muscles went loose and I had to sit back down. "Walker."

"October. Please. Stay away from that new kid. That Trevor. And don't look for Luisa. Sometimes you have to sacrifice the one for the good of the many."

"You're crazy. That doesn't apply here. It doesn't."

But for the first time there were clouds in his blue sky eyes. There was something he wasn't telling me. I stood up again. Touch or no touch, warm, cozy feeling or not, I was out of there.

"Wait," Walker said. "I'm sorry. Sorry. Jed told me Luisa's with her father."

"Her mother doesn't think so."

He frowned, swallowed hard. For once I knew something he didn't. "When did you talk to her?"

"Last night—actually very early this morning. I went over to Luisa's. Her mother's really scared. She thought I might know where Luisa is. Why would she think that? Plus I found Luisa's favorite Frisbee in front of my house. Something is going on and it seems I'm involved whether I like it or not."

"You're not," Walker said. "You can't worry about it. Listen to me."

"Why should I listen to you?"

"Tomorrow at midnight this will all be settled."

"You're not making any sense." In the bright, spring sun, I suddenly got the chills. I put my hands over my eyes. I swayed, nauseated. Walker put his hand on my arm and the nausea went away. Everything went away. I was weightless, floating.

"Oh." Walker said. "I wish… I wish—"

"Leave her alone." It was Trevor. I crashed back to earth, opened my eyes.

"I'm not doing anything." Walker jumped to his feet.

"Then why is she crying?"

I didn't know I had been. "I'm crying for my friend!"

"I heard about Luisa," Trevor said. "Everybody's talking about her. I'll help you find her."

"You will?"

"We can drive around. We'll find her. Come on."

"Right now?"

He nodded and just like the day before I was ready to skip school and go with him. His mischievous smile, his smooth skin, his shiny eyes made me want to go, do, try new things. He shook back his shaggy hair. "Right now," he said.

"Don't go anywhere with him."

"It's none of your business," I said to Walker.

"None of your business," Trevor repeated.

Walker's angry words came out in a growl. "You don't care about her. This is about you and what you want."

"She knows how I feel." Trevor stood in front of me. "Don't you, October? You know how I feel about you." He looked into my eyes and cupped my face with his large hands. His touch didn't make me go warm and relaxed. Instead, my palms began to sweat. My heart began to race. And then the itch returned. My arm, my neck, between my shoulder blades. I put my hand on Trevor's arm. It was like a rock. But I had to scratch. It wasn't attractive, but I had to. I stepped away from both of them and my head cleared although the itch continued. I scratched. I had to.

"See what you did?" Walker said.

Trevor just grinned. "I see what's happening to her. What's about to happen." He turned to me. "October. Let's go."

It was more a command than an invitation and that didn't make me happy.

Walker frowned. "Please stay with me."

That was nicer and he was sweet, but so weird and half the time I couldn't understand what he was talking about. At least Trevor was my age. I'd never had any guy seriously interested in me. Now it seemed I had two. I looked from one to the other. Trevor's face was broad, his hands large, and his fingernails were not exactly clean, but his eyes were like a puppy's and his olive skin was perfect. Walker was so handsome, almost too handsome—he made me feel inadequate—and, as I've said before, he felt familiar in some way. The morning bell rang and everyone began to file into school. I had to go. Walker put his hand on my shoulder. I gave a little jolt as I felt myself flow into him. I can't explain it any other way, but it was as if my blood was a river rushing toward him, impossible to stop or slow down.

"Let go of her," Trevor said.

"Make me," Walker challenged.

"You may be something special in your world—"

Trevor launched himself at Walker, grabbing him around the waist. Walker fell back against the bench. Trevor punched him hard. Walker brought his knee up between Trevor's legs. Trevor yelled. Someone across the quad yelled, "Fight! Fight!" I was livid. I hated both of them at that minute. Maybe I should have been thrilled or flattered that two guys were fighting over me, but they just looked like a couple of stupid idiots.

"Stop it!" I said. "Stop it right now!"

I don't think I had ever stopped anyone from doing anything before, but they pushed apart and both stared at their feet, embarrassed.

Then they each apologized to me.

"I am going to class," I said. "I can't go look for Luisa now. That's ridiculous. I have no idea where she is. And Walker, if you have something to tell me—you can tell me after school."

Trevor started to protest, but I stuck to my guns. "Nope. Don't start. I'll see you in English."

"But, Princess," Walker objected.

"Don't call me that. Do you know how sexist and demeaning that is? Like I'm some Barbie doll." I shook my head. "I am not a princess. I am a person—just like you." He put out his hand and I jumped back. I was not going to let him touch me.

Trevor said, "You won't go with me to find Luisa?"

"You're being ridiculous."

He shrugged and gave his shaggy hair a shake. He looked up in the sky. "I'm going," he said and then he smiled. "You'll wish you had come with me."

I watched him jog to the parking lot and get in his car, a dusty red Prius and I did want to follow him. I bit my lip to keep from calling to him to wait and take me along. The quad was empty. The bell had rung and everybody else had gone into school. Walker stood there. He wanted something.

"What?" I said. I was irritated. "Just say it."

A crow cawed in the distance. Walker looked up. I heard

another crow. Again, my imagination, I thought the crow was saying, "There she is!"

"We have to get out of here," Walker said.

"School."

"No," he said firmly. "No time." He looked at me, and I saw him trying to decide what to tell me. "Those birds—" he began.

"They're just crows."

"Trust me."

Why did he keep saying that when obviously he was not the least bit trustworthy?

There was a sudden swoop above us. A flock or, as they're officially called, a murder of crows flew toward us and circled over our heads.

"Run!" Walker cried. "Into the trees!"

I ran into the park surrounding school as the birds came after me. Southern California black walnut trees are not very big, but they were all the protection I had. The crows were good at navigating through the trees. I kept tripping over sticks and rocks. I was trying to bob and weave, keep them guessing, but they were agile and more practiced at flying than I was at running. Plus the grove of trees was tiny. I was almost out the other side.

"Here!" Walker shouted at me.

I dodged back to him as he picked up a branch and thrust it at the crows. I refused to act like the dumb girl in the horror movie and just stand there and scream. I picked up a branch too. He and I stood back-to-back swinging our sticks. I got a little wild and managed to hit his arm. I scratched him pretty badly.

"Ow!"

"Oh my god. Sorry!"

A great big crow, the seeming leader of the bunch, hovered just out of reach in front of me. It stared at me and if a bird had lips it would have been licking them. I could hear it saying, "Yes. Yes. I've got her. I've got her." Of course that was my imagination, and anyway it was obvious it wanted me bad and thought it had me. But I had a better idea. I pretended I was tired, that my arms could barely hold up my stick.

"I can't do this much longer." I lied.

The bird was interested, puffing up its chest, getting ready for the attack.

Walker believed me too. "Don't stop now. A little longer!"

"I can't."

I slumped and rested my hands—with the stick—on my knees. The bird practically smiled. It came straight at me, wings like an airplane. Quick as I could, I straightened, pulled back, swung, and knocked that bird smack into a tree. It fell to the ground and lay there without moving. It was the most satisfying sporty kind of feeling I'd ever had. I actually understood why baseball players loved to hit that little white ball. I was ready to hit some more home runs.

But I didn't have to. With the leader out of commission the others stopped attacking. They flew over to the stunned—or I hoped, dead—crow lying on the ground and circled randomly like foreign tourists without a guide.

Walker turned to me. I saw the scratch down his arm. It was bleeding.

"Your arm," I said.

He ignored it and pulled me around behind a tree. "You were amazing," he said. He inspected me all over, up and down, my face, my arms. He even turned me around, pushed my hair to one side and scrutinized my neck. His breath was warm. I leaned back into him.

"You're really okay?" he asked.

"I'm sorry about your arm."

"It's nothing."

He felt so good. He didn't make me all jittery like Trevor did and I didn't feel like doing crazy things. Did it mean I was a slut because I was thinking about two guys at once? I turned and he put his arms around me. I breathed in his sweet smell. He patted my back. Then he was kind of stroking. From comforting me, he was progressing toward something else. I was ready. I lifted my face for a kiss. An older guy would be good at it, perfect for my first. And Walker was perfect in so many ways.

"No." He pushed me away. "We can't do this."

"You're not that much older."

"It's not that."

"Do you have a girlfriend?"

"C'mon." He didn't answer my question. He never answered my questions. "Before that crow wakes up." He started pulling me toward the parking lot.

"School's that way," I said.

"Can't go back to school."

"Those crows are done."

"It's not the crows I'm worried about."

As he said that, we both heard footsteps crunching in the gravel at the edge of the park. I turned. Through the brush I saw a figure. Two figures, then three and four. They walked upright, but they were blobby, brown and gray, their bodies and heads indistinct. People in some disturbing costume. One and then another bordered the park.

I stumbled, pointing, backing toward Walker. He nodded. He had seen them too.

"I didn't want to do this," he said. He grabbed my arm, turned abruptly and started running, pulling me, straight for the brick wall of the school building.

I had to run with him or I would fall. "No!"

"Trust me!"

"No!"

He yanked me with him. I was sure we would do a face plant into the brick and I shut my eyes. Just as I steeled myself for serious pain, I fell forward and there was a warm liquid kind of feeling, but dry too, like I was falling through very fine, heated, sand. Walker wasn't holding me anymore. I was swimming, circling my arms. I began to panic and the try to scream and the sand filled my mouth. I was choking. I couldn't breathe. I was going to pass out when I landed on my ass on the ground.

I heard someone laughing. I opened my eyes and was momentarily blinded by the sun. When I could see again, I was shocked to discover I was back in the front of the school, sitting in the empty quad.

"Have a nice trip?" Jacob snorted as he ran by. "See you next fall."

"How original." I got to my feet.

The late bell rang. I was so confused. My head hurt. Where was Walker? How had I gotten here? What exactly was going on?

And then Trevor was by my side.

"That was quite a fall," he said. "I think you were knocked out for a minute."

"I fell?" The last thing I remembered was the wall, and before that those costumed attackers, and before that the crows. The crows.

He pointed at a stone sticking out of the grass. "You hit your head on that. You might have a concussion."

I reached up and felt the bump on my forehead. Great. Just as my crow scratch was going away.

He brushed the hair off my face and smiled at me so tenderly my knees felt weak. I wanted nothing more than to curl up in his arms.

"I wish I'd been here to catch you," he said.

"But I saw you get in your car."

He looked at me like I was nuts. He touched the bump on my forehead and winced. "That is really going to hurt later."

"But—" I turned to the parking lot. There was his car parked where it had been. And Walker was nowhere to be seen. I was having a definite Judy Garland in The Wizard of Oz moment. "But it couldn't have been a dream. It seemed so real. And Walker was there. And you were. And the crows."

"Who's Walker?"

"Wow. I really am losing it," I said.

I thought about the voice I'd imagined the night before. And then I remembered the rest: that Luisa was missing and that Trevor had asked me to go find her with him and Walker had said some weird things and he and Trevor had fought—over me. That really couldn't be true. My eyes filled with tears.

"You hit your head pretty hard."

He kept his arm around me as we went up the steps into school.

"What happened to you last night?" I asked. "You disappeared when Jeb hit my car."

Ms. Tannenbaum appeared out of nowhere. "October Fetterhoff!" she shouted. "Late again?"

"I fell."

"It's always something with you. Detention. Again. Today."

I opened my mouth, but she crossed her arms, daring me to object. I said nothing. She watched as Trevor and I split off to our respective classes, Trevor whispering he'd see me in English. Of course she hadn't given Trevor detention. Only me. What a witch. First Luisa, now Trevor. Tannenbaum obviously hated me.

I made a quick stop in the bathroom to wipe my tears. I looked at myself in the smeared mirror. I looked good despite the bump on my head, no sleep, a very quick shower, and not doing anything that morning but brush my hair. It was shiny and curled softly around my face. My eyes looked larger than usual and my lashes longer even though I wasn't wearing any makeup. My leg itched and I pulled up the leg of my jeans and the flower shaped bruise was almost glowing. It was actually pretty, like a sunflower on my ankle. I scratched and scratched and it was warm under my fingers.

I heard the voice again, but this time it was gentler, friendlier. "You know where Luisa is," it said. "You know."

There was no one else in the bathroom. I shook my head as I sprinted to class. My very loud inner voice was full of crap. Luisa's disappearance was not my fault and I didn't know where she was.

8.

I was surprised when no one in school even mentioned Luisa missing. It was true she didn't come to class very often, but people liked her when she was there. At least no one was talking about my itch anymore. I went from first period to second and then third and thought about Tannenbaum and detention—again. Okay, gym class was lame, but at least I showed up and I never, not once, used my period as an excuse. Personally, I think that sets women back 100 years. I mean it happens every month—time to deal with it, ladies. But Tannenbaum really did not like me and so I didn't like her. It was so nice and easy to be pissed off about something so normal like the PE teacher and detention, because when I thought about Walker and the dream or vision or whatever I'd had when I hit my head on the rock I felt sick to my stomach.

As Ms. Lani, the biology teacher, droned on, I looked through the window and saw Walker's beautiful silver Porsche pull up in the parking lot. I saw him get out of his car. I had to talk to him. Immediately. I had to. I didn't raise my hand or anything, just said, "Excuse me," and ran out of the room.

"Walker!" I was well aware my entire class—including the teacher—could see me in the parking lot. I tried not to look like a crazy person, but I was feeling pretty nuts.

"I want to talk to you."

Walker didn't seem surprised. He turned his startling blue eyes to me and smiled. "Great."

"Don't," I said.

"Don't what?"

Don't be so sweet, I wanted to say. Don't be so cute. Definitely don't touch me and make me feel all loose and Jello-y. But I couldn't say that to him. "Did anything happen this morning?"

He looked puzzled.

"Did we talk? Did you have a fight with Trevor?"

"I just got here." He looked calm and clean, not as if we'd been running through the woods and fighting crows. "Your poor head. Now what?" He reached for my forehead and touched the bump with one finger.

That touch. Like warm syrup running through my veins. I remembered his arms around me in what had to be my dream, the way he inspected every part of me to see if I was okay, the way we almost kissed. Had to be a dream. Had to be. I shook my head. "Sorry," I said.

Then he ran his hands through his hair and the sleeve of his button down shirt pulled back and I saw the long, raw scrape down his arm.

"Your arm," I said.

For a second his face shifted, blanched as if he'd been caught, but returned to normal so quickly I couldn't be sure I'd seen anything. "What?" he asked.

"That's quite a scrape."

"You're not the only klutz around." He laughed and pulled his sleeve down. "I tripped."

He was lying. I knew it. But if the morning had happened, then how did I end up in the grass? I was dizzy. "I have to sit down."

He caught me as I swayed and led me to the curb.

"I don't feel well," I said.

"Take deep breaths," he instructed. "Slowly."

I breathed. I looked up at him, but he was scanning the sky. My stomach lurched. "Looking for crows?" I asked.

He squatted in front of me. "Please," he said, "Please stay away from Trevor."

His face was so serious, so beautiful, almost shining in the sunlight. I thought of Trevor and he was dark and mysterious and yes, kind of sexy in an earthy way. "Okay," I said even though I wasn't sure I should. I wobbled to my feet. "I'll stay away from him—for today—but then you have to tell me what is really going on."

"I will," Walker said. "Trust me."

That again. "When?"

"Tomorrow."

The rest of the day passed uneventfully except Ms. Lani gave me detention for running out of class to "talk to a boy." I didn't tell her I already had detention, and I hoped she wouldn't find out.

The fireflies were out again in the empty lot as I rode the bus home at sunset. They were the highlight of an otherwise sucky day. I did get out a couple stops early so I could see them up close, but I didn't skip or twirl. I apologized for not being as excited as the day before, but I didn't imagine them saying anything back. I dragged my butt down my street. My headache throbbed. I wanted to go inside and collapse in front of the TV, but I still had to write that stupid paper on WWI.

Madame Gold's black Ferrari was in our driveway. I groaned. I was not in the mood. And my mom still wasn't home so it would just be my dad, the loony hypnotist, and me. I couldn't face sitting there listening to her crapola.

I went around the house and let myself in silently through the back door hoping to avoid them. The kitchen was dark. I sniffed. Nothing cooking. Dad hadn't done anything about dinner and I was starving. In fact, the bowl with the pancake batter, the plates, and the dirty skillet were still exactly where he had left them that morning. I saw his uneaten pancake on his plate on the counter. Was it only that morning I'd sat there and watched him not eat? It felt like ages ago. He had never eaten his pancake and there was batter left in the bowl. He was definitely not his old self. I opened the refrigerator and grabbed an apple. I took a jar of peanuts off the counter. It was almost six o'clock, but it didn't seem dinner would be anytime soon. I could hear Dad and Madame Gold talking in the birdhouse room, but their voices were so low I couldn't quite make out what they were saying. I tiptoed out of the kitchen hoping I could get up to my room without being noticed.

"It is more important than ever," Madame Gold was saying, "that you keep her on your side. Keep her close to you."

Dad sounded like he was whining in reply, but I only caught a few words, "family," and "mother," and then, "stolen."

"Luisa was the only choice."

They were talking about Luisa. Without thinking, I charged into the den. "What about Luisa? Do you have any news?"

Dad looked guilty—he hadn't known I was home—but Madame Gold nodded. "I thought I heard you come in," she said. "It is too bad about your friend. I heard about her—on the radio."

"Anything new?"

Madame Gold gave me that simpering, sad, but condescending smile that grown ups use like a pat on the head. And she was hardly a grown up. I really disliked her.

In her low, carefully modulated, hypnotist's voice she said, "I'm sorry, no. But the universe works in mysterious ways, October. Everything happens for a reason."

"Don't spout that baloney at me."

"October!"

I turned and got a good look at Dad. He had lost weight. Already. He looked thinner and his hair was a mess, sort of spiky around his head, not in his usual slicked back, combed and parted immaculate style.

"Dad?" I was worried.

"I feel better than I have in years," Dad said. "All thanks to Madame Gold. Please apologize to her."

"It's not important." She hummed at me. "Join us. Sit down."

My head ached and a wave of nausea undulated through me. I put out my hands to steady myself and they were covered with red welts. I could feel the itch beginning, this time on my chest and stomach. I had to get out of there. "Homework," I croaked. "Lots of homework."

I ran up the stairs to my room and shut the door behind me. I opened the window and gulped in the fresh air. I felt better. I needed to eat, I decided. I hadn't been hungry at lunch and hadn't eaten anything since that one pancake. I shook a handful of peanuts out of the jar and ate them one by one, forcing myself to relax. The blotches on my hands looked like enormous bug bites, only they didn't itch, they burned. I looked in the mirror on the back of my door and saw there were welts on my neck as well. I lifted my shirt and saw them on my stomach too. I peeled off my jeans. There were red stripes all across my legs, as if I'd been grilled on the barbecue. Great, just great. First an itch, now some disgusting rash. Maybe Nurse Raynor was right and it was mange or, I shuddered, body lice.

I threw on my softest, loosest pajama pants and my comfiest T-shirt. I sat down on the floor with my laptop. I ran my fingers over the silly, childish ladybug sticker my mom had given me. I missed her. I knew she loved her work—Dad called her the Queen of Mushrooms—but I was sorry she was so busy right now. I wanted her home. I wanted her to meet Madame Gold so we could hate her together.

My phone chimed signifying a text. I pulled it out of my backpack and read the screen:

Hi October. My name's Enoki. Where are you?

I typed back: Home.

ENOKI: Come out and play?

I'd hung around with my mom enough to know Enoki was the common name of a kind of exotic mushroom. I didn't know anybody with that name and it was definitely odd, but maybe she—or he—loved fungi as much as my mother. Anyway, who was I to say anyone's name was unusual.

Me: Who are you?

ENOKI: Your BFF.

Me: Sorry. That position is empty.

ENOKI: Not anymore. Come outside. I'm waiting.

Me: Outside my house?

ENOKI: Don't let that crazy hypnotist see you leave.

I jumped back from the computer. I turned off my light. Enoki, whoever she/he was, was right outside, possibly able to see in my window. I closed the computer so my room was completely dark and crept to the window. I peeked out. The street looked empty. Where was she/he? How did she/he know about Madame Gold? I sat on the floor and texted.

Me: How do I know you?

ENOKI: Think of me as an early birthday present.

I had no idea what that meant. I was tempted to go out there and meet this person, find out what it was all about, but then I remembered that saying: curiosity killed the cat. And that made me think of the dead cat in my side yard and the crows coming after me, at least once, even if the second time hadn't been real. I typed a reply.

Me: I'm staying in tonight.

No response. I waited and waited, but no more messages came. I figured I had discouraged Enoki and I was okay with that. I really had to write that paper. Then I heard the little chime again.

ENOKI: Trevor sent me.

Me: Really?

ENOKI: Let's go save Luisa. I know where she is.

A shiver went down my spine all the way to my feet. My logical, mature, intelligent self knew I should call the cops. But my reckless, curious, completely stupid self was already putting on my sneakers. We all want to be heroes, right?

I dropped my phone on my bed, opened my window, and popped out the screen. I'd never had a reason to sneak out, but I knew I could. All I had to do was go out my window, side-step across the roof with my feet in the gutter, jump over to the orange tree, and climb down. Without my father or Madame Gold hearing me. And without falling off the roof and breaking my neck. Problem was, I was scared of heights. The glass elevator at the mall made me queasy. A photograph of a person standing at the edge of the Grand Canyon—a photograph—was hard for me to look at. Still, I had to do it. I had to find out if this Enoki person really could take me to Luisa. I tied my Converse extra tight. I swung one leg out the window, then the other. I rolled over on my stomach and wiggled back until my feet felt the gutter. I scuttled along the roof. That part wasn't too hard and my back was to the drop behind. Then I had to turn around and jump to the tree. The branch was close, but not that close. I teetered. I was definitely going to fall. I tottered. I fell, but just in time I caught the branch, scratching my hands and chin as I did. I was breathing hard as I hung there. All I had to do was let go. How far was it to the ground? I wasn't sure, but it felt very, very far. I looked down. Not so bad. And I let go.

I survived. I hit the ground right beside the window where my dad and Madame Gold were still having their session or whatever. I peeked inside. My dad was sitting in a folding chair with his eyes closed and Madame Gold was standing behind him whispering into his ear. He was barefoot—a very rare occurrence—and his narrow white feet with the crazy long toes were tapping and bopping, like mine on the bus going home the day before. And he looked thinner than when I'd first come in. Madame Gold flapped her big sleeves across his face and he smiled kind of sleepily. I couldn't watch anymore.

It was chilly and a breeze blew right up my pajama legs. Pajamas! I'd been in such a hurry I'd forgotten my jeans—and my phone! I started for the tree to climb back up.

"No time for that."

I jumped a foot in the air. A girl stepped out of the shadows right beside me. She was not as tall as me, but in her sleeveless tank top and skintight jeans I could see how strong she was. I understood why they said body builders were 'sculpted' as I looked at her backlit by the street lamp. Her muscular arms almost didn't look real. Then she stepped forward and I could smell her: muddy, moldy—like pond scum.

I must have made a face. "C'mon," she said, "Deal with it."

"Ever heard of showers?"

"Do you want to find Luisa or not?"

"Who are you?"

"I'm Trevor's little sister." She put her hands on her boyish hips and looked me up and down. "I don't see what makes you so special."

She pulled me into the light from the street lamp. She turned me, lifted an arm, almost my shirt.

I pushed her hands away. "Cut it out."

"You look like an average, ordinary, boring human to me."
What a b–i–t–c–h. "Are we going to meet Trevor?"
"Car's this way." She headed off and I trotted to keep up.
Where do you go to school?" I asked.
"Homeschooled," she said.
With a body odor like hers, I was not surprised. She sped up, expecting me to follow, which I did. I noticed that she wasn't wearing shoes and that her feet looked enormous and her toes as flexible as fingers. Like monkey feet. Her hands were huge too. There was something of Trevor in her. Her muscles. Her pointed chin. Her large brown eyes. Her dark, shaggy hair as if she and Trevor used the same dull pair of scissors for their haircuts.
"Where is Trevor?" I asked.
"Moping about you," she said. "He's been a drag all day."
"Yeah, right."
She shrugged. "Doesn't make any sense to me either."
I couldn't believe this girl. Maybe she was disabled in some way. "Is your name really Enoki?"
"Is your name really October?"
That shut me up. We jogged around the corner to her bright red VW bug. She got in. I stood there. It was not very smart to get in a strange car with an even stranger girl who wasn't even wearing shoes. But then I did.
"We are going to drive carefully," she said. I think it was as much for her as for me. "You've already had enough excitement today."
"No, I haven't."
"Oh, right. You haven't. Let's see. You haven't been attacked by crows and you haven't been chased by slobbers and you haven't run through a wall and ended up back in time, back at school."
"I haven't? I mean, I have?"
"You have?"

"Of course not."

"I didn't think so." She turned on the radio and cranked it up. Heavy metal—not a surprise. She screamed along. I rolled down my window. Every stoplight seemed to be green and waiting for us. There was no traffic, no one on the road at all, as if it were the middle of the night instead of the end of rush hour. And it did seem late. It was dark, the sun had set and no moon or stars were visible.

"Where does Trevor think she is?" I shouted over the music.

"Who?"

"Luisa."

"Who?"

"You're taking me to find Luisa."

She turned off the radio and smiled. "No," she said. "I'm not."

9.

When I was nine-years-old, my mom and dad took me on a family vacation. Our only vacation—ever. We had no grandparents to visit, no aunts and uncles, no old college friends. My parents were complete loners who almost never left the house except to work or go to the grocery store. We kept our curtains drawn and didn't even know the neighbors' names. I never had a birthday party, my parents never suggested I have a play date or a sleepover, and consequently I was rarely invited anywhere else. I grew up pretty much solo. But my schoolmates went places like the beach or the mountains or to see the Golden Gate Bridge and I wanted to too. One day in fourth grade the science teacher talked about bird watching at the Morro Bay Bird Sanctuary, only a couple hours away. I whined, begged, and pestered my parents to take me there until they gave in. I convinced them it was educational, told them about the Black Oystercatcher and the Mountain Plover and my dad was psyched to see some different birds. I thought he could watch the birds and I could go to the beach like other kids.

The preparations were extensive. Mom packed the car with most of the house, anything we might possibly need for any scenario. A snakebite kit, a reading lamp in case the motel didn't have one, food, games, even our own silverware. It was as if she didn't believe anything existed outside of our neighborhood. Finally, we were ready to go. I was slathered with sunscreen even though we wouldn't get to the motel until six o'clock that night and who knows how long after that I would actually touch the sand. But I was excited. My mother was a nervous wreck. My dad, not yet truly fat, opened a bag of chips before we left the driveway. "Road food!" he laughed.

About half way there, we stopped at a highway rest stop to use the facilities and stretch our legs. I went to the restroom and my mom slipped off her sandals to walk barefoot in the little patch of grass. She hated shoes, took them off wherever and whenever she could. She had big feet for a woman her size. When I came out of the bathroom I saw three young people approaching my mom. The three, two guys and a girl, looked like siblings. They all had dark, messy hair and dark eyes and they weren't very tall. I didn't see a car in the parking lot other than ours; they seemed to have walked out of the woods bordering the back of the rest stop.

My mother saw them and gave a little scream. My father rushed out of the men's bathroom and stopped. I walked up beside him, but neither of us went any closer. Mom hugged the three people and they hugged her. She was taller and skinnier, but she looked related in some way. My dad grabbed my hand and squeezed so hard it hurt. I looked up at him and his face was sad.

"Ruth." He called to her, but she didn't even turn around.

She began to change, to blend in with them. She seemed to shrink and fill out at the same time. Her mousy brown hair got darker and her legs, in her red plaid mom shorts, got thicker and stronger. My dad let go of my hand and hid his face. I had to do something. I ran to her and threw my little arms around her from behind. She looked down at me and her face was different, more angular, and then it wasn't. She was Mom again.

"This is my daughter," she said quietly to the others. "Mine and Neal's." She gestured back to dad. "Her name is October."

They stepped away from me, and then closer. The girl looked me over very carefully. "Is she?" she asked.

"We don't know," Mom replied.

"When she's eighteen?"

"We don't care." My mom was adamant. "We don't."

The older of the two guys looked at my father and his face was angry, mean. "Your husband is not himself." He laughed.

"Enough!" I had never heard my mother sound so imperious.

He started to say something more, then he bowed his head. "We'll leave you, your lowness."

They all kind of bowed and began to walk away. My mother said goodbye wistfully, with such sorrow in her voice that it hurt me to hear it.

"Wait!" I said.

All three stopped and turned to me. I wanted to say don't leave, or don't leave my mother, or don't leave her so unhappy, but none of that was exactly right. I wanted to ask them who they were and why I felt drawn to them. Instead I just shook my head. The girl bent over me and smiled.

"I see the resemblance," she said. "When the time comes, ask Russula what you should do." She looked up at my mom.

"Her name is Ruth," I said firmly. "Ruth Fetterhoff."

She backed away. My mother put her hand on my shoulder. She was smiling, but tears were spilling down her cheeks. When I looked back, the three visitors were gone. We got in the car and kept driving, my parents very subdued. During the trip, whenever I asked who those people were or why my mom had been crying, she and my dad both said I'd been sleeping and dreamed it. A couple years later, I was spending the day in my mom's lab and I learned Russula was the name of a rare and particularly beautiful family of mushroom. I asked my mother if that was really her name and she just laughed.

That encounter came back to me as I was speeding down Beverly Boulevard in a red VW with a girl named for a mushroom. Enoki looked a lot like those people at the rest stop so long ago. Trevor did too, come to think of it, and maybe that was why he gave me such an anxious feeling in my stomach. Except he wore shoes and went to school and there was no mushroom called a Trevor.

"Where are you taking me?" She didn't answer. "Let me out!"

"Can't," she said. "I have my orders."

The green lights continued. We were going faster and faster.

"My parents will call the police."

She shrugged. I tried another tactic.

"Where's Trevor? I want to see him."

"I know what's best for Trevor. Eenie meenie miney mo and you are not it."

"Are you really his sister?"

She sneered. "A lot of people think you're hot stuff, but I don't." She grunted a kind of laugh. "To me you're just a weirdo. A freak."

"That's funny, coming from you, Stinky."

"Do you have any powers at all?" she continued. "You're not beautiful. Or strong. Nothing special that I can see."

I didn't know what she meant by powers and maybe I wasn't special, but I was not going to be killed or kidnapped or sold into white slavery—whatever this dirty, smelly girl had in mind. Breaking every bone in my body was preferable to that. She slowed a little to turn a corner and quickly I opened my door and jumped out of the car. I expected it to hurt worse than it did. Must have been the adrenalin because I was on my feet in a flash and running down the street away from her. I heard the screech of her brakes and the high whine of her little car going fast in reverse, but I was not worried. I was fast. Faster than I had ever been before. I ran five blocks and I wasn't even tired. Fear, I decided, was a wonderful thing. It made me faster, stronger, able to leap tall buildings in a single—BAM! I was tackled from the side. I hit the sidewalk hard, knocking all the wind from my lungs. Then I was dragged off the sidewalk and down an alley. The pond scum smell was stronger, mixed with dumpster garbage. I struggled, but the two people who had me were strong. I saw their bare feet and hairy toes, shaggy hair like Trevor and Enoki.

"Let her go." It was Enoki's voice. They dropped me hard on the alley cement.

Enoki squatted beside me. "You didn't have to do that. We're here. We have arrived at our destination."

She gestured at a small neon sign reading, "The Underground" over a gray door. She gave me a hand up and even brushed me off. Her two friends or whatever they were waited.

"We're going to a bar? I'm not old enough." Plus it was mortifying to be in my pajama bottoms and a T-shirt.

"Trevor's waiting."

She dragged me behind her through the gray door. Loud heavy metal music pulsated. I was in a club filled with people dancing. It smelled like a locker room crossed with that disgusting pond odor. It was dark with only a couple of red and blue lights moving around in time to the music. Everybody held drinks or bottles of beer. And quickly I realized everybody looked the same. Not like they were all indie or grunge or metal types who shopped at the same stores, but truly they all looked alike as if they were all related. Short, muscled, dark hair, eyes and skin in various shades of olive. Their faces were different and some were taller or thinner than others, but they were incredibly similar. They all looked like the people at the rest stop. And Enoki. And Trevor.

Where the hell was I? A family reunion?

Enoki pulled me toward the bar. A tall, narrow cage, hung in the corner. Inside I saw a skinny, pale, very tall and angular blue-haired girl in a bikini—definitely not related to the people below her—inside the cage. She was in very skimpy clothing and her skin looked lavender, the color of a fading sunset. She would have been beautiful, but the bartender, a giant Enoki-type, offered her a beer and she shook the bars desperate for it. She wanted that beer, badly. I could see it. It was like a drug. She reached between the bars for the bottle. The bartender pulled on a rope, raising the cage higher above the crowd. She kept reaching for the beer.

"After you dance, sweetheart. Dance first. Then beer."

Reluctantly, but obediently she began to dance and the crowd went wild. She was stunning to look at, but so different than the bar patrons and they jeered and insulted her with words like "waif" and "stick" and "fairy." Fairy seemed to be the worst word of all. The girl danced with her eyes closed, opening them only occasionally to make sure the bartender still had her beer.

A cry went up across the room. I fought my way there. Another slim, tall person—a guy with curly green hair and blue skin—was in another cage. He was so drunk he couldn't stand up and everyone stood around laughing at him. They splashed him with beer. Someone stood on a table and poured a drink onto the floor of his cage and everybody cheered as he lapped it up. Like the girl in the cage, he would do anything for that drink.

"Hey," I said. "Stop it."

The group turned to me. They looked me up and down. They frowned. A girl said, "You smell funny."

Me? The place smelled like a hill of fertilizer soaked in beer. "Leave him alone," I said.

"He likes it," the girl said. "We're just giving him what he wants."

"And you wonder why your dad is fat?" A guy spoke in my ear.

I turned. It was Trevor.

"Wanna' dance?"

His face was hard and smooth and not like it was at school. I felt the usual weird pull toward him, but when he took my hand I felt something else—something a lot like fear.

"What did you mean about my dad?" He didn't seem to hear me. He pulled me into the center of the room. He was dancing, but I wasn't.

"Do you know where Luisa is?" I shouted. "Your sister said you know."

"Dance with me." He smiled and his face softened. "Then we'll go. I promise."

He put both hands on my waist and drew me to him. The rhythm of the music was pounding, so loud and deep I could feel it in my feet and up into my stomach. I couldn't help but move to it. Trevor nodded, grinned. Some friend of his danced over and handed him one of the neon drinks. Trevor took a big sip and licked his lips. The drink made his tongue glow in the dark. Then he offered it to me.

"No thanks." I wasn't interested in drinking. Especially after seeing those desperate models.

"Please?"

His friend stayed next to him, watching me.

"No, really. No thanks."

"It's delicious," Trevor said.

"Not tonight."

"You'll like it." He pushed the drink toward me. "I bet you'll love it."

He held it under my nose and I have to admit it smelled fantastic. Like fruit and chocolate and whipped cream and butter cookies, the best dessert in the world, plus the faint scent of the forbidden. It was intoxicating. I looked down into the frothy, electric pink concoction. How could anything that smelled so good be bad for me?

Trevor called to everyone. "She's about to take her first drink ever!"

A girl stopped to watch. And a couple of guys. Pretty soon a whole crowd was gathered. I looked at their faces, all with pointy chins and big brown eyes, all wearing the same expression they had when they watched the girl in the cage. Enoki was there too. She and Trevor exchanged a smile.

"Who is she?" someone asked.

"My future," Trevor answered.

"She's October," Enoki said. "The one and only October."

There were some exclamations, a couple of ahs and ohs. I'd never gotten that reaction before. They backed up, made a circle around us. Trevor held out the drink. I wanted to take it so badly my hands trembled. But I hesitated.

"C'mon," Trevor said. "For me. I just want to see what will happen."

I thought maybe a drink would help me. People said alcohol calmed the nerves. And I was more than nervous.

"Hand it to me," I said to Trevor.

He smiled, the crowd leaned forward, and I brought the glass to my lips.

"Do this," Trevor said, "and I'll be yours forever."

He shook his shaggy hair back and his eyes glittered in the dim light. He put his warm hand on my hip and I got that funny, anxious feeling again. Nervous.

"Then we'll go?" I asked.

"Of course. If you want to." He leaned in and whispered in my ear. "I want you. I want you so much."

It felt good to be wanted. He was cute, strong, and had fallen in love with me the moment he saw me. I never thought anyone would feel that way about me. I lifted the glass. Enoki led the crowd in a chant, "Drink. Drink. Drink." They were smiling, nodding, and clapping and as I looked around I thought they all looked lovely. It was good to have friends. I wanted them to like me. One drink and then I would go find Luisa. One drink just to help me relax. I smiled back.

"No!"

I looked up. It was the girl in the cage. "No!" She said again. The bartender growled and threw a beer at her. It hit the floor and broke. I was shocked to watch her slurping alcohol off the pieces of broken glass. When she looked at me again, her tongue was bleeding. "Don't start," she whispered to me.

Then, all the way on the other side of the room, I saw a small person hop up on a stool. Green! What was he doing here? He was too small and way too young to be in this crowd. He waved and gestured for me to follow him.

"October!" he called.

My head cleared. Following him seemed like a very good thing to do. I handed the glass back to Trevor.

"I have to go."

Trevor was instantly furious, his rage turning his face purple. "We were having so much fun!"

My hands itched. I looked down. Once again they were covered in red welts. I looked across the crowd at Green. He was like an island and I was drowning. I needed to get to him.

"See you tomorrow in school." I didn't listen to Trevor's reply and swam through the crowd toward Green. Enoki tried to grab me, other people pulled at me, hanging onto my clothing, but I brushed them off. I heard the girl in the cage scream. I didn't look back.

Green ran up some stairs leading out of the club and I took them two at a time. "Green!" His shiny black hair flashed under a single hanging light bulb in the dark hallway. "Chris! Wait!" He went through a door and let it shut behind him. I pulled it open, stepped through, and suddenly I was falling blind through warm sand. The same sand I thought I'd been in when I ran into the school wall with Walker. I tried to call Green's name, but my mouth filled and I choked. I coughed and waved my arms frantically. Then I smelled Chinese food.

10.

The smell of Chinese food—that delicious, oily, soy saucy smell—saved me. I'm not kidding. I took a deep sniff, relaxed, and the sand melted away. I opened my eyes and found myself in the booth of my favorite Chinese restaurant. The same red vinyl seat covers, the same thick white tablecloths and squat glass jars of hot mustard and duck sauce. I saw the waiter I'd known since I was a little kid, Mr. Bob, in the back by the kitchen. This was the only restaurant my parents would go to and I had always loved it. Everything looked completely normal, but I knew it couldn't be. How had I gotten there? Where was the club? My mouth was watering. The peanuts I'd eaten back in my room seemed like a year ago.

A dog barked. I knew dogs weren't allowed in restaurants. It barked again and I heard its toenails clicking toward me on the tile floor. "We're here," the dog said. "Hey, hey, here we are." First I'd been able to understand birds, now I was translating dog speak. I loved animals, but no one could talk to them for real. I turned and looked over my shoulder. Walker was walking toward me with a fluffy, black dog at his side. I was so happy to see him. Relieved, safe, all those good feelings he gave me. And then I was just confused. What the hell was going on?

The dog jumped up beside me on the bench and licked my face. "Nice to meet you, happy to see you, isn't this place great?" and its tail was wagging. It had the sweetest dog breath I'd ever smelled.

"Down, Oberon, down, " Walker said. "On the floor. Sit."

Oberon got off the bench and sat obediently, but I didn't need to translate to understand the dog didn't want to. He was wiggling back and forth, his tail going ninety miles a minute. I gave him a pat on the head and I saw that the red bumps on my hand were gone.

Walker sat down across from me. He smiled and his blue eyes were filled with concern.

I didn't want to, but I started to cry. "What's wrong with me?"

"You need to eat." He gestured for Mr. Bob. "Isn't this your favorite place?"

"How did you know?"

"I'm trying."

He took my hands and my breath caught in my throat. That touch. That tingle only he produced.

"Tell me," he said. "What happened to you tonight?"

I tried to stop crying, but the tears kept falling. "I met this girl, Enoki, Trevor's sister, and she told me she'd help me find Luisa, but I jumped out of her car and then she pulled me into a club. A horrible club and everybody looked like her except these poor skinny alcoholics in cages."

Walker spoke quietly and his eyes narrowed. "In cages?"

"The bartender made this poor girl dance before he'd give her a drink. And she did it." I didn't tell him about her licking alcohol off the broken glass, it was too awful. "The guy did whatever they asked too, just so he could have a beer."

Walker squeezed my hands so hard it hurt. He was furious.

"We should call the cops," I said. "It's not right. It isn't. I tried to stop them."

"You did? Oh, October." The way he looked at me made me blush.

"But then Trevor was there, and he and everybody wanted me to take a sip of a drink, this bright, glow in the dark kind of drink. It smelled so good and I almost did, almost, I wanted to, but then I saw Green—Chris Lee, you know, from the experiment—and I followed him out and I fell into this sand." I shook my head, that couldn't be true. "And I ended up here." I looked around. "That club must be nearby. Maybe through the kitchen? In the alley behind?"

Mr. Bob walked up to the table with a tray of food. I was mortified when my stomach grumbled. Mr. Bob put down all my favorite dishes, Kung Pao Tofu and Garlic Spinach and Sesame Noodles. He put a dish of beef and broccoli on the floor for Oberon. Maybe Oberon was a service dog.

"October." Mr. Bob smiled at me. "Eat. Talk later. Eat now."

That's what he had always said when I was a kid. I guess I was a chatterbox. But hearing the familiar phrase just emphasized all the craziness that was going on. The tears began again. Mr. Bob handed me another napkin.

"What is going on?" I said. "I'm hearing voices. I'm falling through sand." I looked around. "None of the people in this restaurant look normal. Except you, Mr. Bob, and you, Walker. And since when do you allow dogs in here?"

It was true. The other tables contained the oddest collection of diners. Skin rusty brown, or gray like a kitten, or almost green, or very pink, wild hair, weird noses and everybody tiny and short or long and tall. There were a few exquisitely beautiful people, something like the poor creatures in the cages, but healthy and happy and drinking tea. It was not a clientele I had seen there before, and my parents had been taking me to Big Wok since I was born.

Mr. Bob said, "I'll get you more napkins. You're going to need them."

Walker spooned food onto my plate. "Here," he said. "Have a bite at least."

I picked up my chopsticks thinking I'd have one polite bite, but once I started I couldn't stop. I was ravenous. It was so good and he was right, the food made me feel better. It was hard to cry and eat at the same time.

"Whose voice?" Walker asked. "Do you know whose voice you hear?"

"It must be me, my inner voice, but it doesn't sound like me. She keeps telling me to go find Luisa and that I know where she is. She also said Luisa is missing because of me."

"Don't listen to that voice."

"It's ridiculous, right? It's just guilt speaking. I wish I could find Luisa."

"But you can't. You shouldn't."

I looked at him.

"They'll find her," he said.

He sounded so sure. I took a deep breath. I put more food on my plate. Walker hadn't eaten anything. "Don't you want something?"

"Save me some noodles."

"Better eat them fast."

He laughed. And, even as confused and worried as I was feeling, I did too. I decided whatever he told me I could deal with. I just wanted the truth.

"Please tell me what's happening here. I know things are not normal. I know it."

Oberon finished his dinner. Sleepily he climbed up on the bench and half into my lap. He looked up over the table at Walker and gave a little humpf. Walker nodded—as if they had communicated somehow.

"Okay. Okay." Walker sighed. "I'm not supposed to tell you

any of this—I could lose my job. I shouldn't tell you; it should be your mom or dad."

"I'm going crazy. Is that it? You're not a psychology student, you're a psychiatrist and you've been sent to take me to the loony bin. Right after my very favorite last meal."

He didn't laugh. "I wish that was it." He saw the look on my face. "Of course I don't wish you were crazy, but this is hard. And I could really get in trouble, but I don't know what else to do." He paused. "You're almost eighteen."

"I wish everyone would stop talking about it."

"It's an important birthday. Think about it. Have you suddenly grown taller? Do you run faster?"

"How do you know?"

"Any marks that weren't there before?"

I thought of the flower-shaped bruise on my ankle and decided that wasn't something I wanted to share. I shook my head. "No. Maybe. Not really."

"October, do you have any idea how special you are?"

I looked up with a mouth full of spinach and rice, swallowed quickly and had to take a drink of water. "Yeah, right," I said. "Average height. Average weight. Plain brown hair, brown eyes. Average—" I stopped myself from going on. It's not a good thing to point out your average-ness to the world's best looking guy.

"Those are human qualities," Walker said dismissively. "They don't mean anything."

"They do to a human. Like me."

He sighed. He pushed his curly blond hair back and for the first time I noticed his ears. They were a little pointy at the top. "Remember the fireflies?"

"How do you know about them?"

"They came for you. Only for you."

He reached across the table and took my hand. I felt that flow between us, the waterway of emotions and thoughts and hopes and fears going back and forth and I know he felt it too. He pulled his hand away.

"I shouldn't. I can't. I don't want to be like him. I'm not like him."

"You mean Trevor?"

"He wants you for one thing and one thing only."

I blushed and then Walker blushed.

"No," he said. "I don't mean that. He thinks… he thinks if he's with you then—" "Then what?"

He took a deep breath and leaned toward me. "You," he whispered with a frown. "I didn't think you would be you. This would be so much easier if you weren't."

Oberon gave a little whine in my lap. I imagined he said, "Oh brother." I looked down. The dog gave a shake, yawned, and closed his eyes. I looked back at Walker and saw him struggling, fighting with himself. I wanted to be out of that restaurant and some place, anyplace, where we could be alone. I wanted my first official kiss to be with him, only him. What had I ever seen in Trevor? Walker filled me up, my chest and my head and my heart. "Let's go," I said. "Where are you parked?"

"Please, Princess," he said.

"You know I hate it when you call me that."

"First listen."

I waited. He looked at me and then looked away. I wanted to touch him. I wanted him to touch me. I reached for his hand, but he pulled his away.

"I need to concentrate," he said. "I know you're wondering why all these unusual things are happening to you. I know you think you're going crazy, but October, listen: none of it is a dream."

If it wasn't a dream, then I had fallen into a Harry Potter book or something. And strangely, I was not completely surprised. This restaurant, the dog on my lap whose voice I understood, the violent crows in the park, running through walls, Enoki, and even the club were almost familiar. My shoulders relaxed. My breath slowed and I nodded. It was almost as if I had been waiting for this moment my whole life.

"Tell me," I said.

"You're not who you think you are," he said. "I don't know how to tell you more gently than that. Your parents are not who they seem."

"I'm adopted?" It had occurred to me, as I think it does to every kid.

"No," Walker sighed. "Your parents are just… different."

"You got that right."

"Do you ever wonder why your dad's so fat?"

"That's what Trevor asked me. He eats too much. Really. It's not his thyroid or anything. I've seen him."

"But do you know why?"

"He loves food."

"He's a fairy."

"He's gay? Oh my God!" I was stunned. "But he and my mom—."

"No, no, no. Listen," Walker gritted his teeth. "Don't talk, don't say anything, just listen."

I nodded.

"Your father is really, truly, honestly, completely a fairy. A magical fairy. Like the kind with wings that flit around and live in the woods. The kind from fairytales."

Dad was the least fairy-like person I'd ever seen. "Where are his wings?"

"He had to give up flying to be with your mother."

"So why is he fat? I thought fairies were little."

"Fairies can't handle alcohol. One sip is too much and then they can't stop. Those poor creatures in the cages were fairies—and addicted. Your father, amazingly, got over his alcoholism. He's one of the very few. But he turned to food instead."

Insane. "What about Mom? She's so skinny she must be a fairy."

"Your mom is a troll. Like Trevor. A troll." He didn't say it like he liked it. "She should be shorter and more muscled. Trolls are very strong. Life as a human has stretched her, weakened her."

"She's a troll and he's a fairy."

"Your parents have a mixed-marriage. The very first of its kind."

"I don't believe it."

But somewhere deep down inside, I did. Little things made sense. The way my father looked up at the trees and frowned on a summer evening. Maybe he missed flying. My mom would get frustrated she was so weak. Once she cried because she couldn't open a jar of spaghetti sauce. Maybe she missed her muscles.

"Your mom is a mycologist because she's a troll. Growing and harvesting mushrooms is what trolls do. Your dad loves birds because he's a fairy. Birds are to fairies like dogs are to people."

I gave Oberon a pat. There was something feathery about the fur around his ears and over his eyes. "If all this is true, then what am I?"

"Unique. You're the only half fairy, half troll in the world."

"But what does that mean?"

"Your powers could be amazing. Fairies can fly, we can do that crazy transplant thing."

"Where we run into walls or out open doors and end up in sand?"

He nodded. "It's called transplanting. It's a way we can travel safely, go where we need to go. We're very smart."

I interrupted. "You're obviously a fairy."

He smiled, shrugged to say of course. "We can talk with animals and we live in the highest tops of trees." Then he posed for me, like an ad in Vogue, until he laughed. "Fairies are also the most beautiful creatures on the planet. All the top models are fairies."

That explained why models were all so tall and thin. "And trolls?"

He sneered. Trolls were obviously not high on his list. "Base, vulgar, shallow, self-serving, self-important."

"Will I be like that?"

"You're not so far. Maybe you'll get their very few good qualities: strength, agility, speed."

I remembered how fast I ran when I jumped out of Enoki's car, how falling on blacktop and rolling to my feet didn't hurt at all.

Walker shuddered. "Trolls spend their lives underground, in the dark. They stink."

I wanted to sniff my own armpit. I had noticed Walker's sweet, floral scent. It was nothing like mine. Maybe I was more troll than fairy. I'd learned about genetics in biology. I knew some traits were recessive, some dominant. I had brown hair and brown eyes like the trolls—mine was a little lighter, but it was nowhere near blond, or blue, or silver. My ears were definitely human ears and my feet were big for my height.

"When will I know?" I asked. "I mean, about my powers, what I can do?"

"When you turn eighteen. At least that's the way it usually works."

If my birthday officially started at midnight, then I had

twenty-six hours to go. I was a little taller, a little thinner, I could sort of understand Oberon, but inside I was still the same old insecure me. Walker went on and on, giving me a crash course in the fairy and troll worlds. I wasn't really listening. It was too much to get my head around at once. Transplanting was running into hard things and ending up somewhere else. Fairies lived above ground, high in the treetops in a special forest. It was only when they came to the human world that they took human size. Trolls lived below ground or in caves or sometimes dense, dark woods where the lower foliage was so thick it kept out the light. Appropriately, many trolls had mushroom names, like Enoki. Like my mom, Russula. Slobbers were those humanoid, blobby creatures that had come after us in the park. They were the pets of the trolls, made from trash and litter found in the forest.

"What about the crows?" I asked. "Why weren't they your friend? And if I'm half-troll, why did those slobbers come after me? Why did Trevor want me to take a drink?"

"That's what I'm trying to find out."

"Is that why you're here?"

"I was sent to watch over you, to keep you safe through the transition. And to see how much fairy is in you. I didn't think you'd be... Look, October, I'm just a regular fairy. You are way, way out of my league."

That was the funniest thing he'd said yet. "This has to be a joke. Where's the hidden camera? Me? I'm just an ordinary, run of the mill, human girl."

"How can you say that?" Walker protested. "Look at you. You're brave, you're smart, you're intuitive and it's not even your birthday yet. Plus, you are beautiful. Truly beautiful. Unusually beautiful. But you're out of my league for another reason."

"Isn't that enough?" I joked.

He gave a sad smile. "The reason I call you Princess is

because that's what you are. Your mother was Princess Russula, only child of the Royal Lownesses, the King and Queen of Trolldom. Your father was a prince, Prince Neomarica, only child of his Royal Highness, King of the Fairy Canopy. When your parents decided to run off together they had to give up being a fairy and a troll and any claim to their royal titles. Now your grandparents are dead and you are the only heir. When you turn eighteen you will be Queen."

"Of which kingdom?"

"Officially you'll be the queen of both. But I hope you'll choose mine." His eyes shone remembering. "It's beautiful. The Fairy Canopy is amazing. Flowers everywhere and colors and birds and squirrels and deer and the air is soft with this perfect smell of pine and jasmine."

"Nice." It was a lame thing to say, but I was too overwhelmed with everything to be clever.

"But I'm worried." Walker went on. "Things have changed since I was there. I hear that after our King died, someone else took over."

"Who?"

"Could be the trolls. Ugly, awful trolls. I hate to think of them in my forest."

"Wait a minute." I thought of my parents, the way they still held hands when they sat on the couch to watch TV, the way they looked at each other when they thought I wouldn't notice, the little things they did for each other. They were still crazy in love. "My mother is a troll. My dad is a fairy. So my parents gave up their homes, their status, their friends and families to be together?"

"They had to. We're not allowed to intermarry."

"Who says? Why not? My parents love each other. What's wrong with that?"

Walker's open face closed down. "Trolls have no business interacting with us. They should stay on their side of the forest. The dark and ugly bottom side."

"But—"

"Think of the trolls in that club, the way they smelled, that black hair, those enormous feet. Disgusting."

"I'm half troll."

"Hardly. I'm not sure you have any troll attributes at all."

I thought of Trevor. He was handsome, even appealing when he wasn't being creepy. I liked the nervous, excited feeling he gave me. I liked all his energy and strength. I even liked the way he smelled. I was sorry he was mean to those fairies, but Walker made me wonder what the fairies did to trolls.

"Do you keep trolls in cages?"

"No. We use more moderate methods to make them work for us. They do the low stuff, take out our garbage, clean up any mess."

"Do they want to do that?"

He shrugged. He didn't care. I was terribly, horribly, sadly disappointed. Walker was not who I had imagined him to be at all. He wasn't open or accepting or as sweet as he appeared. I looked across the table at him and at that moment he wasn't even very attractive.

"Now I know why fairies are so small," I said. "Because they have such very, very small minds."

I stood up, forgetting about Oberon. He tumbled to the floor with a little complaining bark.

"Sorry," I said to him. Then I turned politely to Walker. "Thank you for dinner. I'm sorry I don't have any money to put in for my share." I looked at the empty dishes and Walker's clean plate. My share was all of it.

"You don't understand." Walker stood up too.

"I understand plenty. We've worked hard in my world to make it okay for people to love whomever they choose and get married if they want to. Fairyland sounds like the dark ages."

Walker jumped to his feet. "It's not us. It's the trolls. This is their fault. Why would anyone want to be with a troll?"

"My mother is wonderful. And Trevor doesn't stink. And he's nice to me."

"Trevor wants to be King."

"Fine with me."

"Only you can be the head of Trolldom. He can't be King unless he marries you."

"Fat chance. Why don't you all have elections? Like normal people? Leaders should be trained. They should have some knowledge about politics and the world and the way things work so they can actually do some good."

In my ear, low, so low I almost couldn't hear it, the voice— my conscience, my alter ego, whatever—whispered, "Luisa needs you."

I waved at my ear, like at a mosquito. Walker frowned. "What is it?"

The voice continued, "Half-breed. You don't have any powers. Come to Luisa, that's the best you can do. She told you where to look for her."

"October, what is it?"

"Nothing." And just like that I had a flash, a spark that went off in my brain. I knew where Luisa was. I knew it. I should have known it all along. "I'm leaving now. I am an ordinary teenager. When I turn eighteen I will still be an ordinary human. And I like it that way. So too bad. All you fairies and trolls will just have to govern your petty, backwards, prejudiced selves by yourself. Good luck with that."

"But I—"

"I forbid you to follow me." I decided to use the princess thing one time. "I never want to hear about any of this again. I'm going back to my completely normal life as a plain old high school senior."

The surprise was he obeyed me. He stayed right where he was as I—regally I hoped—strode out of the restaurant.

Outside, I took a deep breath. The sky was a dark ultramarine. Stars were visible, not a usual occurrence in Los Angeles. Were they out for me? Like the fireflies? Every little girl dreams of discovering she is a princess. I was no exception when I was five or six, but that was a long time ago. At that moment thinking about it made my head hurt. And my heart. I was not who I seemed, but neither was Walker.

Then Oberon came running out of the restaurant barking like crazy.

11.

"Watch out! Danger! Danger! Danger!" Oberon barked and growled and his hair stood up in a line down his back. "Slobber over there!"

I saw it slinking behind the parked cars across the street. I heard a crow caw and another crow answer.

"What do I do?" I asked the dog.

Oberon took off after the slobber. A bus was heading my way. I started running to the bus stop.

"Princess!" Walker ran out of the restaurant. A crow swooped over my head.

I looked over my shoulder. A slobber leapt down from the roof onto Walker. It pulled him to the ground and sat on him, pummeling his head and face. I hesitated. The bus had almost arrived. Mr. Bob rushed out with his tray and wacked at the slobber. The tray was not a very effective weapon. Walker was getting his ass kicked. The creature was twice his size and a hundred times nastier.

"Use your powers!" I yelled at him. "Fly away."

"I won't leave you."

"I'm getting on the bus."

A crow swooped down to me and landed on my shoulder. I writhed and jumped, trying to shake it off, but it held on and pecked at my head and neck. Out of nowhere, Oberon leapt up and grabbed the crow in his jaws. Blood squirted all over me as the crow exploded under his teeth. It was gross, but the other crows fell back.

"Go help Walker!"

Oberon ran to his master and leapt at the slobber. And then a slobber grabbed me from behind. I wriggled around and tried to push its face—or where a face should be—away. It was slimy like one of those sticky, stretchy wall-walker toys. Gross, but I tried to find its eyes with my fingers just as I'd been taught in self-defense class. The whole time I was thinking, "stop it" and "let me go" and "I hate you," not on purpose, but because naturally that's what I was thinking. What I didn't realize was that each time I thought, "let me go" I was growing stronger and larger. "Go away!" I finally shouted and to my shock the creature whimpered and disintegrated into a lot of unconnected trash.

I couldn't believe I had done that.

I wanted to try again. I ran to the slobber on top of Walker, put my hands around its throat and demanded it leave too. "Go away!" It crumbled into junk.

Walker lay on his back staring up at me. "Your eyes just turned this wicked shade of green. You got bigger."

"I couldn't."

"You did," he assured me, wheezing and struggling to get up.

Oberon barked. More slobbers were coming down the street. I had to lead them away from Walker and Mr. Bob and Oberon. "Hey!" I shouted to the slobbers. "Here I am! Over here!"

Walker cried out, but the slobbers turned away from him and Mr. Bob and galumphed after me. They were fast. They were catching up. Walker ran after them. I heard him yell, "Transplant! Think of home. Transplant!"

He was crazy. I couldn't do that. Not by myself. I was too scared. But the bus was stopped blocks behind me at a red light. The slobbers were getting closer. I looked for a blank wall and saw the side of a Chinese market with a painted picture of a smiling child holding a bowl of ramen. He looked a lot like Green and he seemed to beckon me. He wasn't moving exactly, but his eyes were telling me "this way."

I hesitated.

"Do it!" Walker shouted.

A hipster couple in skinny jeans, flannel shirts, and matching fedoras, were walking into Chinatown under the beautiful dragon arches.

"Now!" I heard Walker's desperation.

I ran right across the hipsters' path, the slobbers on my trail, as fast as I could toward the painting. "You can do it," the kid in the painting seemed to be saying. "Right here." The hipsters stopped to stare. I was sorry to upset them but I shut my eyes and ran as fast as I could and smack into the wall. And through it. And into the thick, warm sand again. The third time really is the charm—I knew to keep my mouth shut and my arms still and just go with it.

Something was dead. I smelled the sweet, pungent odor of decomposing flesh. I gagged and tasted regurgitated tofu. I rolled over, opened my eyes and stared right into the half-eaten eyeballs of the dead cat in my side yard.

I squealed and sat up, scrambling away from it. I was home, but I had landed in the worst possible spot. That cat was swollen with maggots. I wondered why Dad hadn't buried it or thrown it away or something. It was right under his favorite birdhouse. I looked up at my bedroom window. The screen was lying on the porch roof. I really had climbed out that window, but I didn't think I could climb back in.

Or maybe I could. I was a princess after all. I stood. I bent my knees and jumped up and to my complete surprise, easily grabbed the tree branch. Just a few hours earlier it had seemed so high. Like a gymnast I swung myself up to standing on the branch and with perfect balance walked to the end and gracefully leapt to the roof. I was stronger. I was more agile and as I looked down I realized being high up didn't bother me at all. I climbed in my window and peeled off my blood soaked clothes as quickly as I could. I found my jeans and a clean black T-shirt in my drawer. Halfway through getting dressed, I realized I'd forgotten to turn on my light. I could see perfectly well in the dark. Maybe my troll side was finally surfacing. Strength, agility, able to see in the dark. I wondered if I would be more troll than fairy, if anything else about me would change, how I would end up, but I pushed the thoughts away. I had to go. I had a plan. I would sneak out again and take the car to where I was sure Luisa was hiding. She was obviously part of this. Maybe Walker could have told me who or what Luisa was, but it didn't matter. She was a friend. She'd been in school with me for the past four years. She wasn't like Walker or Trevor—she didn't like me just because I was about to be a queen. She was really, truly a friend. And if she were my friend, then the slobbers and the crows would be after her too.

"Exactly," the voice in my head said. "Now you're getting it."

I was finally making my conscience happy. I put my hair—it felt longer and thicker—into a quick ponytail. So much to think about and so much I didn't know. I have to admit it was not an unusual feeling for me. Too often I learned only what I needed to learn—like for a test—but no more than the required information, so the peripheral edges were always fuzzy. I could recite the facts, but I had no context. For example, I knew WW I had begun in Austria with the assassination of Archduke Franz Ferdinand and I knew he was in line for the throne of both Austria and Hungary. I didn't know who killed him and why. Which suddenly sounded very familiar: I was heir to two kingdoms and somebody was after me but I didn't know who or why. I only knew I didn't want to end up dead like the Archduke and I didn't want to start World War III.

I opened the closet to get my hoodie and caught a glimpse of myself in the full-length mirror. What was going on? My jeans were like capris, my T-shirt showed an inch of stomach. I stopped and looked, really looked. I was a lot taller and slimmer and my hair was thick with loose curls I had never had before. It was just after midnight. In twenty-four hours—less!—I would be eighteen. I was changing, I could feel it all over—not an itch, but a tightening as if I'd been swimming in the ocean and the salt water was drying on my skin.

There was no sound from downstairs. My dad was probably in his birdhouse room. I could skip climbing out the window. I carried my Converse and tiptoed down the stairs. The living room, the whole house, was dark. I switched on the lamp by the couch and practically peed in my pants. My dad sat there.

"Dad?"

His eyes were open, but he wasn't looking at anything.

"Dad!"

His eyes shifted up toward me vaguely and went back to staring at nothing.

"Are you all right?" I turned on another light. He was thinner. Much thinner. Thinner by 100 pounds than he had been that morning when I left for school. Thinner than when I got home from school. But he looked terrible. He sagged all over as if he was a balloon that had collapsed, as if he'd had all the air sucked out of him. His face was a deathly shade of gray and his blue eyes were like dark holes in his head.

"What happened?" I knew it was Madame Gold. "What did she do to you?"

I shook him. He barely responded. I hugged him. He didn't hug me back. I ran to the kitchen, retrieved the cookies from their hiding place and brought him the entire bag. He was unin-terested. Then a single tear rolled out of his left eye and down his cheek. He looked up at me again and I saw that he was trying, trying hard to tell me something. She'd given him a stroke or a brain aneurism or something.

"Dad. Say something," I got right in his face. "I'm calling Mom."

I took out my phone and called her cellphone. Straight to voice mail. I texted her, "Dad Emergency."

"I'm calling an ambulance." Dad didn't look like a fairy prince, he looked like a zombie and I was not ready to add zom-bies to the crazy day I'd already had. I thought of calling Walker until I remembered how dismissive he was of my parents and their choice to get married. I dialed 9-1-1.

"I need an ambulance," I said into the phone. "My father's had a stroke or something." I gave the dispatcher my address. I explained my father's condition. Her voice was calm and normal as she said the ambulance was on its way.

I sat down beside him and held his hand. My phone chimed, a text had come in. "Must be Mom," I said to him. "Don't worry."

But when I looked at my screen it was from Luisa.

"L.A. River, under the Los Feliz Bridge."

And immediately she sent another text. "Plz. I need you."

She was exactly where I thought she would be: the LA River. Her favorite place. Now I had to help her and for some dumb reason I was sure I could. I texted, "Coming."

She texted right back, "Hurry."

I knelt down in front of my dad. "I have to go. Luisa is in trouble."

Dad groaned.

"The ambulance is on its way," I told him. "I'll leave the front door open." I ran around the living room turning on every light.

"I have to go."

As frozen as he was, he seemed agitated; I could see him panting, his chest moving up and down.

"It's okay. I know about the trolls and the fairies and you and mom. I know who I am."

His eyes widened and then he slumped and sagged even more than he already was. His head fell forward.

"Don't worry, Dad. I'm strong. A lot stronger than I used to be. And I'm quick and I know how to transplant. I'll be fine."

I could tell he didn't want me to go but I had to. As I drove away, I heard sirens getting closer. The doctors would take care of him. I sent another text to my mom, illegal as it was to text and drive, telling her Dad was at the hospital.

I got a chill down my spine as I zipped through my quiet neighborhood so I hit the door lock button. I kept my eyes peeled for slobbers or crows. Nothing was what it seemed and bad things were happening and I couldn't help but wonder how Madame Gold fit in. She wasn't a troll and she wasn't a fairy. What was she?

The Los Feliz Bridge wasn't far. Luisa had said the LA River was where she went to get away. That was the flash of insight I'd had. That's how I'd known that's where she was—even before I got her text. I was different and it wasn't only my appearance. Yes, my hair was thicker and my eyes looked enormous. I hadn't moved the seat up in my dad's car because I didn't need to. But I was different inside too. I knew things and I trusted what I knew. That was what was really different—I trusted myself. I knew I could help Luisa and I knew Walker was wrong about trolls and fairies intermingling. I was the living proof that it could work out just fine.

And I was starving. Had I really eaten plates of tofu, spinach, noodles plus two egg rolls? It had barely been an hour and

I was ravenous. It wasn't just because of the old saying about Chinese food; it had to be because I was growing so fast. Had to be. I hoped I wasn't going to be the second obese fairy.

I didn't take the freeway because I wanted to stay around normal people. At least I thought they were normal. I stopped at a red light and looked over in the car next to me. The driver was hunched over the wheel. He had an enormous hooked nose and ridiculously long fingers. And he was a lime green color. Across the street, a girl was laughing high and musically as she came out of a restaurant. She was stunning, black with silver hair and graceful, tall and thin. Her friends came out after her and they all looked like the loveliest Disney kind of fairies: shiny, slim, and fluttery for lack of a better word wearing skin tight clothing and gauzy scarves. They were only missing their wings. The homeless guy on the corner looked like he was talking and gesturing to himself, but that night I could see little creatures buzzing and dive-bombing around his head. There was a woman with an earpiece who seemed to be talking on her cell phone but she was really talking to an elf sitting on her shoulder. I no longer thought I was losing my mind. For the first time I was seeing the world as it really was.

My phone pinged. I hoped it was my mother. And it was. "Go home," she texted. "I'll meet you there. I'm on my way."

It was tempting. Maybe I could go home and she would tell me what to do or come with me or recommend I call the police. But I didn't really want her to do any of those things. I wanted to help Luisa all by myself. I wanted to test my new self. Stronger, taller, smarter, and more confident. For once I wanted to be special, more than average or ordinary. For once I wanted to be extraordinary.

"Yes," the voice said. "Ignore your mother."

I turned my phone to silent. The really stupid thing is, I was only thinking about myself, about what I might be able to do. I never thought about what kind of trouble Luisa could be in. Slobbers and crows had definitely tried to hurt me, but I didn't think about something dangerous or deadly being with her. It wasn't very smart to just go running to the L.A. River, a big cement trough that was home to gangs and taggers and people hiding from the world. I could have called the cops to meet me there. I could have asked Walker, or at least Oberon, to come with me. But that is all stuff I'm thinking now. Then I wasn't thinking about anything but getting there and saving the day.

I parked in the parking lot of a restaurant right near the Los Feliz Bridge. It was as close as I could get in the car. I walked toward the chain link fence and the gate leading down to the bike path. A family came out of the restaurant and walked to their car. The Dad was carrying a sleepy little boy who raised his head and pointed at me.

"Look," he said. "A fairy."

I was stunned. What did he see? I was in my jeans and hoodie. Before his parents turned around, I darted through the gate and disappeared into the dark.

12.

I walked down the gravel path leading under the bridge. Streetlights from the road above made the discarded soda cans and shards of broken glass glitter almost like Christmas lights. Or fireflies. But not. There were long grasses and scraggly bushes throwing spooky shadows along one side. On the other there was a steep cement retaining wall and a sheer drop to the river. Some gang had tagged the wall with graffiti, but I couldn't decipher the elaborate script. I called Luisa's name as softly as I could.

"Luisa?"

I was glad that crows were diurnal and usually slept at night. Slobbers I wasn't so sure about. Gang members and psycho murderers were out at all times. I listened and held my breath as I walked. I stayed on my toes, ready to run. It was darker under the bridge but it didn't take long for my new troll eyes to adjust. I turned in a circle. It seemed a very odd place for Luisa to be hanging out for a few days. It was eerie, almost claustrophobic with the sharp drop to the river on one side and the bushes encroaching on the other. I felt both totally alone and as if I was being carefully observed. Plus the water in the river was smelly and there was no place to sit. Luisa might have found this spot relaxing, but I did not.

Across the river in the opposite retaining wall I saw a round portal with the door open. The round portal-like openings appeared intermittently along the river walls—I'd noticed them ages before on a bird watching trip with my dad—but always with the heavy iron door shut. They were circular like some kind of big pipe and I assumed they were conduits for when it rained and the river threatened to overflow. I was about to head back to the car when a light blinked on and quickly off deep inside that open portal. I froze, held my breath. It happened again. A yellow flickering light, not the blue of a flashlight, but more like a flame. A cigarette lighter? I had no way of knowing it if was Luisa or some mass murderer.

The voice in my head spoke. "Luisa needs you."

Anybody could be through that door. And I wasn't looking forward to climbing down the cement wall on this side and fording the river and struggling up the other side. Plus I was worried about my dad. I could head right to the hospital and ask my mom what to do. Besides, if Luisa was sending me signals with a lighter then how much trouble could she be in? I could just text her. Tell her to cut it out and come home.

"Trust yourself." The voice again. I hadn't asked Walker if this loud, combative inner voice was a fairy thing or a troll thing.

And then, to seal the deal, a text from Luisa. "Help!"

"Okay," I said out loud. "I'm coming."

I climbed over the embankment, crouched down onto my butt, and slid down the retaining wall. It was gritty and when I put my hands down to slow my speed, little rocks stuck in my palms. The stink of the water got stronger the closer I got—not unlike Enoki's odor, ha ha ha—and I could see trash, an old tire, some boards. The good news was I could use those as stepping-stones across the murky water.

I almost lost my balance on the first board. It wobbled and I windmilled my arms to keep upright. I looked down into the water. I saw things that were not fish and not snakes and not normal. Lizard-like, but with flippers and teeth. Perfect, I thought. More weird creatures. No matter what, I could not fall into that water. I took a deep breath and tried to think fairy thoughts, like I was light, lighter than air. Even if I couldn't fly, I could tread so lightly on these boards they wouldn't move or sway. I took two quick steps to the old tire. It seemed to work. I hopped to a rock. I jumped to the next and gasped. I'd almost landed on one of those lizardy creatures. Its mouth was open as if waiting for my ankle.

"Watch out," I thought.

"Me?" it said. "You're the one skipping all over the place."

Before I had time to process that I had understood what it said, it slid back into the water. I sprang from rock to old shopping cart to a board across the remaining strip of river to the slope on the other side. I rested for a moment. Cement had never felt so good under my feet, so solid and dry. I looked up. The incline wasn't as steep as the other side and the open portal was not far above me. I half-crawled up the wall using my hands while trying to be as quiet as possible. As I got closer I could feel the cold, damp air spilling out and I smelled rotten eggs. Sulfur. If I wasn't walking into a den of psycho rapists, I would probably be asphyxiated by lethal chemicals.

I stepped into the dark. "Luisa?" I peered into the blackness. So much for troll vision, I couldn't see an inch in front of me. The dark was like a blanket absorbing all sight. Where was the flickering light?

My phone chimed. Automatically I looked down and the light from the screen blinded me. I blinked frantically, rubbed my eyes, stumbled, and someone grabbed my arm. Someone strong. I smelled dirty water and mold. Enoki.

She flicked on her lighter and I saw her grinning.

"I knew it was you by the smell," I said.

"I knew you'd come to find Luisa." She laughed. "We both knew it."

"You and Trevor?"

"Trevor is an idiot. He still thinks we can do this his way. We know better."

She grabbed my cellphone from my hand and threw it into the river. She yanked me deeper into the tunnel. I resisted, but she was much stronger and her hand on my arm squeezed until it hurt. She flipped off her lighter and it was as if a thick black hood had fallen over my face. I wished Trevor was there, or Walker, or even little Green. Someone who would be on my side.

I tried my royal blood. "I'm your Queen," I said as majestically as possible.

"Not for twenty-two more hours," she said. "Right now you're nothing. Who knows what will happen when you really turn eighteen. Probably nothing. Nothing."

The way she said 'nothing' was like a stone hitting my chest.

"You know nothing." She went on. "You're the queen of nothing. You can do nothing. You are nothing."

Each time she said it was like another hit. It was hard to breathe. I was upset—over nothing. Stop it, I told myself. Nothing is fine. I had been happy being nothing. I had my parents. I had college to look forward to and studying the animals I loved. In college I always hoped I would make friends with people like me. But as Enoki pulled me down lower and lower, darker and darker, I realized there was no one like me. I was the only one and I would never have a friend.

"Where is Luisa?"

She smiled and her teeth were pointier than Trevor's. "Don't think she cares about you. No one cares about you."

It made sense that Luisa wasn't my friend. She was in on this, just a way to get me here, into this dungeon leading under the earth.

"Walker!" I shouted his name.

"You shot him down pretty hard. He's not coming to save you."

"Walker!" I screamed again.

"You were just a job and his job is done. He doesn't care about you anymore."

I couldn't listen to her. I had to fight back. I thought if I could get out of her grip I could run into one of the walls and transplant. But she held on tight and I couldn't see anything and the tunnel was getting shorter and narrower. I bumped my head and my shoulders against the rough, bumpy walls. I had to stoop. There was no room to get the running start I needed. I wanted my mom. I should have listened to her. I should have gone home and explained what was happening and asked for her help. My poor mom. Her husband was a zombie and her daughter was nothing.

If I could only see. I thought about how we take light for granted, how we flick on a switch and the lights go on and in the morning the sun always comes up. We're so rarely in the dark unless it's by choice, at the movies or to sleep at night. I thought about the fireflies, the beautiful, twinkling fireflies in the empty lot near my house. I was happy I'd seen them once in my life before I died. Because I was sure Enoki was taking me somewhere deep beneath the earth to kill me. I tried to concentrate on the amazing fireflies instead of what Enoki had in store.

I heard a gentle swoosh and there they were. A thousand fireflies all around us. They blinked and sparkled and twinkled. I felt instantly better. Their light wasn't bright but it was enough for me to see the walls of the tunnel and the path under my feet. And they flustered Enoki. She swatted at them with her free hand, but they flew in her face and in her hair and down the collar of her shirt. She hopped and wiggled. She let go of me to flap both arms at them and that was my chance. I took off. I couldn't get around her to go back up to the river, so I ran down. Some of the fireflies flew with me to light my way. "Thank you," I whispered. They were incredible in so many ways. "Thank you." They brushed my face with their soft wings.

I scurried around a bend in the tunnel and saw a dim light ahead. Maybe it was another way out. Maybe a big enough space so I could transplant. I ran as fast as I could in my hunched position. And then I was free. The tunnel spilled into open air and room to stand up. I was outdoors. A light drizzle was falling and the rotten egg smell was worse and the scene before me was not pretty.

I stood on the edge of a forest of enormous trees like the giant redwoods in Big Sur and Yosemite, but these trees were dying. The ground at the bottom of each one was dug up and the roots were exposed. The trees leaned, close to falling over without the earth holding onto them. They were huge, and a golden color instead of reddish with no branches until way up high, but their leaves had turned brown and there were streaks of gray up and down the trunks. They must've been beautiful once, but on that dark, cloudy day they were sad and ominous. I looked back to the tunnel opening, a small black hole in a boulder. Enoki couldn't be too far behind. I ducked around the far side of a tree. A small wooden plaque with a picture of a hyacinth was fastened to the tree. I looked up and through the leaves I could just see the bottom of a platform or tree house of some kind. I ran to the next tree, and the next and the next. There were plaques with pictures of flowers or pinecones or leaves on every one—like house numbers—and tree houses up above, but they all looked old and faded and frayed. The wood was cracked, a lot were broken apart. I remembered Walker telling me that fairies lived in the forest canopy, way up high, but he said it was bright and colorful and this looked so dismal. I couldn't hear a voice or a sound. No one was living here. The sulfur smell was definitely coming from somewhere nearby. I knew this couldn't be the Fairy Canopy. Walker had said it was exquisite. There were no flowers and everything was gray. Strangest of all, there were no birds. No squirrels or even insects. Empty. Post-apocalyptic.

I heard Enoki yelling and pounding down the tunnel toward me. She had gotten past the fireflies. Quickly I ran to another tree, further away. At my feet was a channel of yellow water. It gurgled and bubbled and when a bubble popped the sulfur smell made me gag. The trench was manmade—or fairy made or troll made—but it was hard to imagine fairies dumping toxic sewage.

I took a quick glance around the tree. Stupid Enoki was looking the wrong way. She ran off in the opposite direction. "I'll find you. I will!"

I almost laughed. I ran from tree to tree, light on my feet, my sneakers making no sound at all on the dug up earth and fallen leaves. The trees weren't sick. Someone had done this to them. In the distance I heard a powerful machine attempting to start. It revved and died. Revved and died.

I went from tree to tree, hiding and peeking out, as I moved toward the noise. I saw a yellow backhoe, a digging machine, through the healthier trees ahead of me. The machine started and roared so loudly I wanted to cover my ears. The big shovel in the front lifted and fell into the earth below one of the giant trees making it shudder as if it had been punched. It dug and I saw roots torn up in its claws. Was that a fairy driving? It was so gray and slumped that it couldn't be a fairy. I circled away from the backhoe and saw a dilapidated industrial warehouse. It was made of corrugated steel, rusty and falling apart. Out the end I saw the disgusting yellow sludge pouring into the trench.

I heard a voice yelling something that sounded a lot like "timber!" There was a loud creaking and I looked up to see one of the gray and dying tall trees rocking back and forth. As it rocked forward I saw a little house, a fairy home, plummet from the top spilling beds and dishes and chairs that broke into a thousand pieces against the forest floor. Poor fairies. The tree hit the ground with such a tremendous crash the earth shook. Then I saw movement through the trees, lots of people swarming over the fallen giant tree. I crept closer and closer.

Slobbers formed a line with their backs to me. They guarded prisoners who were falling on their knees to dig with their hands in the ground turned up by the fallen tree. Most of the prisoners were tall and impossibly thin, but like the one driving the backhoe, they were all as gray as the coveralls they wore. I couldn't believe these unhappy beings were fairies. One of them turned away and threw up. I saw tears—she didn't want to dig. She didn't want to hurt these trees. A slobber slapped her hard and knocked her down. It stood over her threateningly. Her neighbor helped her up and she went back to scrabbling in the dirt. When they found something—I couldn't see what—they dumped it in a bag they each wore over their shoulders. None of the skinny prisoners seemed to be finding much. They weren't strong and whatever they were looking for was gross—more than one found whatever it was and gagged.

A slobber sent a prisoner into the woods to tag the next tree. He trudged in my direction, thick ribbons of black material in his hands. He checked the wind, the path the tree might fall, and to my surprise flew up into the canopy. It looked like he was checking the little house to make sure it was empty. It must've been. He came down and tied one of the black strips around the trunk. Like a mourner's funeral armband. He slumped further and further into the woods, marking tree after tree. I snuck over to him and let him see me. He stared, and then pretended to keep working.

I whispered to him, "What are you doing?"

"Searching for mushrooms," the fairy answered.

"Why?"

"For her." He wouldn't say her name.

"Why?"

He shrugged. "It's killing the trees and without these trees, we fairies will die. We're already weakened because so many have come down."

I heard a woman, Madame Gold, shout, "Work harder, my lovelies!"

The fairy jumped as if struck. He hurried on to the next tree.

Madame Gold. In her flowing dress of rusty orange and red she was the only spot of color in the dreariness. She looked like an enormous flame burning on top of the platform where she stood. A dangerous, undulating, wicked flame. There were crows perched on the railings beside her, crows circling above. They did her bidding, swooping down and pecking at prisoners who weren't working hard enough.

Madame Gold, I thought, of course.

Of course it was she who had sent the crows to attack me. She who had sent the slobbers. But what could she want from me? She walked to the edge of the platform and I gasped. Behind her my dad sat on a stool drooping and thin and not moving. She truly had zombie-fied him. Had the ambulance ever really come? I knew she was evil. I had known it from the beginning. I looked at my hands, red welts were appearing. The back of my neck felt hot and tight. I touched my cheek and felt a rash there too.

The voice in my head said, "October. Come out now. I know you're there. "

The voice in my head, the voice I'd been hearing all along, was Madame Gold's.

13.

I leapt out from behind the rock so angry I didn't even think to be frightened of the crows or the slobbers or her. "What have you done to my dad? What are you doing to these people?"

"They're not people," she said. "You know that."

She was perfectly calm, her voice as soft and low and controlled as when I met her. It set my teeth on edge. My stomach threatened to return all the Chinese food I'd eaten.

"Dad!" I shouted. I ran toward the platform. Crows launched themselves toward me, ready to attack. I pointed at them. "Stop it!" They stopped in mid air. I pointed at the slobber running toward me. "Go away!" It disintegrated. The noise of the saw stopped and it was quiet. The prisoners were watching me. I put my hands on my hips and stared at Madame Gold. "Give me my father. Now."

"You are not Queen yet," she said. "For now, I am in command of this place. I have much work to do in the next nineteen hours."

She clapped her hands. The giant backhoe started up again and another tree rocked back and forth. The prisoners were forced back to work. I made another slobber and another disintegrate, but Madame Gold was creating new ones as quickly as I was destroying the old. I had to make her go away. That was the only way to save my dad and stop this destruction.

I jumped, almost flew, right over the fallen tree and ran to the platform. Even though I wasn't eighteen yet, my abilities seemed to be expanding. She backed up as I clambered to the top. My father didn't even look at me. I advanced toward Madame Gold. I was going to kill her with my bare hands. She wasn't a fairy. She wasn't a troll. And I was both.

I heard her voice in my head. "Don't bother. It won't work."

"Shut up," I said. I leapt at her and grabbed her neck. I squeezed but she only smiled at me, flapped her stupid sleeves and somehow twisted away, out of my hands. I came after her again, but at the last minute she stepped to one side and I almost fell off the platform. Again I ran at her and she pushed me—with one hand—and I went flying back and crashed into my dad. I looked up at him.

"Help me."

I could see him struggling, see that he wanted to, but he was trapped. She had locked him in this new skinny body. His hair was curling, the angles in his face had returned, but his eyes weren't blue anymore, they were a dark, murky gray.

I stood. "I am almost Queen. My powers are growing stronger."

"Your powers?" She laughed, a terrible screeching sound like a dog in pain. "We'd know by now if you had any real power. You can't fight me."

"I will be powerful. I had a powerful itch."

"Yours was nothing compared to mine." And she laughed again.

She had experienced the itch? But she couldn't be a fairy. If she was, why did she want to destroy the trees? They had to be as necessary to her as to any other fairy. I couldn't understand what made her different, what made her so big and strong and beautiful and red-haired, green-eyed. She was right though; I couldn't fight her. Not physically. I looked down at the poor prisoner fairies.

"Where's Luisa?" I said to her. "What have you done to my dad?"

"Once your mother is gone—any moment now—your father will marry me and I will be officially queen. I just have to get you out of the way—before you turn eighteen."

She came toward me slowly, a horrible smile on her face. For a moment her straight white teeth looked pointy like Enoki's, pointier than Trevor's. Just for a moment.

She waved her sleeves back and forth slowly as she spoke. "So young," she said. "So special. They say you're the only one of your kind." She nodded. "We'll stuff you and put you in a museum."

I couldn't move. She had frozen me like Dad. "St…stop it." She kept coming. Help, I thought it as hard as I could. Like the fireflies, someone had to come help me.

Bam! That someone leapt onto the platform and scooped me up in his arms. Trevor! He held me tight and jumped, landed on his feet and looked back up at Madame Gold.

"Trevor!" she said. "You will pay for this. We had a deal."

"Screw the deal." He took off with me still frozen in his arms.

"After him!" Madame Gold commanded.

The slobbers and the crows came after us. Away from her, my trance broke and I could move again. I disintegrated as many slobbers as I could. I commanded the crows to leave us alone. I looked over his shoulder. I could stop the crows—they listened to me more than her—but more and more slobbers were coming from all directions.

"Can you fly?" I asked him.

"You mean like a fairy? Are you crazy? We don't need to fly. Hang on."

I put my arms around his neck and he took off, jumping,

leaping, turning somersaults in the air and literally bounding off the trees. It was exhilarating. It was great. I hoped that a minute after midnight I would be able to do it too. We easily left the lumbering slobbers behind.

We continued more slowly through the stumps and then the remaining tall trees until Trevor jumped down a hole under a bush. It didn't look big enough for him with me in his arms, but inside it opened up into a smooth walled tunnel. It was like a rabbit warren with multiple passageways and burrow rooms. We were going quickly, but I saw beds and rugs, tables and chairs, like a troll apartment building. I tried to ask him about it, but he wasn't stopping and too soon we went up and up a darker, empty shaft until we were back in the real world right by the parking lot. The moon was out and the bushes that had seemed so forbidding glittered in the silver light. It had been daylight in the Fairy Glen. Time was all screwed up. How long until I was eighteen? Without my phone, I had no idea.

Trevor set me down gently.

"Thank you. Madame Gold is going to be furious with you."

"You're my Queen. I had to save you."

He took my arm and tried to drag me toward the gate into the parking lot. I was tired of people dragging me around.

"Stop," I commanded. And he did. "I know what you are, Trevor. I know what your sister is and why her name is Enoki. I know who I am."

"Did Walker tell you?" he asked. I nodded. "He could lose his job over that."

"Doesn't look like he has a job anymore—thanks to Madame Gold."

He sighed and then he bowed, actually bowed to me. "Your Lowness."

"Not yet. I don't think. Not until midnight. But then I will be Queen and I want—I demand—to know what's going on. First, what is Madame Gold doing in the forest?"

"She's harvesting mushrooms. She needs them. For something. Some plan."

"Why not use trolls? Trolls love mushrooms."

"But trolls might steal them or eat them. They're hard to resist. They're very special mushrooms."

It made no sense to me. None of it did. "Okay. Second, what kind of deal did the two of you have?"

He kicked a rock gently and it landed all the way across the river. "No one had even heard of her until a month ago. All the trolls started talking about your birthday and wondering if you'd come back and rule the fairies or us. And then our King—your grandfather—died and the Fairy King—your other grandfather—died too and she just showed up and took over. She made Enoki her ally. She tried to make me…" He stopped and sighed. "You see how powerful she is."

"But what does she want from you?"

"She wants to be Queen."

"How can you make her Queen?"

"I'm next in line after you. My father was your grandfather's third cousin."

I understood. If she got rid of me, then he would be King. The deal was he'd have to marry her. "But what about my dad? She said she was going to marry him."

"Marry him first." He sighed again. "She'd be Queen of the Fairy Canopy. Then—when he's gone—she'd marry me. She'd be Queen of both kingdoms."

I knew what 'gone' meant. Like my mother would be 'gone.' She was one sick hypnotist and there were so many things I didn't understand. "She hates the fairies." That was obvious. "Why does she want to be their queen?"

"She doesn't like the trolls much either."

So what was she? And what did she really want? Because being Queen was not going to make her happy, of that much I was sure.

"You're in trouble," I said to Trevor. "Saving me was a bad idea."

"I had to. I don't care about her. I had to save you."

He held my shoulders and looked into my eyes. His hands were large and strong and his eyes were warm. He was so easy, so normal—for being a troll. My breath caught and I rose onto my tiptoes even though he was not much taller. We were eye to eye, nose to nose, practically lips to lips with just the thinnest column of air between us. Nothing really keeping us apart. Maybe he didn't like fairies much, but he liked me and he knew what I was. Walker had said it was only because he wanted to be King, but it didn't feel like that. Not the way he was looking at me. Not the way he was making me look at him. After all, he could have let Madame Gold kill me and then he would be King. His arms went around me. His eyes closed. I had wanted to kiss Walker—before I knew his true personality. Was it terrible that now I wanted to kiss Trevor?

We kissed. My first official kiss. It finally happened only hours before I turned eighteen. Other girls tried to lose their virginity before they went to college. I was happy to be kissed. And it was a good kiss. A warm and friendly kiss. I'd read first kisses were often awkward. You don't know which way to tilt your head, where to fit your nose, how open your mouth should be, tongue or no tongue. No tongue. It was nice. I didn't feel much more than that, but when we opened our eyes and looked at each other, I was ready to try again. I closed my eyes and leaned toward him.

"October," he said more seriously than I'd ever heard him.

I opened my eyes. He held both my hands.

"October," he said again. "Will you marry me?"

"Are you crazy?"

"You kissed me."

"I was just trying it out. One kiss. Are you some kind of fundamentalist?"

He looked confused. "You're almost eighteen. I've been eighteen for a while. It's time."

He hadn't mentioned love once. "And you don't mind that I'm half fairy?"

"It doesn't thrill me. But it's okay. It makes you...unusual. As long as our children are brought up to be trolls. As long as you stay in Trolldom and we rule together."

Walker was right. Trevor wanted to marry me so he could be king. "What makes you any different than Madame Gold?" I shoved him away. "You want to marry me just because you want to be king?"

Trevor looked at me sharply and I saw a hunger, lust in him, but it wasn't for me.

"I will be King," he said. "I'm next in line. I am a cousin."

"I don't want to get married."

"Madame Gold wants to kill your whole family. Marry me and we can stop that. I don't want your family to die. I'd rather be King with you."

He looked at me proudly, as if he was some superior being because he didn't want to kill me and my mother and father. He just wanted to marry me and make me miserable. Make us both miserable.

"I think you're nuts."

"I will be King. I've been preparing for it my whole life. Then I heard about you. That you existed. It's just lucky you're female so we can propagate."

"How lovely you make it sound. Is there anything about me you actually like?"

"I like your feet," he said looking down at my muddy shoes.

"I'm getting hair on my toes," I said. "Troll feet."

"But still fairy-sized," he said. "I've never seen feet so small."

They were pushing against my shoes, growing as we spoke. I wasn't sure how big they would eventually be. My legs and arms and hands, on the other hand, were longer and slimmer and way more sensitive. I put a finger on his arm and I could feel his blood moving through his veins.

"I have to go." I looked toward the parking lot. "I still haven't found Luisa."

"Too late," Trevor said. "She's…gone. Madame Gold knew she would get you to the portal to the Fairy Canopy. She was just a decoy." He shuddered all over, like a dog shaking off a bath. "Luisa was a fairy, but she'd been in the human world too long. Other than her Frisbee skills, she didn't have any powers." As if that made killing her okay. "Your grandfather hired her. She looked after you for years."

"What?" I heard the truth in his voice. My legs wouldn't hold me; I collapsed on the path. Luisa was dead. And it was because of me. Because Madame Gold didn't want me to be Queen. Poor Mrs. Flores. Poor, poor Luisa. It wasn't fair. I hated Madame Gold more than ever.

"We have to go. She's coming after you. Get up," he said. "Come on."

I struggled to my feet. Trevor lifted me easily and carried me to my car. He set me down and put his arms around me.

"I know a safe place."

I pushed him away. Nowhere in the world was safe anymore.

"I know this is a lot to take in," he said. His smile was sweet, his eyes the color of dark chocolate. "I do like you, October.

Something about you makes me want to take care of you. I never knew a fairy before, even part fairy. Everyone I know is just like me." His voice lifted, what he was saying was a revelation to him. "You can make me a better troll. We will be the best King and Queen ever. Trolldom will rule."

"But I'm not a troll," I said. "I'm not a fairy either."

"That's the thing." Trevor lifted my chin. "Nobody knows what you are. Maybe you will be the most amazing Queen ever."

My car keys were still in my pocket. My phone was gone, but I had my car. I had to find my mother. I had to tell her she was in danger. She had to tell me what to do to save my father, save the fairies, and the trolls.

"I don't want to be Queen," I said. "Why didn't Madame Gold just ask me? Why is this happening? I want to stay in the human world."

His eyes went cold. "You will be Queen. You must be. You were born a Queen. You will be one when you turn eighteen whether you want to or not. And you will take me with you."

"No! I'm going to college. I'm going to study animals. Now that I can understand them, I'll be a superstar. This is what I've planned for my whole life."

"But you didn't know this isn't your real life."

"This is my real life. You and Walker and Madame Gold and the rest are not for me. None of you. Out there." I pointed to the houses and buildings and all the humans in them. "Out there, people run governments and organize the world and do important work. I want my mom and dad and Luisa and the rest of my senior year. I want to go to prom and graduation. Nobody even believes in you anymore."

Trevor did not disagree. "That's why we need you. Our world is changing. Fairies and trolls are leaving our world to live in the human world. Why not? Humans don't believe in a little pixie dust. Parents give their kids money before the tooth fairy even has a chance. Even little children won't clap to keep Tinkerbell alive." He looked at me and his eyes were glittering coldly. "But you, as our new Queen, someone who has lived out there, can return us to glory. You can make us more modern. And with me beside you, we will secure our borders. No troll will leave to live in the human world. And nothing, not a goblin or a gnome and certainly no more fairies will get in."

"No, thank you."

"Our line will be pure."

"Except for me. And meanwhile Madame Gold will keep digging up mushrooms and enslaving fairies while we do nothing. I don't like you—any of you—very much." I opened my car door. "You killed Luisa for nothing."

"I didn't do it."

"It doesn't matter who actually did the deed. It was you and Madame Gold and your sister and Walker and all the other creatures who want to keep everything so pure."

"Trolls are good!" Trevor protested. "We protect the soil and the groundwater and the shrubs and the mushrooms."

"Goodbye."

"What?" he said.

"I command you to never bother me again."

"Wait a minute..."

"You know what? I do want to be Queen." His face lit up. "I want to be Queen just so you and Madame Gold are not." I got in my car and slammed the door shut.

"Where are you going?"

"Home," I said.

"That's the first place she'll look."

"I'm ready for her."

14. Two Hours Until My Birthday

The clock in the car said it was 9:47. Just a little more than two hours until my birthday. I pulled up in the driveway, glad to see lights on in the house. Mom was finally home. Together we would figure out how to save Dad and stop Madame Gold.

"Mom?" I ran up the porch steps and through the front door. "Mom?"

Oberon trotted out of the kitchen wagging his tail. Walker came out next. I sighed. The last person I wanted to see. "Where's my mom?"

"She's missing," he said.

"What do you mean?"

"She came home right after she got your text about your father. But then she went outside and disappeared. Trolls are good at that."

I ignored his disparaging tone. I wanted my mom—I wanted her badly. "Luisa's dead," I said. "They used her as a decoy to get me to the portal."

He nodded. He knew all about it.

"Madame Gold has your… kind, you know all the fairies, under her control. She's digging up your forest. Searching for some kind of mushroom."

He nodded again. He knew everything.

"We have to stop her," I said.

"That's easy." But his face looked anything but easy. "All we have to do is keep you safe until midnight and then you marry

Trevor. You and he will be King and Queen of both worlds."

"Trevor? Why would I marry him?"

"It's okay. I get it. He won. You kissed him." Walker's shoulders slumped. "Maybe you marrying him will make Madame Gold go away."

I was horrified he knew I'd kissed Trevor. But more importantly why did that mean that Trevor had won? Won what?

"It wasn't a competition," I said. "And I am not a prize."

"But you kissed him. You belong together now."

"What is it with you magical beings and one kiss? Most girls I know kiss a whole lot of guys and don't marry any of them."

"That's not why you kissed him?"

"No. I just… I just… wanted to see what it would be like."

"What was it like?"

"Oh Walker, none of your business, but it was fine."

He was quiet. "The earth didn't move?"

"It stayed absolutely still." I could see his relief. "How did you know I kissed him? How did you know I'd come home?"

"I always know where you are. Don't you feel our connection?"

I did. I didn't want to, but I did. I changed the subject. "I have to find my mom."

He didn't say anything.

"I have to find my mom, save my dad, and kill Madame Gold."

Walker looked shocked. "Fairies don't kill."

"Good thing I'm not really a fairy." I waited, but he didn't try to talk me out of it. "What is she?" I asked. "She said she had an itch. But she can't be a fairy."

"Not like any fairy I've ever seen."

"There's something she's hiding. I think she has a secret and secrets make people vulnerable." I was hungry again—always—

and started for the kitchen. "If we can figure it out, it might be a way to get to her."

"October." Walker's voice was low. "October. October, please. Look at me."

I turned to him and he looked so sad it worried me.

"I'm sorry," he said. "About before. I've been thinking about it and you're right. None of this would have happened if we had allowed Princess Russula and Prince Neomarica to stay together in our world. They would be Queen and King now. Madame Gold would have no power at all."

"That's true. None of this would've happened. But would you really be okay with a troll as your queen?"

"I'm trying. I am. I look at you and I see the best of both worlds." His voice was so quiet I had to lean in to hear him. "If you want to marry Trevor, I understand. I just want you to be happy."

He was very considerate and very ridiculous. "I'm not marrying anybody. I'm certainly not marrying Trevor." I told him the truth. "I'm sorry I kissed him."

"I thought it was different between us," Walker said. "I thought you felt it too."

I had felt it. I was still feeling it. When I was with him it was exactly right, like the banana pancakes my dad made me. Slightly exotic, mostly sweet, warm and delicious. But he had let me down. I couldn't be with someone who had such deep-rooted prejudices. He said he was trying, but I would have to wait and see.

I put my hand on his arm, just to comfort him. Touching him made my whole body glow. And before I knew it, he grabbed me and kissed me. From having never been kissed, I had kissed two guys in less than hour, but I didn't have a chance to feel like a slut. Walker's kiss was a real kiss. It was a perfect kiss. My first perfect kiss. An electric current started in my chest, swelled and radiated out to every part of my body. It made the backs of my knees tremble, the soles of my feet warm, and finally the ground seemed to vibrate beneath us. The earth really had moved. I never wanted it to end.

He broke away first. "I shouldn't have done that."

"Yes, you should have." I pulled him to me.

"No, I shouldn't. I can't. You can only be with royalty."

"Another of your stupid rules?" So much for all the changing he was supposedly doing. "Even the future King of England was allowed to marry a commoner. Besides, I thought I was the only royalty left. Other than Trevor."

He looked up, down, anywhere but at me. "There's a distant fairy nobleman."

"Noble-man?"

"He has no claim on the throne, but he's from an important family. I think he's still alive. By now he'd be close to 120 years old."

"Wow. That's so appealing." I stepped away from him. And another step. The further I got, the more my head cleared. "We have to go. We have a lot to do." I hurried into the den. "Enoki threw my phone in the river, but I bet my dad's is here somewhere. Just so you and I can stay in touch—in case we get separated."

"We should stay here."

"We have to stop Madame Gold."

"We should just stay here." Walker came to the doorway. "Lay low, stay safe for two hours until you're Queen."

I ignored him. The phone was on Dad's worktable next to his latest birdhouse project. I checked it was charged and quickly texted my mom. "It's me, not Dad. I know everything. Where are you?" I hit 'send'. I would go upstairs, get my backpack and take a few essentials this time, like a flashlight and some money and a knife or something.

Walker stopped me at the bottom of the stairs. "We have to stay," he said. "Oberon and I can protect you here."

I knew the look on Walker's face. I could feel his determination. He and Oberon would tie me to a chair if they thought it would keep me safe. Somehow I had to get rid of him. I wanted him with me, but I would find Madame Gold and save the day without him if I had to.

"Make me a sandwich?" I asked. "I command you to make me a sandwich."

He looked so completely flummoxed I had to laugh. No one had ever asked him that before.

"A sandwich?"

"Two slices of bread. Lettuce, tomato, cheese, mustard, no mayonnaise in between. Or maybe peanut butter and jelly. No. Make it cheese and avocado. I think there's some cream cheese. And raisins. That'd be good. Whole wheat. No, white. No, whole wheat." I was trying to confuse him. It was working. "Oberon can help you."

"Sandwich, sandwich, sandwich." If it was food then Oberon—typical dog—was excited.

"I think there's turkey for Oberon."

"Turkey! Come on, Walker. Come on!!!" Oberon dragged Walker into the kitchen.

My mom's keys were on the table by the front door. For a brief moment I debated waiting the remaining sixty-eight minutes until I was really, truly Queen, but I couldn't be sure it would help. Maybe officially turning eighteen would kill me. Maybe I'd lose my mind and become a babbling container of pudding. Walker had told me no one knew exactly what would happen. With my luck, it would all go bad. I needed to act now.

I picked up the keys and silently, like the good sneaky teenager I was, went out the front door.

It was chilly, but the stars were brilliant and there were a zillion of them. More than I had ever seen. The leaves in the trees and bushes rustled in the breeze. It sounded like whispering and giggling. In the distance I heard a pack of coyotes crying and howling just for the joy of it and I saw an owl swoop across the sky and a mouse scurry under the leaves. There was a lot of urban nature I was suddenly able to hear and see. Or had I just ignored it before? I opened my mom's car door and got in. I didn't close it, didn't want to make any sound, and I put the car in neutral and coasted out of the driveway. Then I turned the car on and drove. Drove as fast as I could. I looked in the rearview mirror surprised no one was chasing me. Asking Walker and Oberon to make me a sandwich really had them stumped.

All the lights were with me as I drove back to the L.A. River. Every red turned green as I approached. I remembered that had happened driving with Enoki and I wondered if it was part of being a troll. I was thinking more clearly and I was wide awake, but I was a little sick to my stomach, queasy and jittery like after too much coffee. Except I hadn't had any coffee. The skin on my hands on the steering wheel seemed to sparkle as I passed under the streetlights—like Walker's skin did, but not as much. I was not as pale as he was either. I checked my arms. I was a more ruddy, golden color. I'd never had a tan, never outside enough, but I looked tan now. Or something. Turning eighteen was only forty-two minutes away.

I got out in the same parking lot by the restaurant, now closed, and hurried through the gate to the trail by the river. I had my dad's cell in my pocket, thank goodness, but I'd never filled my backpack with those things I thought I might need. No flashlight, no sweatshirt, no knife. But it was fine—I didn't need any of them. I was perfectly warm. I could see fine. And if I actually had a knife, I knew I'd only end up cutting myself.

I came out from under the bridge and I stopped. The river was amazing. A full moon had risen. In the distance the buildings of the Los Angeles skyline were glittering against the night sky. The river reflected the moonlight in a thousand shining ripples. Reeds and cattails swayed in the soft breeze. This way, they seemed to call to me, come down and be with us. Madame Gold frightened me, but not this place. Not at all. I felt at peace with all the plants and the animals, birds, and fish, even with the scuzzy water on its journey to the Pacific Ocean. I knew what Luisa must have felt when she came here. It made my chest hurt to think she would never have that again.

A dog barked. I knew that bark. Oberon. "Over here," he was saying. "She's here."

Walker ran up to me out of breath, his face more pale than usual. "Don't ever do that to me again."

I felt safer having him with me, but I stepped back out of his reach. I didn't need his touch messing with my mind. "Took you long enough," I said.

"I have six different sandwiches in my car."

I laughed.

"We should have waited at your house." Walker chastised me.

I looked at my dad's phone. "I'll be Queen in thirty-seven minutes."

Oberon began to growl—and then bark his danger bark. Walker and I turned.

"Not soon enough," Walker said.

Out of the shadows from under the bridge strode Madame Gold in her long flowing dress. Her hair was long and wild and a lustrous red even in the dim light. She looked angry. A black panther slunk out of the dark to her side. It hissed at Oberon, then looked at me and growled. A panther. Where did that come from?

I could understand Oberon's barking, "Get out of here, Cat!" but I couldn't understand the panther, couldn't hear the words in its growling. I saw some images, but they didn't make sense. The freeway rushing by. A blanket in a cold, dark room. I got an odd feeling from it too, as if it weren't an animal at all, not even a dumb one like a crow. I could understand the crows—they just didn't say anything worth listening to.

Walker gave Madame Gold the smallest of bows. "We've been expecting you."

"Why are you bowing to her?" I said to him. "She's a monster."

"So are you," she said. "Half-breed. Neither nor."

"I don't want to hurt anybody."

"Didn't you say you wanted to kill me?" She nodded at the phone in my hand. "Too bad I have your father. And your mother has gone AWOL."

I was dizzy all of a sudden and stumbled a little. Blotches and big red welts covered my hands and arms.

"Not feeling well?"

Her smirk turned my fear into anger. "I'm glad I have an allergic reaction to you. It just proves how disgusting you are."

I held up my hands, willed the welts to be gone, and they were. I didn't know how long I could keep them that way, but it had the desired effect. Madame Gold frowned and took a step back.

"She's powerful," Walker said. "She's going to be very powerful."

"October?" Madame Gold recovered and gave her terrible laugh. "Oh Walker. You're so cute when you're funny."

How did she know him? It seemed she knew everything. Or Walker did. Or they both did.

"Come on, Miss Fetterhoff." When Madame Gold turned to me it was with all her previous confidence. "I said I want us to be friends."

Yeah, right.

"I'm impressed at how hard you're fighting this. We really are two peas in a pod, aren't we? We fight for what we want."

"I'm not a thing like you."

"More than you know. We really could be very good friends." She took a step closer. "I could learn to like you. Enoki on the other hand…"

That's when I saw Enoki standing behind her. She was seething. Her face was flushed red and her hands were balled into fists. Her lips curled back from her teeth. She wanted to rip me open and I wasn't sure why.

Then two slobbers came after her half carrying, half dragging Trevor. He was bound in thick rusty chains and one eye was swollen shut. His nose looked broken. Dried blood caked his shirt and pants.

"Not so pretty now," Madame Gold said. "Is he?"

"What did you do?"

"We had a deal. He disobeyed. He knew the consequences." She gave her frightening laugh. "You've done it again, October, you've done it again." Her voice was low and breathy, the voice I recognized too well. I heard her speaking out loud and at the same time I heard her inside my mind. My head throbbed. "Your dad. Luisa. Now Trevor. All because of you. All dead or dying because of you. Think you're worth it? Worth their lives?"

"Not me. You did this."

"For you. It was all for you. Marvelous you."

"Stop it." I directed my thoughts at the slobbers. I had

stopped them in the Fairy Glen and outside of Big Wok. I had made them disintegrate. Go away, I thought as hard as I could. Dissolve! But she had made them stronger somehow. I shouted at them, demanded they disappear, but the slobbers held Trevor so tightly I could see his skin bruising under their fingers.

Madame Gold laughed. The welts returned on my hands. More burned my neck, popped out on my face.

"This is your doing," she said. "October, this is all your fault."

"Don't listen to her," Walker said.

She smiled a strangely beautiful, welcoming smile. I took a step toward her. I was nauseated. The path beneath my feet undulated as if I stood on the back of a snake.

"Don't," Walker said again.

I took another stumbling step toward her. I couldn't fight it. I couldn't think anything but about the mess I'd made, about what a mess I was.

"Let me." Enoki came forward. "She did this to my brother. Let me at her."

Instantly Walker was at my side. "Don't even think about it, troll."

He grabbed my hand and squeezed. Calm filled me, starting at my hand and flowing up my arm and through my entire body. The despair subsided, my strength returned. I looked at the creatures facing me. First, the panther. As I studied it, I could actually begin to see a person inside the animal, a girl, and I could feel that she was less sure of herself than I expected. A black panther is a terrifying image and that's why she was in that form, but in reality the girl didn't want to fight. She especially didn't want to fight Oberon. His sharp, white canines looked deadly.

Enoki worried me. I could feel her anger emanating from her in hot waves along with her hatred. But then I saw she was sad too and very concerned about her brother—more than anything else. If she could get him away from harm, she wouldn't bother with me. Walker could help her save her brother. I would demand that he did.

Then I would stop Madame Gold.

When I looked at her, she wavered as if I was looking down at her through a swimming pool. She was so lovely, so perfect. She had amazing strength. If she wasn't a troll or a fairy, then what was she? Why did she want to marry Trevor? Why not just take the throne for herself? She certainly had the power. But there was something wrong with her, some little dark worm I could sense deep in her center that she had to hide and somehow overcome. It couldn't stay hidden forever. As I let my power—or whatever it was—dig down in her soul, I saw her secret swelling, expanding, and demanding to be let out.

She felt me. "Stop it!" she said.

"What's wrong with you?" I asked. It wasn't very nice, but it just came out. "What are you hiding?"

"Nothing!"

"There's something about you. Something nobody knows."

The others turned to face her, wondering what I was talking about. Enoki looked Madame Gold up and down.

Madame Gold waved her arms as if shooing me away. "You're pathetic. That's all you've got? Telling me I have a secret? Everybody has secrets."

"I don't."

"Not a surprise. You're nothing, practically human."

In that crowd, human didn't seem like such a bad thing to be. "At least I'm not hiding who I am."

Walker said, "She'll be eighteen very soon. Less than twenty minutes." He walked toward Madame Gold. "And then she will be Queen no matter what you do."

Madame Gold squinted her eyes at me. If looks could kill,

I would have been eviscerated, my guts lying on the ground. Instead, she turned toward Trevor, leaned over and whispered in his ear. I couldn't make out what she was saying, but Trevor began to writhe and groan.

Enoki wailed. "Stop!"

I grabbed Madame Gold and tried to pull her away from Trevor. The panther leapt at me, sinking its teeth into my arm. I screamed. Oberon charged and tackled the panther forcing it to let go of my arm. Walker caught me as I fell back. Blood bubbled from my arm and slobbers surrounded us. Walker stood over me, slowly circling to watch each slobber. I pushed to my feet and we stood back to back. The panther and Oberon rolled across the path and through the weeds. They knocked into the fence, growling, squealing, making the most horrible noises. The panther fought hard but ultimately was no match for Oberon. He grabbed the panther's neck and shook. The panther cried out—a very unpanther-like sound—and went limp. Oberon panted and licked his wounds. My arm hurt, but I couldn't complain when I saw what Oberon had suffered for me.

"Stupid dog!" Madame Gold said.

"Stupid lady!" Oberon returned. "Dogs beat cats every time!"

The panther lay in the weeds without moving, breathing with difficulty. It was dying. Its form shimmered. Something was underneath, some other creature. But I had to focus. I made a slobber disappear. And another. Madame Gold hissed at me and bent to whisper again in Trevor's ear. He began to scream in pain.

Enoki hollered. "Madame, please!"

"It's all October's fault." Madame Gold turned to me. "What's the matter, Princess?" She said it like it was a curse. "Can't you save him?"

I could. I had to. I left the slobbers—there were too many

of them anyway—and concentrated on Madame Gold, on that dark spot inside her. I saw her arms lowering, imagined her powerless and Trevor strong and whole. It almost worked. Then I heard her voice whispering in my ear. "He's going to die and you can't stop it. He will die because of you. Just like Luisa."

I fought against her. None of it was my fault. I hadn't asked for this. I tried to block her voice, but it filled my head. I heard her everywhere.

"You killed Luisa. Trevor will be dead because of you. And your father."

I couldn't concentrate anymore. I sat down on the path and hid my face.

She continued. "Look what you've done. And why? You're nothing. Absolutely ordinary in every way."

She was right. And as I thought that I lost all the power I had. I couldn't make her stop and Trevor was getting weaker. His head flopped strangely, his hands shook and his legs twitched. He stopped screaming, the slobbers let go of him, and he fell to the ground, shuddering, gasping for breath.

"Let's transplant." Walker whispered in my ear. "There's nothing you can do."

"Yes, there is. There must be." I ran to Trevor. I got down on my knees and pulled him into my lap.

Enoki tried to pull me up. "Leave him alone."

"Look!" I said. "Look what she's done!"

We both watched as the color faded in Trevor's face leaving him the awful gray of an old bruise. He opened his mouth, desperate for air, trying to speak but unable to. He was almost gone. I looked up at Madame Gold. There was only one thing to do. "You can be Queen," I said.

Her eyes widened. I had interested her. Trevor trembled in my arms.

"I'll go away," I said. "I'll go back to the human world. Forever."

She gave an ugly, twisted smile. "You promise?"

Walker tried to pull me to my feet. "Don't," he said. "Don't do it. Promises must be kept."

"I mean it." I ignored Walker. "I will not be Queen. But I have a couple of conditions. First, stop hurting Trevor."

Madame Gold shrugged. Trevor went still and the chains fell off him. He took a deep breath and another.

"I'm sorry," I said to him. "I'm so sorry."

His eyes were solid black and shiny as wet tar, without pupils, not even a little bit human. He clutched my arm. "Marry me." That was not what I expected to hear. "Right now," he said. "We can stop her."

It was tempting. It was very tempting.

I saw Walker hang his head. I saw Oberon bleeding from multiple wounds. I saw the look on Madame Gold's face, interested in what I would do, but not very concerned. I was only minutes from being Queen, but she knew I was powerless and I would probably continue to be, Queen or not.

I looked at the panther struggling to breathe. The black fur wavered and shimmered and changed form until it became lovely, shiny, dark hair. The body curled on its side became a girl's body in jeans and a black T-shirt. The panther was Luisa. Luisa! She was still alive. Barely, but alive.

"Luisa!"

"I thought she'd last longer than that." Madame Gold dismissed her.

She was breathing, not dead yet. I looked at Madame Gold. "Save her," I said.

"Marry me." Trevor said again.

But I couldn't see how that would fix anything. All this hate.

Madame Gold's desperation. She would find a way to kill my mother, marry my father, and then kill me. "I can't," I said to him. "I can't."

Madame Gold laughed as he passed out. A trickle of blood spilled from his mouth. Bruises were appearing on his face and torso, on every bare patch of skin.

Enoki pushed me away. She lifted her brother in her very strong arms and glowered at me, her eyes bright darts of hate. "Promise her. Just promise and go away forever."

"Will he be okay?"

"What do you care?" Enoki ran across the river and through the portal carrying her brother.

I staggered to my feet. Walker put his hands on my shoulders. I felt the calm, the warmth, and for the first time, it didn't matter.

"You can't do this," he said. "You are Queen."

I pulled away and walked over to Madame Gold. I was not a queen or even a princess. Still, I could do something good for other people.

"Here are my terms." My voice was small and Madame Gold had to bend down to hear me. "One: you will make my father better and return him to me. Two: you will leave my mother alone. Three: you will leave Trevor alone. Four: You will free the fairies and all those slaves. And…" I could barely speak. My throat was so dry and my tongue felt like a piece of sandpaper in my mouth.

"And?" she asked with a sneer. "Speak up when you talk to a future Queen."

Queen Witch! My anger gave me strength and I practically shouted, "Five: I promise to go if you will save Luisa's life."

"October!" Walker cried. "Her promises are no good."

"I always keep my promises," Madame Gold said.

Walker took my arm. He tried to turn me around to face him. "Six minutes until you're eighteen. Wait. Wait and see what happens."

"I don't think Luisa can last that long." Madame Gold closed her eyes and Luisa wailed and began to shake.

"You promise me first." I could insist on that much.

She took a deep breath, waved her arms and said, "I promise."

I looked around at Oberon and Luisa and across the beautiful river to the open portal. I looked back at the wide, human world. I did not look at Walker.

"I promise I will return to the human world forever and when I turn eighteen, I will not be Queen."

"NO!" Walker shouted. "No."

Before I could even say goodbye, a clock somewhere, a big fairy, troll, magical clock with a deep bell struck the hour. Bong. It was midnight and I was finally eighteen.

Bong. The world went black and the chime reverberated and I was nowhere and Madame Gold and Walker and Oberon and Luisa had all disappeared. I was floating in the dark. Bong. I counted one—two—three. With every toll of the bell, a new part of my body throbbed. I was stretching and growing too fast and it hurt. I heard voices, a million voices, not just people and fairies and trolls, but the voices of animals and birds and even trees and plants. A symphony of life, but too loud, too demanding. My senses were expanding, becoming more acute. The entire life cycle of a flower and a bird and a mouse, from seed or egg or birth through baby and seedling and learning to fly and youth and bud and flowering and mating to old age and death and decay, maggots cleaning the mouse and bird bones, passed before me in seconds. I saw my mother and my father young, meeting each other for the first time. The smiles, the joy. My own birth. Moments of real happiness in my childhood. Moments of fear. I saw the three trolls at the rest stop when we went on vacation and I knew how sad they made my mother. On and on. Middle school. The people I knew, strangers on the bus, the fairies and trolls I had thought were human, I felt their sadness, their worry, their excitement and anticipation. Whatever anyone was feeling, I felt too. I saw Luisa laughing with Jed and knew how happy they were together. I knew Trevor's desperate desire to be king and his fear when he crossed Madame Gold. I felt the pain she had caused him. Then there was Walker smiling at me. Walker's admiration. Walker's warmth reaching out to me. I felt how hard he had tried to protect me and I felt his despair that he had failed. I saw his fear of what I had promised and what it would bring. I saw his disappointment. I felt it all. Every emotion that anyone anywhere had ever felt poured through me and puddled in my chest, in my heart. My limbs ached. My brain too. It was too much. I give up, I thought, I don't want this. If that was what it meant to be a queen, to feel everything and still be powerless to help, I was glad I turned it down. As the clock struck its final clang, I let it all go black.

15.

A bright light was shining in my eyes.

"That's quite a fall you had," a woman said.

It was Nurse Raynor from school. She checked my eyes with a little penlight, then carefully touched a very painful spot on my forehead.

"You have a nasty bump. I don't think you have a concussion," she said, "but I'll call your dad and give him a report, just in case."

I watched her pick up the school phone and dial my house. It was bright daylight and I could hear kids in the hall. I started to stand, then sat down again. Every muscle in my body was sore as if I'd taken an extra hard yoga class the day before. Which I definitely had not. Gingerly I touched the enormous goose egg on my forehead and bit my lip so I wouldn't cry. The clock said it was eleven minutes after noon. Hadn't I just been on the path by the river? I remembered the promise I had made. But how had I gotten here and what had happened to the last twelve hours?

Raynor was speaking into the phone, "Okay, Neal, I'll tell her... No, I don't think it's serious, but you might want to watch her tonight in case of nausea or headache..." She laughed at something my dad said. "Thank you. I'll see you at the meeting tomorrow. Right... bye." She hung up.

I knew it! She was a fairy too and they were having a meeting about getting rid of Madame Gold. Maybe I couldn't do it, but if the fairies all joined together...

"What meeting?" I asked. "I want to go."

She went red and flustered. "Oh, October, don't be silly. This isn't your kind of meeting."

"Yes, it is. I'm involved."

"Of course you are, but you should go to a meeting for family members. This is a regular AA meeting." She sighed, resigned to tell me the truth. "I'm a recovering alcoholic just like your dad and he's my sponsor."

"Oh." I clapped my hand over my mouth. "I'm sorry. I won't tell anyone. I know I'm not supposed to know. I mean, of course. I...I thought it was something else."

I stood up slowly, but stayed bent over like an old man. It hurt too much to straighten up completely. I was wearing my jeans and my tall, lace up boots and my favorite hoodie. Just like always. I started to shake my hair back, but it made my head pound. I staggered and I grabbed the bed frame.

"You okay? You can lie down a little longer," Nurse Raynor said.

"No, no. Thanks. Guess I'll go to class."

I shuffled for the door as she called out. "October?"

"Yes?"

"I forgot to say—happy birthday."

"What day is it?"

She laughed, thinking I was kidding. So that meant me turning eighteen was that weird pain and nausea, hearing the voices of every kind of creature, and having visions of myself and other people and animals. And after all that, this feeble, twisted, painful body was me being eighteen. So much for remarkable powers. I was definitely not a queen.

I trudged down the hall in a daze. No one paid any attention to me or to the enormous bump on my head. Back to usual, I was practically invisible. I walked into English class and Ms.

Campbell didn't say a word about me being late. She frowned a little and then nodded for me to take my seat. The desk behind me was empty. After class I asked a girl if she'd seen Trevor and she didn't know who or what I was talking about. Had Madame Gold wiped everybody's memory clean? Or was none of it real? I have to admit I was sad and disappointed. Everything was back the way it had been before Walker first appeared, before the itch. Nurse Raynor had talked to my dad and he seemed completely fine. I was glad my dad was okay. I'd made my decision and I knew it was the right one, but for a moment I had been someone special. Now I was nobody again.

After class, I ducked into the bathroom to splash some cold water on my face to keep the tears away. I studied my reflection. The lump on my head was huge and black and blue, but my hair was thick and shiny and curlier than it had ever been. It was also reddish rather than plain old brown and my eyes looked large and warmer than before. My eyelashes were long and thick. My jeans were still short on me under my boots and loose around my waist. My boots had gotten very snug. I had definitely grown.

All of that could be explained as a normal, human growth spurt, but if my toes were hairy I would know what I remembered was real. I was about to unlace my boots and take them off to check when the door opened and the most popular girls in school, Rose and Belinda, sauntered in chatting a mile a minute. They ignored me, of course.

"She just disappeared," Rose was saying.

"Dropped out?" Belinda was shocked.

"Henry told Jacob who told me she ran off with Jed. He's not answering his phone either."

Then they saw me at the sink and wrinkled their perfect noses.

"Another itch?" Belinda giggled.

So the itch had actually happened. "Are you talking about Luisa?" I asked.

They both looked at me as if it was none of my business, but the gossip was too good for Rose not to tell. "Luisa and Jed ran off and got married. Eloped! Now they're gone. No one knows where. Poof. Like magic!" She snapped her fingers.

"How do you know?"

Belinda chimed in. "Jacob talked to Henry who talked to Jed. Jed told him that he and Luisa were getting married and leaving town."

I smiled. I even laughed I was so happy. That meant Luisa was alive. Madame Gold had kept her word.

"What are you smiling about?" Belinda asked.

"You think that's funny?" Rose confronted me, hands on her hips. "Do you?"

A week earlier Rose would have intimidated me, but not anymore. "Relax," I said. "I just think it's so romantic. Don't you? Two lovers taking off like that?"

Belinda kind of nodded, but Rose frowned. "What's romantic about dropping out of senior year, three months from graduating? Now she's screwed."

"Luisa's smart," I said. "They'll let her graduate."

"You think so?"

I really had no idea, but I didn't think fairies needed high school diplomas. "I'm sure you know." I was making it up as I went along. "There's that special program for graduating early."

"Oh, right," Rose said. "Sure." She didn't want me to know anything she didn't.

"What happened to your head?" Belinda finally asked.

"I tripped." I laughed. "I am such a klutz. Always was. Always will be."

Belinda laughed with me. "I know, me too! It's these heels."

I looked down and sure enough she was wearing four-inch spikes. As it was she barely came up to my shoulder. She was tiny. "I'd kill myself in those shoes." I said.

"I almost do. Every day." Belinda giggled again.

Rose looked me up and down. "You look good," she said. "What are you using on your hair?"

I stood next to them in front of the mirror. We all three gazed at our reflections. I was taller than either of them and my cheekbones more pronounced. My face had an angular quality it hadn't had before.

"You've lost weight," Rose said.

They both looked at me expectantly, waiting for my secrets.

"I've been running," I said. That was certainly true. "And drinking lots of water. Lots."

I smiled at them and for the first time in my whole high school career they smiled at me.

"Cool," said Rose.

Belinda said, "Water is the best."

I backed out of the bathroom before I blew it and said something stupid.

The rest of the day passed uneventfully, no itches, no falling, nothing. I kept watching for Walker, wondering if he would come by to check on me. But he didn't. Of course he didn't. I was exhausted by the time the last bell rang. I got on the bus and collapsed into a seat by the window. I couldn't wait to get home and talk to my parents about everything that had happened.

I hoped Trevor was okay, that he had healed and returned to the troll world with Enoki. I hoped Walker was not too angry with me. I hoped he understood I had to do it. As the bus bumped along I stared out the window at a completely normal, ordinary world. A woman walked by with an earpiece, chattering away. There was no elf on her shoulder. A homeless man was nodding and talking—to himself. There were no creatures fluttering around his head. I sighed. Maybe none of it had been real. Maybe it really was like The Wizard of Oz and I had traveled to another land in a dream. I caught a glimpse of my reflection in the bus window; I was prettier than I had been, but maybe I'd been getting that way all along.

Luisa.

I sat up straighter. I smiled. Real or a dream, Luisa was alive and she and Jed were together. I looked out the window as the bus passed the empty lot. At first I was disappointed the fireflies were gone, but I decided I didn't need fireflies anymore. They didn't belong in Los Angeles, just as I didn't belong in that other world, the one I'd given up. I was a plain old high school senior. I'd been through a lot and I could be glad it was over. I had things to do, college to look forward to, a life to live. I didn't need fairies and trolls and magical kingdoms. I continued to convince myself all the way home.

My mom's car was back in the driveway next to my dad's. I hoped that meant she was home. We could talk about everything that had happened. She and my dad would understand. They wouldn't care that I wasn't a queen. They'd be glad.

"Mom! I'm…" I started and stopped. Dad came out of the kitchen with his apron on. He was really, honestly, truly thinner. He had probably lost 125 pounds.

"Birthday girl!" He hugged me. "Happy, happy birthday."

It felt as if my birthday, the clock striking midnight, had been long ago, eons ago, another lifetime ago. How could it possibly still be my birthday? I couldn't stop staring at my father. "You look… great."

"That's a good sized bump on your head," he said. "Betty, the nurse, said you took quite a fall."

"I'm fine. But you… is this all because of Madame Gold?"

He looked puzzled, as if he didn't know what I was talking about. "I've been going to Overeaters Anonymous. You know that. For over two months."

Wait. What was he saying? "Not a hypnotist?"

"Load of hogwash. Hypnotism is a scam." He chuckled, not his usual belly laugh. "Dinner's almost ready. All your favorites. Nothing too good for my birthday girl." He headed back to the kitchen.

I followed him, expecting to find my mom sitting at the kitchen table with a cup of tea and a scientific journal. But she wasn't there. "Where's Mom?"

"Remember? The conference?"

"She's still there?"

"She is so sad to miss your birthday." He gestured to the table. "Sit down."

"I need to talk to you—and Mom too. About the Fairy Canopy and Trolldom and me being Queen."

He kept chopping vegetables.

I tried again. "I know what you and Mom gave up to be together. I just have a few questions. I mean everything has changed because of my promise." It didn't seem as if he was even listening. "Listen to me! Why won't you listen?"

He turned around. "Calm down. You've had a bad accident. Betty said you could be a little disoriented."

"You were a zombie. The hypnotist, witch, whatever she was, Madame Gold, turned you into her slave."

He shook his head as if I wasn't making sense. "It's been a rough few days."

"I know what you are," I said. "I know what I am. Or what I was. Or what I was supposed to be."

"Sit," he said. "We will eat when you calm down."

"I don't want to calm down!"

"Do not shout at me."

My dad never talked like that, but I had never yelled at him before. "C'mon, Dad, you were supposed to be King of the fairies. King!"

He gave another weird dry laugh. "You haven't been yourself," he said.

"Me?"

"I think turning eighteen and graduating and college ahead of you has been more stressful than your mom and I expected."

He looked sad and worried. My head was pounding. Maybe Luisa had really just eloped and Trevor and Walker had never existed and I had hit my head and imagined the last three days. I knew my dad would never lie to me.

"Okay, Dad. Okay."

I could feel his relief. "Thank you, Pumpkin." He smiled and straightened his shoulders. "Dinner in two minutes."

"I'm not hungry," I said. For once, eating sounded impossible. "My head hurts and my stomach too."

"Maybe I should take you to the emergency room."

"I just want to talk to Mom." My eyes filled with tears.

"She said she's too busy to talk." He looked at the clock. "Plus it's the middle of the night where she is."

"Where is that?'

He kind of smiled. "You know? I can't remember."

He'd never said that before, but she did travel a lot. "I'm gonna lie down. I'll eat later."

I went upstairs and shut my bedroom door behind me. It was a relief to be back in my room. The sun was low in the sky and the last rays shone through my window and turned my white walls golden. I took off my boots and tossed them in the very back of my closet. I never wanted to wear them again. I didn't want to be reminded of the itch and the day I dreamed

I met Walker and all the things I was not and would never be.

I heard the ice cream truck coming down the street, playing the same song as always. "You are my sunshine. My only sunshine." Over and over again, some awful electronic version. I heard kids calling to each other as they ran to the truck. I wished I was nine again, or ten, eleven, even twelve—a long way from my eighteenth birthday.

College. That's what I had to think about now. Colorado was going to be great. Far away with mountains and cowboys and lots of snow. Snow. Cold weather. Both would be all new for me. I counted the months, April, May, June, July, and August, until I'd be gone. I could start over, a new person. Maybe I could finally change my name. Annie, I thought. I had always liked that name, kind of pretty but innocuous too. Anybody could be an Annie. I had to shower. I could smell myself, the sour tang of sweat and dirty hair. No hint of flowers like Walker or clean earth like Trevor. I was all human and I stank. As I undressed I noted how short my pants were. I'd grown an inch or two for sure. And food was beginning to sound good. I wasn't sure when I'd eaten last. I figured the Chinese food hadn't been real and before that I couldn't remember. I threw my jeans in the hamper and then took off my tall socks, first the left, then the other.

There was something on my right leg and when I tried to brush it off it wouldn't go away. I turned to the window and the fading sunlight and gasped. A tattoo, a beautiful and intricate tattoo started with a blooming flower above my ankle and continued with vines and leaves and smaller flowers twining around and up my leg. It was absolutely gorgeous, in rich, true colors I'd never seen on a tattoo before. And it started right where I'd been scratching the most, where the itch had been the worst.

I knew I had not gotten a tattoo. Never. No matter how crazy or out of it I'd been, I would remember the pain and the hours that took. And a tat this complicated would have cost a fortune, way more than I could spend.

That meant it wasn't all in my imagination. It couldn't be.

16.

Mom. I had to talk to her. She'd never been under Madame Gold's spell, she was far away at a conference. Even if I woke her up, she would have some answers. And sure enough, there was my cell phone on my desk as if I'd left it there that morning. As if Enoki had never thrown it in the river. Something was happening—had happened—and I had to find out what. I flicked it on and waited impatiently for it to warm up. I typed in "Mom" but she didn't come up. Same with Dad, and Luisa, and Walker and the main school number. My phone had been wiped clean. There were no numbers, no old texts, even my photos were gone. It was more proof I had not lost my mind or slipped into dreamland: I knew I had not erased everything on my phone. Someone did not want me getting in touch with any of those old contacts.

I knew my mom's number by heart and I called her. It rang once and went to voice mail. She had probably turned her phone off to sleep. I sent her a quick text, "I miss you. We need to talk." I also sent a text to what I thought was Luisa's number, but it bounced back, "Undeliverable."

Dad knocked on my door and almost scared me to death.

"Dinner's getting cold," he said.

"Quick shower. I'll be right there."

In the shower I decided that after dinner I would sneak out, take the car, and go to Luisa's house to talk to her mom or to the Chinese restaurant to talk to Mr. Bob. I needed some answers and I couldn't wait for Mom to get home. As I toweled off I admired my beautiful tattoo again. Then I noticed that my toes were in fact a little hairy and my feet definitely wider. Like smallish troll feet attached to skinny fairy legs. Gross. I ran my razor over my toes and the hair was wiry and uncooperative, but I finally managed to get rid of it. Hairy toes did not work for me.

I put on clean flannel pajama bottoms—as if I was going right to bed—and a tank top. I went downstairs and into the kitchen.

"This looks great," I said to Dad and it did. He'd made veggie lasagna and a bright, colorful salad filled with all my favorites, spinach and mushrooms and tomatoes and cucumbers and yellow peppers. "Thanks for cooking."

Whatever was going on, it was good to have this moment with Dad. He was not jovial, he didn't make a single bad joke, but he seemed more like himself. A much thinner self. His cheekbones were emerging and his eyes were bigger in his face. They'd returned to their usual bright blue—close to Walker's color and my heart gave a surprising wrench. I missed him and it hurt. Troll-hater, bossy, and opinionated as he was, I missed him. I thought about never seeing him again, about his life continuing without me in the Fairy Canopy, imagined him with his friends, a girlfriend who would make him laugh, and I slumped and pushed my plate away. I longed for him. Like in the old fashioned poems, I yearned. I had been a job to him and he had finished that job—or I had finished it for him—but he was much more than that to me. It was a new feeling and not a good one. Unrequited love sucks.

At least Dad didn't notice. I didn't want to try to explain anything.

After we ate—and I noticed my dad had some of everything, but normal sized portions—he pushed my presents toward me.

"They're not much," he said. "I'm not working as you know, but I think you'll like them."

"You didn't have to get me anything." I knew money was tight and college was coming up.

He pointed at the largest box. "That one's from your Mom. Wish she was here."

"Me too."

I opened it and was really surprised. It was a soft, dark green sweater I had fallen in love with in a catalog. I didn't know she had paid any attention to me drooling over it. I held it up. It was better than in the picture.

The next was a book. I always got a book and this was one I had really wanted to read about a werewolf and his human girl-friend. Seemed pretty tame after what I'd been through.

The last was in a smaller box. The card was from my dad. It read, "Because you are special." It was an odd, formal sentiment coming from him. I unwrapped the box and took the lid off revealing a smaller dark orange velvet box inside. I knew that color, like flame, like a pumpkin, but I couldn't remember where I'd seen it recently. Typical Dad to give me pumpkin-colored things. I opened the velvet box and froze. Inside was a necklace more exquisite and delicate than anything I'd ever seen. Incredible. My parents had never given me jewelry before. I didn't even have my ears pierced. I looked at Dad. "Where did this come from?"

Without hesitation he said he had bought it at the jewelry store in the mall. I knew that wasn't true. My dad did not go to the mall and this was higher quality and more unusual than anything that discount store offered. The pendant was my ini-tial, "O," in silver, but a kind of silver I had never seen; when it caught the light it changed color. There was some intricate etching on the surface too, almost like writing, but no words or letters I recognized. Even the chain was exceptional.

"I love it! It's amazing." I hugged and kissed him.

He hugged me back. "Put it on. Now."

"I'm going to bed," I said. "I'll wear it tomorrow. I can't wait."

"You can sleep in it," he insisted. "It's made to be worn all the time. It's a special metal that gets better the more it's worn. Even sleeping. All the time." He looked so serious for a moment, and then he kind of laughed. "I bought it for you. I want to see it."

"Okay." I actually couldn't wait to put it on. I was so taken with it I couldn't stop staring at it and nothing he said seemed weird to me. It was obviously a special kind of silver, and I thought it made sense that the oils from my skin would somehow make it more radiant. I clasped it around my neck. It was so light it was like wearing nothing, except the metal was oddly warm. The "O" rested snugly right between my collarbones. It was very warm. Any warmer and it would burn me.

"Perfect," my dad said. "Just right."

I ran to the hall mirror to look at it. It was gorgeous and subtle and as I moved it gave off little sparkles.

"Thank you. Thank you."

"Promise me you'll wear it always."

"I will."

"Time for dessert."

Dad went to the fridge and took out an enormous home-made birthday cake, chocolate frosted, decorated with my name, and pre-spiked with eighteen candles. He grinned.

"Brand new recipe," he said. "Let me light the candles."

I didn't eat birthday cake. He knew that. I didn't think I liked birthday cake anymore, certainly didn't think I could choke this one down. I was shaking my head, but he ignored me.

"I have to sing to you."

He sang to me, badly, and I made a bunch of silent wishes as I blew out the candles. I wished that I could talk to Walker. I wished for Trevor to be healed. I wished for my mom to come home soon. I wished for Luisa to be fine and for Madame Gold to go away forever. I had tears in my eyes from wishing so hard.

I anticipated the giant piece he'd cut for himself, but he cut a regular sized piece of cake for me and none for himself.

"You're really doing this diet thing."

"Just not interested anymore."

"That's great."

"But you should try it. I worked hard."

"Looks like it." I took a bite just to be polite. The cake was incredible. I hadn't had cake in so long and I really did still like it. I liked this one. "Wow, Dad. This is fantastic."

I ate and ate and ate. The piece of cake was never ending and I had never tasted anything so good. When I finally pushed my plate away I thought I might really, truly explode. My stomach hurt and I was dizzy from the sugar. I closed my eyes and when I opened them, everything was out of focus. The room blurred around me. Was it the food that had made me so sleepy? I was afraid I would pass out at the table. I tried to push my chair back and stand up, but my legs were like rubber.

"Bed. Need to go," I managed.

"A good long sleep—all night—that's what you need."

Dad smiled, but even in my haze his smile looked fake, his eyes were dull and serious.

"I can't think." I couldn't help but slur my words. "What is…?" I couldn't concentrate long enough to remember my question.

Dad lifted me easily and carried me upstairs to my room. He tucked me into bed as if I was eight, not eighteen. I tried to protest, to tell him I needed to brush my teeth, I think I even said I needed to find Walker, but he shushed me and told me to let it all go.

"I want you right here with me forever."

I put my hand over my necklace, growing warmer against my skin, and sunk into the deepest sleep of my entire life.

17.

My alarm went off and I struggled to open my eyes. I was groggy and disoriented. I knew instantly that my dad had drugged me. He had put something in my birthday cake to knock me out and keep me home all night. Did he think I wouldn't notice? This was not normal parent behavior. He could have just asked me to stay home; it was a little extreme to slip a pill in my frosting. I felt like I was underwater, but I had to go to school and I was eager to get out of the house and away from him.

I pulled my phone off the bedside table. No messages. I called Mom again. No answer. This time not even voice mail. I texted her, "Where R U????" It said my text was not delivered. She was talking about the benefits of mushrooms at some conference out of cell phone reach and I needed her. At that moment, I hated those mushrooms of hers. Which made me think of Madame Gold forcing the fairies to dig in the dirt like truffle pigs. Whatever kind of mushroom Madame Gold was searching for seemed really important to her. Important enough to enslave all those fairies and turn fairyland's flowers and grass into mud.

I dragged myself out of bed and trudged to the bathroom. I washed my face with cold water and that helped a little. As I brushed my teeth, I saw my necklace in the medicine chest mirror. I had forgotten it, but it really was perfect. It looked like it had been made for me. My eyes had flecks of gold in the morning sun. Those hadn't been there a week before. My hair was shiny and definitely more red than brown. I pulled up the leg of my pajamas and my tattoo was still there. Maybe I wasn't Queen, maybe I had no real powers, but I was not the same old me. Most importantly, I was not going crazy imagining things that hadn't happened.

I searched my closet and found a short, flirty skirt I had never worn. It still had the price tag on it. I'd bought it at an after Christmas sale hoping I'd have a reason to wear it. That morning the time had come. I cut off the tag and put it on. It was a little big around the waist and definitely shorter than when I'd tried it on in the store. Short, but not too short. I put on my brand new sweater and it fit perfectly. I slipped into my pretty little flats. Some mascara and a dash of lip gloss and I looked pretty good.

I came down the stairs into the kitchen hoping for a cup of tea to help wake me up and caught my dad sitting at the table, not eating, not reading the newspaper, just staring at the wall. Okay. That was flipping odd. On a regular day he was cooking while he was reading the paper and complaining about the bad news, the politicians, the state of the world. He jumped up as I came in and put on a smile—as if it was a mask from the Halloween store.

"Good morning, Pumpkin. Sleep well?"

"You know how I slept," I said.

He ignored me and went to the stove where he stirred something in our biggest pot. Without looking at me he said, "You look nice."

No line about how short it was. No terrible joke about my wrinkle-free skirt ironing out my problems. And nothing about my very obvious tattoo.

"Gotta go," I said. "Don't want to miss the bus."

"But I made oatmeal." He turned from the stove and came toward me with a big bowl.

"No way!" I practically knocked it out of his hand. Then I backpedaled. "I mean, after all that food last night—I'm still full."

"Breakfast is the most important meal of the day."

I waited for him to finish by saying, 'All day.' I waited for him to laugh, but he was completely serious. That was when I knew the creature in front of me either wasn't my dad or that my dad had been possessed by a demon. That stupid breakfast joke, he always said the whole thing. He had to.

"Really?" I hoped he was waiting for me to finish our joke.

"Delicious oatmeal with raisins." He was not.

"I said I'm not hungry." I started for the door.

He—whoever he was—frowned. "Why don't you I take you to school? I'll get my keys." He put the bowl down. He'd lost even more weight overnight.

"I'm good." I had the front door open. "See you later."

I picked up my backpack and tried to look as if I was fine, happy, just rushing for the bus. I definitely did not want him to think I was running from him. What was going on? Madame Gold had not kept her promise. My father was not "back to normal" and I was no longer convinced that Mom was at a conference. She hadn't even called to wish me happy birthday.

I was sure Imposter Dad was watching me from the living room window, so I walked briskly down the sidewalk in the direction of the bus stop. As soon as I turned the corner and was out of sight, I took off running. I had to run. I had to get as far away from my house as possible as quickly as possible. I wanted my life and my family back the way they were before flowers started appearing on my skin and crows wanted to kill me. Everything was so completely and totally wrong. I couldn't reach my mom, but could I find Walker? He said he always knew where I was. Did he know at that minute that I was running down the street? Did he know I was scared that Madame Gold had not done anything I asked? Was Luisa fine? Was Trevor okay? Had she let the fairy prisoners go? Maybe I had given up being a queen, but I hoped I wasn't a fool.

I got angrier and angrier as I ran and the anger focused me. I could look for Walker at Henderson Park or I could—I shuddered—go back to the L.A. River. It seemed pointless to go to school. Trevor wouldn't be there, or Luisa, or… Green! Green would know how to find Walker. He had appeared in the club and guided me to him. He had fought the crows and he had kept me from kissing Trevor. He was somehow connected, involved and he was probably at school. I picked up my pace. I could have run all the way there, I wasn't even winded after twelve blocks and honestly, truly my feet seemed to leave the ground longer than humanly possible, but the bus was just stopping so I hopped on.

I waved my pass at the bus driver and headed for the back. There were only two other riders and in my suspicious mind they couldn't be who or what they appeared to be. A woman sat up front near the driver in nice go-to-work clothes. I saw her on the bus most mornings, but when she looked up and smiled hello I jumped away from her. The other passenger was a guy sitting in the middle. He wore a green windbreaker and a stocking cap and he was humming and rocking in the seat. He most definitely was not normal, but whether he was supernaturally abnormal or just your average crazy bus rider I could not determine. He stared at me from under bushy eyebrows. He could have been a troll with his dark skin and eyes. I tried to see his hands clasped in his lap, but I was afraid to look too hard. Whatever he was, I didn't want to encourage him. I sat down a few rows behind him where I could keep an eye on him.

I texted my mom again. Again it didn't go through.

At the next stop an old woman got on carrying three beat up and overflowing plastic shopping bags. I saw clothes, twigs and branches, and who knows what else in those bags. She wore a long, flowered dress over baggy red and yellow striped pants and two sweaters. She smiled at me. All my life, wherever I went, the homeless, whacko types loved me. Especially the old women. They always talked to me. I was not in the mood. I ignored her and looked out the window but even with all those other empty seats, of course she sat down next to me. She smelled like tomato soup and rusty metal. I didn't want to be rude, but I turned sideways to face the window, putting my back to her. She started pulling things out of her bags and talking to herself.

"There's the bunny. Cute little hopper. Where's your carrot? Ah here you go."

I had to look. I was relieved to see it was a stuffed rabbit, pink and filthy, but a real carrot so old it was as limp as a cooked noodle. She pulled out a pair of impossibly long green tights.

"Dancing, dancing. I want to go dancing." Her feet tapped on the floor as she waved the tights back and forth as if she were one of those ridiculous ribbon dancers in the Olympics. Another stuffed animal, without ears or eyes, so dirty and misshapen it was impossible to know what kind of animal it was supposed to be. Then she took out a big gray coat and shook it so that dust covered both of us. She laid it down across her lap—and mine.

That was it. I didn't want her disgusting stuff touching my new skirt. I spun around and spoke to her through clenched teeth.

"Excuse me. Do you mind?"

She was looking down in her bag, and turned to me slowly. She had surprisingly bright, blue eyes. Brilliant blue, as if she were wearing contacts.

"I'm sorry," I said. "Could you sit somewhere else? You'd

have more room over there."

In retrospect I guess I could have gotten up and moved. But I wanted her to move. Actually, I think I just wanted to yell at her. I wanted to yell at someone and she was handy and annoying. "Please go!" I practically shouted.

The guy in the stocking cap turned around to look at me. He didn't look friendly and for a moment I worried the blue-eyed bag lady was a friend of his and I had really pissed him off. But then he faced front again, obviously uninterested in the fight happening in the back of the bus.

"Why?" she said. "Why should I?"

"The whole bus is empty. Why do you have to sit here?"

I expected her to tell me I was in her usual seat and that she always sat in this row.

"Never mind," I said. "I'll move." I grabbed my backpack and stood up, but she put one dirty hand on my arm. I pulled my arm—in my new sweater—away.

"I have something for you," she whispered. "I can't let anyone else see."

Just what I needed, a diseased, filthy stuffed animal or something. "Thanks," I said. "But no thanks."

I tried to squeeze past her but she yanked on my skirt, and wouldn't let me pass. "Where'd you get that necklace?" she asked.

"It was a gift."

The old lady nodded. "They certainly make tracking devices pretty these days."

"What are you talking about?"

"Nothing, if you want someone to be able to follow your every move."

She looked up at me with those blue eyes and smiled. Her skin was smooth and rosy between the wrinkles, as if she was a fresh peach that had been squished. She tucked her matted gray hair behind one ear and I saw the top of that ear was pointed. Like Walker. The bright blue eyes. The pointed ears. She was a fairy. My heart beat faster. Maybe Walker had sent her.

"I… Are you?" I started to ask, then stopped. I couldn't trust her; even my dad was not my dad. I felt as if I was encased in Plexiglas, a box separating me from both the human and the supernatural worlds. I belonged in neither. I was neither. I could not trust anyone. I sat back down and my eyes filled up with tears.

"Perfect," I said out loud, meaning that the one day I'd chosen to wear mascara it was going to smear all over my face.

"Yes, you are perfect," she said and patted my leg. "I would have known you anywhere. You are your mother's daughter. And your father's. Don't be sad. I do have a present for you."

"I hope it's a Kleenex." I sniffled and pressed my fingers to my eyes trying to keep the tears from spilling. "A new one."

She dug around in her third bag. This bag seemed to be filled with shoes, single shoes. She handed them to me to hold. Not what I wanted to do, but the alternative was probably having her lay them in my lap on my skirt. In no time she had filled my arms. No two shoes were the same; she didn't have a pair in the bunch.

"Where are all the other shoes?" I couldn't help but ask.

"Oh, I don't know," she sighed. "I don't care about them."

"What good is one shoe?"

"You know how you always see one shoe on the side of the road?"

I nodded. I knew exactly what she meant. I saw a solitary shoe lying in the gutter or on the shoulder of the road all the time as I rode the bus or in the car. I always wondered how people could lose one shoe—so many people.

"I put them there," she said. "I'm the shoe fairy."

"Shoe fairy?"

She nodded. What possible use could there be for a shoe fairy? Tooth fairy, yes. Fairy godmother, of course. But a shoe fairy? Blue eyes and pointed ears notwithstanding, she probably was just a crazy old bag lady.

She pulled out more shoes, more and more, hundreds of shoes it seemed like, piling them on the floor around our feet, tossing them over her shoulder into the back. Her plastic bag was like Mary Poppins' carpetbag—more fit inside than seemed possible. Finally, she gave a little "ah ha!" and brought out a boot exactly like mine. It could have been mine, if I didn't know they were both home in my closet. She reached inside the boot all the way down to the toe and shook the shoe. I heard a faint, metallic tinkling.

"Got it," she said. "Here."

She pulled something out of the boot in her closed fist. She turned to me and opened her hand. I know my mouth fell open. In her open palm was a necklace exactly like my necklace. Exactly.

"Look familiar?" She cackled. "Let's trade."

"No." Hers had to be fake or something. It had come out of an old shoe.

"They're just the same." She dropped hers into my palm. "See? Except yours means they know exactly where you are at every minute. Mine will protect you."

"Protect me from what?"

"Your dad thinks you're going to school, right?"

How did she know? I held up the other necklace. It looked just like the one I had around my neck, but the one in my hand was cool, and the one around my neck was warm and getting warmer.

The old lady tapped my shoulder. "Excuse me, your Highness. Look out the back window. Someone wants to keep track of where you're going."

I ignored that she had called me 'your Highness' and twisted around to look back. A large black crow was flying along behind us, not too close, but definitely following us. As I watched, another one swooped in beside it. And through the window I heard the crow in front saying, "Look! Shiny things!" and the one in back say, "Don't get distracted. Follow the necklace." I looked at the bag lady, the shoe fairy, with alarm.

"What do I do?"

"Change with me," she whispered.

The man in the stocking cap turned around to look at us again. I tried to hide behind the seat, but the shoe fairy shook her head. "He's nothing special," she assured me. "Unless you think petty crime is special." Then she looked at me. "You would know that if you tried. Look at him. Really look."

I stared at the back of the guy's head. I began to get pictures, his donut for breakfast. His girlfriend sleeping. The pile of wallets and cell phones and crap he had stolen. He was a purse snatcher, not a troll. I could see his thoughts—and if I listened I could hear them. I smiled at the shoe fairy, but she nodded behind us.

There were five crows behind us now. My hands were shaking as I took off my necklace and handed it to her. I put on hers and she put on mine. The new necklace was cool against my skin. The shoe fairy winced as she fastened the old one around her throat. "Hot, hot, hot," she said.

"Thank you," I said. "But…" I had so many questions I didn't know where to begin.

All the shoes and clothing and stuffed animals were magically back in her bags as she smiled at me and patted my leg again, "Tell Walker hello."

"Walker. You know Walker. Oh, tell me, how do I find him?"

"You know."

"I don't."

"You know exactly how." She tapped her forehead. "Think about it." The bus slowed and stopped at a corner. "This is my stop!" She wheezed as she stood up.

"Wait," I said. "Please."

She nodded at the crows. There were more of them, a small flock circling the bus. "Thank goodness those birds aren't very smart." She waddled up the aisle.

"Thank you," I called to her, "Thank you. Is there something I can do for you?"

"Survive," she said.

She got off the bus slowly, as if her knees were bothering her, like any old woman. She started down the sidewalk and stopped and tottered over to the curb. I watched, curious, as she reached in her bag and pulled out a beat up green sneaker and dropped it on the side of the road. One shoe. The bus pulled away and I turned to watch her walk in the opposite direction. Miraculously, the crows followed her.

18.

School. It sounds just plain wrong to say it, but I was thrilled to be there. There was no way every student, teacher, administrator, guidance counselor, secretary, janitor, and cafeteria worker could be a fairy or a troll or possessed by demons. In fact, as I walked up to the big double doors, I reveled in the tedium and predictability. The ugly brick building was the same as always; the same cliques were gathered on the lawn out front; the same grass was dying trampled under their feet. I grinned as I started up the stairs, then I noticed that my fellow students seemed to be looking at me. All of them. The girls were watching me and whispering to each other. The boys were definitely checking me out. Jacob the jock whistled long and low.

"Whoa, girl," he said. "What happened to you?"

"Nice ink." A skater dude commented looking at my leg.

"Your parents let you do that?" A nerdy girl couldn't help but ask.

I answered honestly. "Nothing they could do about it."

"Awesome," Jacob said.

"I love your skirt." Rose sidled up next to me and linked her arm in mine.

"Yeah. Great…skirt." Jacob actually blushed.

"Down, boy." Belinda laughed at him.

Okay, after being invisible for most of my school life, it felt surprisingly good to be getting so much attention. Of course looks don't really matter and being a couple inches taller, a few pounds thinner, and even having flowers tattooed on my calf, did not change who I was as a person. If they liked me now, they should have liked me then. But in high school, that's not the way it works. In my experience, to be noticed and popular you have to have all the shallowest attributes: clothes, hair, figure. I'd gone through twelve years of school mostly anonymously and I can admit I liked the envy and the admiration I was seeing on everyone's face. Plus, the sensation I created wasn't because I was a princess of anything or about to be a queen, it was just because I was hot.

"See you at lunch," Rose said as we split to go to our respective classes.

Another popular girl, Audrey, appeared at my side. "You've been hiding out," she said. "But now we can get to know each other."

She was very pretty and I knew she was smart too—in all the honors and AP classes—but she had snubbed me in English the beginning of the year and laughed at an overweight girl in gym class and generally been awful to everybody and I wasn't going to let this opportunity go by.

"Sorry," I said. "I really don't hang out with high school students."

The look on her face was priceless. The other students tittered. I sauntered down the hall. Jacob panted after me.

"Hey," he said. "Wanna ride home after school? I have my car."

I raised my eyebrows at him. Was he kidding?

"Or get together to study tonight?" He tried again. "We both have to do the WWI paper, right?"

"What's your name again?" I watched him deflate. "You still go to school here? Weren't you supposed to graduate last year? Or the year before?"

He was crushed. His jock friends whooped and laughed and I have to say I felt lousy. I mean he really was a jerk and a cliché jock, but he didn't deserve that. And my mom had been saying all year that the reason he was so mean to me was because he liked me and didn't know how to say it.

"Hey." I touched his arm and he jumped. "I'm sorry, Jacob. I'm busy today. But thank you."

"Okay. Another time." He grinned.

My mom would've been proud.

My mom. Thinking about her reminded me of everything going on in my real life—whatever life that was. At school I had slipped into every girl's fantasy, but it was time to snap out of it.

The first bell rang. I scanned the group once looking for Green, but figured I'd find him at lunch for sure. As I hurried through the halls, kids stepped back for me. The crowds seemed to part. There was something about me that height and a new skirt did not explain. The tattoo—which wasn't a tattoo—was part of it, but there was more than that. I tried to smile at everyone and felt like a queen smiling at her subjects. I slipped into my first class just as the second bell rang. I was grateful for fifty quiet minutes to be alone with my thoughts. I checked my phone. Nothing from anybody.

"I know graduation is only three months away," Mr. Fleming was saying, "but this is no time to slack off. C'mon, people!"

He went into a boring story he had told us before about someone who got their college acceptance rescinded because of lousy second semester grades. Whatever. I tuned him out. What had the shoe fairy meant when she said I knew how to contact Walker? I couldn't remember him telling me anything to do—except giving me his cell phone number like anybody else. The windows were open in the class and I could hear some birds outside. Really hear them.

"Pretzel crumbs," one twittered.

"Corn chips," another peeped.

"I love eating at the high school."

I laughed out loud and Seth, the guy in front of me, turned around. I smiled at him and he blushed. I'd known Seth since second grade, but he looked at me as if he'd never seen me before.

The assistant principal, Ms. Garcia, knocked and entered. I held my breath, remembering when Trevor had come into class behind the principal, but Ms. Garcia just whispered something to Mr. Fleming and waited.

"October?" he called. "You're needed in the office."

The class did not look surprised. Any girl with a tattoo and an attitude like mine (even for one day) was obviously looking for trouble. I left my backpack on my desk and followed Ms. Garcia, and this time thirty-one pairs of eyes watched me go.

Four days ago I had run out of class because of an itch. That itch was the beginning of the end of my old life. That itch had turned into this tattoo. And four days ago in this hallway, scratching my bare foot desperately, I had met Walker. Where was he now? Would I ever see him again? I tried to summon him with my mind, but I saw only a swirl of colors and heard only silence. I thought of his arms around me, the kiss I had felt in my knees, in my whole body. The kiss that had truly made the earth move. His blond curls, his ultra blue eyes, the v created at the neck of his button down shirt. That was all coming in loud and clear. I put one hand on the wall to steady myself.

"Come along," Ms. Garcia said. "Don't dawdle."

I blinked back to reality. Her little feet in sensible black pumps clicked against the floor. I shuffled along behind. She was the academic assistant, the one who called your parents when you were flunking and gave out the awards when you won. That reminded me of Green. He was always winning some award or other.

"Hey Ms. Garcia," I caught up to her. "Do you know which lunch period Chris Lee has? Or what class he's in now?"

"Chris? He has first lunch."

"Thanks. He's…helping me with my biology."

"He's a very good student."

We had reached the office door. As she pushed it open, she smiled at me. Her eyes were kind and she reached for my hand and gave it a squeeze as I went past her. My stomach did a flip-flop. In tenth grade Aaron Goldsmith had been called out of class because his dad died in a car crash. I was going to be sick. Could my mom be dead? Was that why I hadn't heard from her?

Dad got to his feet when he saw me. "October, thank God you're all right."

"Is Mom okay?"

"What? Sure. Uh… you didn't answer your phone…" He trailed off.

"I turn my phone off in school." I smiled at Ms. Garcia. "I'm supposed to."

"Of course you do." Dad didn't smile. "You forgot your lunch." He thrust a brown paper bag toward me.

I wanted to give him a hug and squeeze my father back into this body—because that was definitely not my dad. He hadn't once called me "kiddo" or "pumpkin." He never brought me my lunch if I forgot it. And blotches, those same red welts, were popping up on my hands. I stepped away from him and noticed him staring blankly at my necklace.

Ms. Garcia noticed it too. "That's quite beautiful," she said.

"Thank you. It was a birthday gift—from him." I couldn't quite bring myself to say 'Dad.'

"Did you take it off for any reason?" the Dad-thing asked me.

"Oh," I said as if I just remembered. "Right. I took it off to wash my face. My make-up smeared." I lied, but I wanted him to think it was still working. "Left it in the ladies room. Thank God it was still there when I went back."

"Leave it on," he said sternly. "I mean it. Do not take it off. Do you hear me?"

"Okay, okay. I—"

"Well, then—all cleared up," Ms. Garcia interrupted, trying to avoid an unpleasant family moment. "I understand your worry, Mr. Fetterhoff." She walked us to the office door. "We have lots of parents calling to check in." She turned to me. "You could check your phone between classes, just to set your father's mind at ease."

"Good idea." I turned to go. "Bye, Dad. See you later."

"Wait," he said. "Your lunch." He handed it to me. "Be sure to eat every bite."

In your dreams, I wanted to say. Instead I took it, smiled, and waved as I left.

The hallway was deserted and I leaned against the wall and breathed deeply the sour smell of school. The hives on my hands disappeared as quickly as they had come. The shoe fairy had been right, the old necklace was a tracking device because obviously the Dad-thing had lost me and gotten worried. My phone—in my backpack in the classroom—was on. I knew he hadn't tried to call or text me. He was keeping close tabs on me, but I didn't know why. I had made my promise and I hadn't broken it—so far.

It wouldn't be long before he figured out the necklace wasn't working anymore. If I was going to find Green and then Walker, I had to hurry. I thought about the fairytales I'd read as a kid, Cinderella, Snow White, the Snow Queen, hoping for some clue how to solve this mess. I wished I could just kiss Walker and we would wake up in a world without Madame Gold, but

I had kissed him and he had kissed me and nothing had happened except to get me all hot and bothered. The shoe fairy, like a witch by the side of the road, had given me a gift, but unlike the princess in a fairytale I hadn't done anything in return. I'd been mean and told her to move. "Sorry," I whispered. "Survive," I thought I heard her say again. I would do my best.

I threw the lunch bag in the trashcan and headed for the science rooms. Green could be there with the other smart kids taking AP Chem or something-ology. My cell phone vibrated. Already, I thought. The dad-monster was checking on me already. I got out my phone and looked at the number. It was one I didn't recognize. I took a deep breath and answered anyway.

"Hello?"

There was static. I almost hung up, but then I heard my mother's voice.

"October?"

The connection was terrible.

"Mom!" I almost started to cry I was so relieved to hear from her. "Where are you?"

Every other word was dropping out. "…Helping… a special mushroom… Madame Gold…" Then she said something about meeting her somewhere.

"Where? Where?"

"You know…"

"I can't understand you."

"You … out…. Danger here… Have to go." And she hung up.

I didn't have a clue where to meet her. She said I knew, but I knew nothing. Being taller and having red hair didn't make me any smarter. I had to find Green, and he would help me find Walker and Walker would help me find my mom. He had to.

I ran to the chem labs. Empty. It was hours until the first

lunch period. I went up and down the hallways looking in each classroom. What if Green wasn't at school? What would I do?

As I ran past the school's front doors, I saw my father getting out of his car and heading back in. He had already figured out the necklace wasn't working. I looked around. There had to be somewhere to hide. Obviously not in a classroom. Not outside under the breezeway where I was likely to be seen. I ducked into the library and forced myself to walk nonchalantly past the librarian and turn into the stacks. Then I bolted to the shelves farthest from the door. The fluorescent light that had gone out over my and Trevor's heads was on again. For once, the school had fixed something right away. And I really wished they hadn't.

The light flickered, gave a pop, and went out. Just as it had before. Had Trevor done that before? Had I just done it myself? Was it some troll ability to make the world as dark as possible? I looked at the next light and wished it would go out too. I concentrated. It went out. Awesome, I thought. Truly awesome. I began to concentrate on the next one.

"If you make them all go out, it'll look suspicious."

I jumped. Green stood behind me with another armload of books. I should have thought of looking for him in the library—the perfect place for a nerd to spend his time.

"You can make them go on, too." He smiled up at me. "Hello, October."

"Green. I mean, Chris. I'm happy to see you."

"You are? Nice to see you too. We have to leave now."

"I'm supposed to meet my mom."

"That's a good idea."

"But I don't know where."

Green cocked his head and looked at me with a funny, quizzical expression—like a dog. "You don't?" he asked.

"The phone kept dropping out. And there was a ton of static. I couldn't understand her."

He continued to look at me, puzzled.

"I didn't hear what she said."

"But she's your mother."

"So?"

"You two have always had a good connection." When I frowned, he continued. "Think. October, you know exactly where she is. Just think about it."

That was exactly what the Shoe Fairy had told me about Walker. I closed my eyes. I tried to concentrate on my mother. A picture began to emerge. She was standing shin deep in water and there were cattails and grasses all around her. A marsh of some kind. It looked vaguely familiar, but it could have been any marsh in the world.

"I knew you were thinking about me. That's why I'm here," Green said. "You've been thinking about Walker too."

I blushed. I had been thinking about Walker. Earlier I'd been wishing he could see me in my skirt and I'd been imagining being alone with him.

"Uh oh," Green said.

The doors to the library opened and I heard the dad-thing call my name. The librarian shushed him, but he ignored her. He was coming our way.

"Transplant." Green grabbed my hand and started running toward the back wall of the library. "Transplant!"

"Where to?" There was no time for him to answer.

19.

The warm sand. The claustrophobia. I wasn't scared until I landed with a bump and things with sharp corners hit me in the head and jabbed my shoulders and legs.

"Ow." I opened my eyes. Books. Green's stack of books had also transplanted and fallen on me as they came through. Green himself was nowhere to be seen. And I was the last place I expected to be—in the middle of the mall behind the kiosk selling baseball caps. I had to laugh. It was perfect; my dad would never think to look for me at the mall. Strangely, no one paid any attention to my abrupt arrival. Moms with strollers. Senior citizens in sneakers doing laps. It was a school day, but I saw kids my age hanging in front of the pretzel place. This was where people went to skip school, I'd obviously been right about that. I stood up, brushed myself off, and collected Green's books so he could find them again. Didn't want him getting a hefty library fine. Ha ha ha. I put the books on a bench and sat down. I closed my eyes and concentrated on my mom. Again I saw her standing in a marsh, bent over, feeling for something in the water. But what marsh? I wondered if I could transplant there even if I wasn't sure where it was. So far I hadn't done very well at planning my transplant destinations. I opened my eyes, and my breath caught in my throat.

Walker stood in front of me. Walker. I jumped up and wanted to throw my arms around him, but then I didn't. He looked sad and remote with his hands in the pockets of his jeans. He gave me an unhappy smile and then looked at the floor between us. I had never been so glad to see anyone. My chest lifted. I grinned. He wore a blue button-down shirt, very normal and very nice, and he was more handsome than ever.

"Hey. It's you," I said. "At the mall. Cool. New shirt?" Ugh. I was so lame.

"You look...amazing." That was really nice to hear. He gestured at my tattoo. "Your fairy mark is excellent. Perfect. Deserving of you."

"Fairy mark." So that's what it was. "It's getting me a lot of attention at school."

"I bet."

There was an awkward silence. So much to say, so hard to say it. We both started at the same time.

"I'm sorry," I said.

"I'm sorry," he said.

We stopped, started, stopped, and finally I said, "You have nothing to be sorry about."

He did not agree. "I should have explained it to you better, made you see how complicated this all is."

"Things aren't working out."

"No."

"My dad is still under her spell." He nodded, not surprised. "What about Luisa? Trevor? The Fairy Canopy? Are they okay?"

"Depends what you mean by 'okay.'"

"But she promised me. I thought we had to keep our promises."

"Fairies do," he said. "But Madame Gold must not be a fairy. Whatever she is, lying is just fine with her. I should have made that more clear."

"Oh, oh... I'm an idiot. An idiot. I'm so stupid."

Walker spoke bitterly. "Stop. This is not your fault. You tried to do the right thing. Your only mistake was thinking she was an honorable being."

He looked miserable. I agreed things were bad, but my heart was lighter just seeing him. Maybe it wasn't suitably coy and blasé, but I wanted to tell him how I really felt. "I…" I couldn't go on. I couldn't stand it if he laughed at me, or told me to get lost. So I only said, "It's great that you're here. Really great."

It wasn't enough. I took a step toward him.

He stepped back. "I'm not supposed to see you anymore. I can't. She's forbidden me to even be in the human world."

"But you're here."

"Because I knew you'd be here."

"How did you know? I didn't know I'd be at the mall."

"Don't you get it?" He had tears in his eyes and they turned from sky blue to the color of a stormy sea. Actual tears. He reached for me, but dropped his hands before he touched me. "Princess."

"I'm not a princess anymore."

"No. You're the Queen."

"I'm not. I gave that up, remember?"

He wiped his eyes with the back of his hand. "You are the Queen. My Queen. Our Queen. No matter what." He looked at the baseball caps, at the floor, at the ceiling, anywhere but at me as he said, "I'm in love with you."

I stopped breathing. If there were other people in the mall, shoppers going past us on either side, I didn't see them anymore. The whole world—both worlds, the real and the supernatural—had become only the two of us. "Walker." I said his name as if I had just learned it.

"Fairies aren't supposed to feel this way," he said. "We don't do this."

"Say it again."

"I love you."

"You can't." I thought of my hairy toes. "I'm half troll, a weirdo, a half breed."

"I don't care. I really don't." He looked as surprised as I felt.

I took his hand. The touch was electrifying as always. My whole arm buzzed as I pulled him toward the closest doors out of the mall. "Let's get out of here."

"Wait," he protested.

"Come on." I didn't want the most romantic moment of my life to happen at the Westfair Mall in front of Forever 21.

"Fairies aren't supposed to fall in love." Walker tried to smile. "It's different for us. We make sensible choices, we regard all creatures equally, our marriages are often arranged. Not like trolls. Trolls fall in love twenty times a day."

"I don't." I pushed through the glass doors.

"I'm not sure how this happened," he said. "I think about you all the time, the way you laugh, that little thing you do with your thumb when you're angry, how strong and kind you are, how you smell like toast and cinnamon. When I thought I'd never see you again it hurt. It physically hurt in my chest, as if I'd been punched. Seeing you today, even knowing you don't feel the same way about me, makes me happy. I'd do anything for you. Is that love? It's wonderful and terrible all at the same time."

We were outside in the parking lot. The sun was shining and the tears on his cheek glistened and his eyes were a beautiful deep sapphire. I wanted to tell him I felt the same. I wanted to tell him not to be sad. I wanted to tell him so many things and I didn't know where to begin so I kissed him. He was surprised, I could feel it, but then he put his arms around me and kissed me back. This was different, bigger, fuller somehow than our first kiss. This was real and true and deep and absolutely right. We belonged kissing each other. It was like a roller coaster ride, slow at first, then more and more exciting, up and up and over the big drop and it took my breath away.

"October," he said when we finally broke apart.

"Walker," I said.

We kissed again and again I felt that roller coaster rising and plummeting down to my toes.

"I think I love you too," I said to him. "I do. But I promised. I promised."

Walker wilted. "I know. It's fine. I'll never go back. I'll stay here with you."

"You can't." I knew how much he loved his fairy world.

"Your mother and father did it. Now I understand why. Nothing compares to this—to you."

"Mom," I said. "My mother and my father..."

"What is it?" he asked. "What else has happened?"

I pulled the necklace out from under my sweater.

He slammed the wall with his hands and started looking around, behind us, up in the sky.

"Don't worry," I said. "This is a copy. The Shoe Fairy gave it to me."

I could hear his relief. "She found you."

"She told me to tell you hello."

"Do you see?" he asked.

"See what?"

"How much we all love you. How much we need you."

I thought about Green and Luisa and Jed and the Shoe Fairy. Luisa turned into a panther because of me. Jed worried out of his mind but telling me to stay inside and lock the doors. The fairy in the cage telling me not to drink. Green appearing just when I needed him. All of them protecting me, helping me. And I had let them down. I looked at Walker. I wanted nothing more than to be his girlfriend, his ordinary human girlfriend.

I wanted us to go to the movies together or on a hike or to Ricky's Tacos and talk and talk long into the night. But it wasn't possible.

Suddenly I was furious. Who did Madame Gold think she was? She was ruining my life. Who the hell did she think she was? "This has to stop," I said. "I'm going to stop her."

"You promised."

"You forget, I'm not a fairy either—not completely. I have a mostly human mind, a good one, and I can change it any time I want." I swear that as I spoke I grew taller, that I became stronger thanks to my determination. "I will fix this."

I concentrated on my mother in the marsh and in a flash I knew what she was doing. Five years earlier she had been part of the team that discovered a new species of river mushroom. She was looking for that mushroom. I didn't know why, but it was important. And I knew where she was: the L.A. River. Not far from the portal. We could pick her up on the way.

"We have to go back to your world. Now."

Walker didn't argue. "My car is this way."

We walked quickly across the parking lot. The sky was a brilliant spring blue. The air smelled sweet. I wanted Walker to take my hand and he did.

"What's happened to Luisa?"

"She's with Jed."

That was good.

"In jail."

That was bad.

He continued, "Madame Gold doesn't trust them."

"And is Trevor in jail too?"

"Ha. Trevor is her betrothed."

"She's still going to marry him?"

"She can't be queen without him."

"But she's so powerful."

"She has no royal blood. He does. In our world that's the way it works. If he was out of the picture, then it would be his younger sister and Enoki doesn't want that—for lots of reasons." He paused. "Without Trevor, Madame Gold can only rule the trolls by force."

I thought about Trevor and got a clear picture of him. I saw him in a troll style palace bedroom—fancy but dark with unfinished dirt walls. He looked mostly healed and he was pacing angrily, wearing down a path in the moss carpet. When he felt me in his mind he stopped. He looked up, right in my direction, and nodded. Then he went over to the only window. It looked out on roots that were as twisted and thick as a jungle. There were metal bars across the window, but he was strong and with very little effort he bent the bars open. I watched him climb out and disappear.

I felt guilty for thinking of Trevor, but I was happy he had escaped even if it seemed he could have done it at any time without me. Run, I told him in my mind. Run away from Madame Gold. Walker was still talking, telling me about the fairies and all the horrors going on his world.

"And, if you are alive," he said, "somewhere, anywhere—no matter what you promised—she cannot sit on the fairy throne. She can imprison the fairies, make them work, punish them, she can even rule them in a way, but literally, magically, she cannot enter the castle. Those doors are forever locked to her."

Everything became clear to me. Why she was still following me. Why she still had control of my father. And why my mother had stayed away and hidden.

"Why didn't you tell me that?"

"I tried."

"You know what?" I said wearily. "Your world is totally

screwed up. This system is ridiculous. Ultimate control is always a bad idea. You need a better method—like a president that people vote for."

"We need you."

I opened my mouth to disagree as a lone crow soared over us. Walker's grip tightened. Another crow appeared, high in the sky circling, looking for me. We ducked under the cover of some oleander bushes beside the parking lot. We crept along the edge until we came to a beat up, faded blue Honda. Walker opened the passenger door.

"Get in," he said.

"Where's the Porsche?"

"You are such a snob." He laughed, but his eyes were worried, searching the sky. "I'm on my own here. Not official business."

I got into the passenger seat. It was an old car, the dashboard was cracked and a Disney store Tinkerbelle hung from the mirror.

I pointed at it and raised my eyebrows as he started the motor, with difficulty.

"It's a loaner, okay? My friend's car."

"I'd like to meet this friend." It was definitely a girl. There were hair bands around the gearshift and clothes in the back and a pink hairbrush rolling around on the floor at my feet. "What's her name?"

"Okay, okay. I stole it."

"This? You stole this?"

"You don't care that I stole a car. You're just upset it's not a Porsche."

He drove out of the parking lot. The engine had a very unhappy knock. I wasn't sure we'd make it to the corner, much less all the way to the river. I laughed out loud.

"I wish you'd take it seriously," he said. "Those crows could be after you."

"I don't care." I leaned over and kissed his cheek. He smelled like flowers and better than that, he smelled like him. "Anyway, look. The sky is completely clear. They have no idea where I am."

I expected him to disagree, but to my surprise, he sighed and pulled the car over on the shoulder of the road. Then I did get worried. I thought he had seen something and that we were in trouble. "Slobbers?" I asked.

He turned to me and took me in his arms and kissed me. If a thousand crows had attacked the car right then, broken through the windshield and killed me, I would have died happy.

20.

We didn't kiss for long. First, the front seat of a 1992 Honda Civic is an awkward place for making out. We were too far apart and the gearshift and the brake and a couple of crusty Slurpee cups were between us. Second, and yes, more importantly, I heard my mother calling to me, telling me to hurry.

There was a clatter on the hood of the car. A giant crow stared at us through the windshield. Its little eyes were like black marbles as it turned its head one way and then the other. Terrifying eyes, no pupils, no color, blank and unfeeling. I heard it thinking, "Here you are. Here you are."

Then it looked as if it were choking, it bobbed its head and gagged. When it looked up again it dangled something from its beak, something that sparkled in the sun.

"My necklace!" I gasped.

"Shiny," the crow said. "Pretty."

If the crow had my real necklace, it could only mean that the Shoe Fairy had given it up. And she would have given it up only if she had to.

"Oh no," I whispered. "The Shoe Fairy." I clapped my hand over the necklace I was wearing. Did she really sacrifice herself for me?

Walker turned to me and held my shoulders in his two warm hands. His eyes were sad, but his voice was urgent. "If you tell me to, I'll take you right back to school," he said. "If the Shoe Fairy couldn't fight them off, I don't think you—or even I—can.

Tell me to take you to school. You'll be safe. I don't want you to be hurt. Just choose to go on with your human life. I'd rather never see you again than have anything happen to you."

"Then the Shoe Fairy will have fought for nothing!" I practically exploded. He was sweet, romantic, and I loved that he was worried for my safety, but I couldn't sit by and do nothing while Madame Gold ruined his world and Trevor's. "And Luisa and Jed will be in jail forever. Is that what you want?"

I had to fight. I had more reason than ever to defeat Madame Gold.

"Okay," he said. "Your choice. Okay."

I didn't know why it seemed important to him that it was my choice we go back to the fairy world, but I didn't get a chance to ask. He landed on the horn with both hands, startling me almost as much as the crow. It cawed loudly as it flapped away. He put the car in gear, stepped on the gas, and the tires squealed against the asphalt.

"We can't out run it," I said as I fastened my seat belt. The crow was following, and gaining on us.

"I want it to catch us."

"It has my necklace. My father and Madame Gold know I'm not at school."

"Trust me."

"Don't say that. Please, don't say that."

He turned onto a winding road through Griffith Park and had to slow down. Way down. The crow flapped up beside me.

"What are you doing?"

"Roll down your window."

"Are you insane?"

"Do it."

I did and Walker whistled—a high, sharp blast.

Oberon leapt out of the brush on my side of the car and

caught the crow in his mouth. Snap! Squish! The crow exploded in a mess of blood and feathers. Walker pulled over, got out, and opened his door. Oberon trotted up proudly carrying my necklace in his mouth. He dropped it into Walker's open palm. Walker threw the necklace as far as he could—which was very far especially considering his skinny fairy arms—into the woods. Then Oberon hopped in the backseat.

"Good boy," Walker said.

Oberon wiggled all over, pleased with himself. He had feathers stuck in his teeth.

"Hello, Oberon," I said. "Thank you."

"Hi, October. Didn't I do a good job? Didn't I? Pet me! Pet me!"

I patted his head, scratched behind his ears. His tail wagged, making a swooshing noise against the backseat. He licked my hand. I thought of where that tongue had just been. Yuk. Oberon wiggled up between the seats and licked my face.

"Is that necessary?" I asked.

"Guess we both like kissing you," Walker said.

"Very funny."

"Love me, love my dog."

I started to laugh, then I remembered the Shoe Fairy, and she led to Luisa and Jed, and then Trevor beaten almost to death, and of course finally to my poor demented dad, and I started to cry instead. Oberon whined and licked me again. Walker took me in his arms. He patted my back and smoothed my hair off my wet face.

"It's okay," he said. "It's okay. A week ago you thought you were an average, human, high school senior. Now you're one of a kind, half troll, half fairy, and Queen of two kingdoms. Crows are chasing you, your dad's a zombie, and we're trying to find your mom. To say nothing of some fairy showing up who just wants to kiss you all the time." He demonstrated, kissing my forehead, my eyes, my cheeks. "You're amazing. I wanted to quit, but you're still fighting, still thinking, still wanting to save everybody else. You're incredible."

I buried my face in his blue shirt. I wanted him to keep talking. I wanted to be with him forever. It was more than just his blue eyes and curly blond hair. More than the way he kissed. It was the way I felt when I was with him, both protected and strong. He helped me feel as if I could do anything. He had so much confidence in me that I almost believed it myself. The tears stopped and my shoulders straightened. I could do this. I sat up and told him I was fine. Walker pulled a U-turn and we headed toward the river.

"Thank you for finding me," I said.

"I didn't find you. You found me."

"But you came to the mall."

"Because you sent me a message."

"I did?"

I tried to remember sending anything. I didn't even have a cell phone.

He gently touched my forehead. "You have a power," he said. "A very strong power. And you have been thinking about me."

I squirmed, thinking of some of the things I'd just been thinking. "Really?"

"I can't get the specifics." He smiled at me and raised his eyebrows. "Too bad." He took my hand. "But when you want to see me, it's clear."

I thought of Trevor and the way he'd felt me watching him. It was wild to think that my thoughts could travel. "Can all fairies do that?"

"We have some ability. Nothing like what you can do. You can call us, and I bet you can see us and even communicate with us."

He was right; I saw my mother as clearly as if I was standing next to her.

Walker said, "I've never felt the call so strong and so unmistakable. You just have to practice."

"What about trolls?"

"Definitely not a troll trait."

I wanted to try it out. I closed my eyes and pictured my dad. Instantly I saw him in an industrial warehouse of some kind, subdued with his head bowed. Last I'd seen him, he'd been coming for me at school. I'd known exactly how determined he was. Now his thoughts were confused, in a swirl of muddy water. I couldn't send him a clear message. He was standing beside Madame Gold. My thoughts went to her, but she felt me looking and her head came up and I felt her mind drilling into mine. I shut down. Thought about school. Homework. WWI. "Madame Gold," I said.

"Did you see her?"

"Worse. She saw me." I tried not to think of her. "She's very powerful. What is she? She can't be a fairy."

"There have been a few Red Fairies in the past," Walker said. "Also what they call White Trolls, trolls with potent magical capabilities. Neither are the good guys."

"So which is she?"

"We don't know. She appeared in our world fully grown. She attached herself to Trevor, so we all assumed she was a troll of some kind. But her powers, using the crows, the hypnosis, are more like the abilities of fairies. She tried to ingratiate herself with both worlds, but once she learned about you everything changed. Plus she's crazed about those mushrooms. She wants more, more, more."

"There has to be something she's not good at. Some way we can beat her."

"For now," he said, "better not to think about her."

Of course the minute you're told not to think about something, it's all you can think of. An orange car reminded me of her orange dress. A driver with red hair reminded me of her red hair. I forced myself to think of something else. I tried a technique they'd taught us in Sex Ed class: every time you think about the bad thing (i.e. sex), immediately replace it with a picture of something good (i.e. not sex). So when I thought of Madame Gold, I pictured ice cream cones. I was thinking about it so hard, I expected ice cream to be falling from the sky. And I couldn't be sure it was because of me, but as we passed the frozen yogurt place there was a line of people out the door. At the same time, I tried to find my mom. The L.A. River is forty-eight miles long.

But then I saw her in the rain. Standing among giant rocks. She was thinking of me, hoping I wouldn't come to wherever she was. She was hurt. Her face was bruised and she was limping. It wasn't just raining, it was pouring. That couldn't be. I looked out the car window. There was not a single cloud in the southern California sky.

"Walker," I said. He heard the change in my voice. "My mom is somewhere rocky and it's raining. And she's hurt."

He put one hand on my thigh. "I think your mother has been captured. I figured it was just a matter of time."

First my dad. Now my mom. I would kill Madame Gold. I really would. And the moment I thought about her, she thought about me. I saw her smile her evil, sick smile. Ice cream. Ice cream. Ice cream.

We had arrived at the L.A. River. We parked and I jumped out. Walker and Oberon followed me through the gate and down to the river. I had no problem going down the retaining wall and this time I actually sort of flew over the trash in the water to the other side. Oberon bounded across. I turned to ask

Walker if I was able to fly and saw him hopping clumsily from piece of trash to piece of trash. One foot splashed into the water.

"What's up with you?"

He didn't answer. I strolled as he slipped and slid and clambered up to the closed portal door.

"You okay?" I asked.

Again he didn't answer. He stood before the enormous circular iron door. He touched it with both hands and shut his eyes. Nothing happened that I could see. His eyes opened wide and his face went whiter than it already was.

"Do we need a key?" I asked.

"It's the way home. Fairies have instant access."

"Maybe it's because you were forbidden to come out here."

"No. I'm still a fairy. This can't be." He banged on the door. "I'm still a fairy." For the first time he looked rattled, desperate, and even afraid. "I'm still a fairy."

Oberon nuzzled up against his leg. "You are, you are," the dog said. "And I'm your bird—uh—dog."

"Of course you're a fairy. We'll just transplant."

"What if it doesn't work?"

If it didn't work, it would hurt. A lot. I had transplanted to the mall so I knew it was possible for me. I had promised not to return, but it didn't seem as if my promises meant anything. Or maybe Madame Gold wanted me to come find her. I was happy to oblige. Time was wasting. "I'll go through and then open it for you. How does it work?"

"A fairy just has to close his eyes and press on it. You'll go right through. But you—you're not a fairy."

"Hey. I'm the flipping Queen. That's what you said." I tried to make him laugh. He didn't. I stepped close to the door, put my hands on it.

"Wait," Walker said. "You don't know the way. You don't

know what's down there."

He'd forgotten I'd been there before. The only way was down. I pressed hard on the door, closed my eyes—and opened them inside the tunnel. Easy as pie. I could see fine in the dark, even without the fireflies. My eyes had definitely gained more troll abilities when I turned eighteen. I tried to turn around and open the door for Walker, but first I couldn't find a knob, then I realized the door wasn't there. It was just another wall of rock. I tried closing my eyes, pressing hard, and going back through it the way I had come. It didn't work. I should have asked him how to get out.

"Walker!" I shouted. "Walker!" I pounded on the rock.

Fairyland was so difficult it was beginning to get to me. There were too many rules and too many odd magical stupidities. No, I told myself, no. I only had to follow the tunnel down and when I got the forest I would find a way to bring Walker in. There was another way in and out, Trevor had taken me back that way. I turned and started walking quickly down. The tunnel got smaller and narrower, just as I remembered. The walls were rough as I remembered. The only thing missing was the light I'd seen at the end. I assumed it was because my eyes were doing so much better in the dark and therefore the contrast was not as great. I had to crouch lower and lower. I couldn't really look over my shoulder. Just as I remembered.

And then there was water under my feet that I knew had not been there the last time. I continued. The water got deeper and deeper until I was splashing through it up to my knees. Not good. What was going on?

I tried to find Walker in my mind, or my mother, or even Trevor, but it was like the line was busy. I couldn't get through. Walker couldn't hear me and I had no idea where I was. I stopped but the water kept getting deeper. Up to my thighs. Up to my waist. Up to my chest. I wasn't a very good swimmer and there was barely room to swim anyway. The water kept rising. It was up to my neck. I tried to turn around and go back up to higher ground, but there wasn't room. The tunnel was like a terrible capsule, holding me, preparing me to drown.

I tried to scream for Walker one last time, and the water rushed into my open mouth and filled my nostrils and I went completely under.

21.

I came up sputtering and choking in a deep crevasse filled with water. It was pouring rain and sheer rock walls surrounded me. "Help," I called out weakly. I treaded water, but I wasn't very good at it and I knew I wouldn't last long. Fairies and trolls are not water entities. Or at least it was not my strength. I paddled over to one side and felt my way along it, searching for a ledge where I could get a grip. I went all the way around looking for any place I could hold on. I would not allow myself to cry. I had come so far and I was not going to let a little water pull me under. Ha ha ha. That was a Dad joke. I wished he were there, my old dad, not the new one. I tried to imagine him throwing me a rope, lowering a ladder, reaching his long arm over the side, but I couldn't feel him or see him in my mind at all. It was as if someone had unplugged my Internet. My inter-mind connection had gone black, blacker than the tunnel had been. I continued around the perimeter of the water-filled chasm. There had to be a way out. In Ms. Tannenbaum's P.E. class we had done a rope climb that at the time seemed impossible. We tried it every single class, day after day, week after week, until one by one each and every girl figured it out. It took strength, sure, but also balance and determination and optimism. If I could do that, I could climb up these stupid rocks. Rocks had to be easier than a rope. I went slowly around the edge again and again and on the third time around, as my arms were just about to give out, my fingers found the tiniest of outcroppings above me. I held on. I pressed my waterlogged shoes against the rock below and pulled myself up. I reached with my other hand to find another place, no matter how tiny, where I could hold on. There. My toes found an indentation. I pushed with my legs. I was climbing. I was doing it. Hand over hand, achingly slowly, my arms screaming with pain, slipping and sliding and almost falling back in, I made it up the side. Luckily it wasn't very high. I made the final ascent over the edge and onto my belly. I lay there panting. I had done it and I didn't think I could stand up, but I was exhilarated.

I lifted my head. I had climbed to nowhere. Nothing in any direction but black rocks and piles of black rocks. The rain continued, the drops enormous, each one like a cup of water falling on my head and shoulders. The sky was an awful shade of greenish gray, like the ocean under an oil spill.

"Walker!" I shouted, but my voice was swallowed, as if I was shouting inside a helmet. All the sounds were very strange. I knocked my fist on a rock and it thudded as softly as if I had knocked on a carpet.

I turned slowly, looking for a flat, wall-like surface. Transplanting seemed the only reasonable way out. I concentrated on a boulder with a mostly smooth side. I could definitely run into that. I took off, but the wet rocks beneath me were slippery and I couldn't get up any speed. My feet kept sliding out from under me. It was like running in a nightmare, jogging through peanut butter, working so hard and getting nowhere. I headed for the flat side of the rock as quickly as I could, but it wasn't fast enough. At the last moment, I put my hands out to protect my face and sure enough, BAM! I smacked into the rock. I bit my tongue and my mouth filled with blood as I fell backwards.

Oh man, that hurt. I'd worried if Walker couldn't transplant running into the portal would hurt him and I was right. I hoped he wasn't trying it on his own. Okay. I blinked back the tears. I could figure this out. There had to be another way out and I was going to find it. If I couldn't transplant through the big boulder, I could still climb it and get a look around. I stood up on top and spit out a mouthful of blood. The rain instantly washed it away. It was a silly thought, given everything, but I was sorry my clothes were ruined, my shoes were a soggy mess, my new sweater had stretched down below my butt, and my cute skirt was clinging to my thighs. I wiped the water out of my eyes and searched through the rain. Nothing as far as I could see except rocks. Piles of rocks. I turned slowly and saw nothing. And turned again. Still nothing.

But wait! There in the distance were lights. I blinked and wiped the water from my eyes for the umpteenth time and stared. Yes! Warm, inviting yellow lights just forty or fifty rock piles away.

I didn't want to scoot off the boulder on my butt and damage my skirt more than it already was, so I tried to climb down and I slipped and landed hard on my right ankle. Hard enough so it buckled beneath me. When I stood up, it hurt a lot to put any weight on it. Again, I refused to cry. "You're wet enough already," I said out loud. Ha ha ha. I wasn't laughing as I limped toward the lights. Or in the direction I thought they were. Unfortunately, I couldn't see the lights from the ground.

Thirty minutes later, I still hadn't reached anything but more rocks. I had to stop frequently and rest my ankle. I found a place to sit on the nearest rock. I was tired and tired of the rain and tired of the pain in my ankle. I wished I were home in bed— but when I thought about home and my dad-not-dad I knew it was no refuge. Really, I wanted to be back in that dirty little car with Walker. Walker. Where was he? Why hadn't I listened when he told me to wait? So much for my good, quick mind. "Pride goeth before destruction, a haughty spirit before a fall."

Shakespeare had used that proverb in Macbeth and I actually remembered it from English class. I hadn't known how true it was. My pride had brought me here and thanks to my haughty spirit I had both literally and figuratively fallen.

I picked myself up. I had to get to those lights. I climbed to the top of another pile of rocks to see where I'd gotten off track. I felt Madame Gold searching for me. I felt her laughing at me. I concentrated on Walker. That would make me feel better and maybe some tiny bit of my thinking would get through the rain and the rocks to him. I thought of his warm arms around me. The way he kissed me. The way he looked into my eyes.

Then I thought about how he had to give up being a fairy for me. How his friends, Luisa and Jed, had been hurt. How he no longer could fly or transplant or do any of his fairy things. That was my fault. And I felt terrible.

But then I wondered how he had already known my dad was still a zombie. How did he know Jed and Luisa were in jail? Why, when we met her on the path, had he bowed to Madame Gold? I wondered why he had let me go through the portal. He could have stopped me. He could have grabbed me and pulled me away from the door.

He wanted me to be in here. Without him.

If pride is bad, self-doubt is worse. My heart shrank in my chest. That's what it felt like, as if it had turned into a small, hard, rock—like any of the rocks surrounding me. I was a fool to believe Walker loved me. What an absurd idea. Gorgeous fairy him and half-breed me. Never! He hated trolls so much. He had to hate the troll in me.

I crumpled and sank to my knees on top of the rock. He was a liar and a manipulator and I had bought every line he'd thrown at me. Fairies don't fall in love, he said, but I fell in love with you. I was an idiot. A complete idiot. I shouted "Idiot!" as loud as I could, even though I knew no one would hear me. "I hate you!" I yelled. But I wasn't sure if I hated him, or myself.

I crawled to the edge and looked down twenty feet to the rocky ground. I would dive headfirst. If I landed right I could definitely break my neck. What difference did it make? Nobody cared. My dad was brain dead, my mother was hurt and jailed somewhere, and I had no friends. If I was gone Madame Gold could make everything right again. My tears were almost as large as the drops of rain falling on my back. I allowed myself to cry and I sobbed and sobbed.

Oh my God, I was making myself sick. "Snap out of it," I hollered. I was having a big stupid pity party and letting a guy ruin my life. I had sworn I would never do that, never be like a girl on a television teen melodrama beating herself up over some boy. "I am not that girl." I said that out loud too, although I didn't shout it.

Gingerly, I stood up on my sore ankle and slowly turned searching the distance. There they were! I gave myself a virtual pat on the back. I was going in the right direction. I could see the lights. I was doing something right. I even laughed a little. I'd show Walker. I would do this by myself. Only a few more piles and I would be there. I marked the piles, memorizing unusual features of each one that I was sure I could see from the ground. I sat down and very carefully, not caring about my skirt or sweater, slid down the rock and landed gently on the ground. My ankle felt a little better. Maybe. Even if it didn't, I was going to keep walking. I had no choice.

I rounded the last bunch of rocks and saw a cluster of little huts made mostly of rocks with some very weathered wood. Their front doors all faced a big pile of empty liquor bottles and rusty beer cans.

"Hello?" I called.

The door to the closest hut opened and a man emerged. He was a fairy, or had been, he had silver hair, pointed ears and blue skin, but he was wearing ugly, dirty, rough clothing that barely covered his enormous unfairylike belly.

"What are you?" He sneered. "Not a fairy. Not a troll either. Some weird creation 'she' made." I knew he meant Madame Gold.

"No. She didn't make me."

He whistled and surprisingly the whistle carried through the sodden air. Other doors began to open and others emerged, men and women. Most of them carried a bottle or a can, and my heart sank when I realized they were all drunk. They pulled the bottles from each other's hands and threw the empties in the pile, cheering at the crash of broken glass. Was this what my father had been like? And my mother had fallen in love with him anyway.

"Hey. Hi. Can you help me? I'm lost."

"And now you're found!" One of the men chortled.

"Where am I?"

"This is The Pits," a woman said.

"I can see that."

"That's what it's called." She took a long drink of whatever brown liquor was in her bottle.

"Why are you doing this?" I was surprised at my own imperious tone. "You're fairies. Pull yourselves together."

They looked chagrined. For a millisecond. And then one of them, a woman who once was stunning and now was missing teeth and hair and had blue skin covered in sores, looked me up and down. "I know who you are," she said. "You're the half-thing that decided not to be our Queen. You did this to us. You left us to rot in hell."

The group roared in agreement.

I asked the woman, "Are you the fairies who were digging for mushrooms?"

She nodded. "Some of us."

"Madame Gold promised me she would let you go."

The woman shook her head. A man spoke and his words were so slurred I could barely understand him. "Yeah. She let us go. She let us go down here."

"But—" I tried to remember her exact promise, but it didn't matter. She didn't have to keep her promises.

The woman said, "This is all your fault."

"I didn't know. I didn't mean for this to happen."

I had tried to save Trevor and Luisa and my dad and only ended up destroying so many others. The fairies came at me. They surrounded me, grabbed me, and began to pull and tug me in all directions at once. I screamed. They would pull me into pieces.

"Enough!" A familiar voice cut through the throng.

The fairies dropped me on the ground and stepped away. I looked up—and into the face of Luisa. She was bruised and had a long red scar down her beautiful cheek, but it was Luisa. And Jed was right behind her. Once again she had showed up at exactly the right time. "Luisa!"

She helped me to my feet. "Stay away," she told the group.

Battered as she was, they listened to her. She should be Queen, I thought. So much more regal than I. She led me away from the fairies. They muttered and complained, but they let us go. When we got around behind a pile of rocks, she hugged me. "Are you all right?"

And Jed said, "What are you doing here?"

"I'm fine," I assured them both. "I went though a tunnel and ended up here. By mistake. Why are you here?"

"It was you know who." Luisa's soft brown eyes went hard

and cold. "She tricked me and Jed, told us she'd send us home and she sent us here."

"I was trying to find my mom. I have to find her."

Luisa frowned. She and Jed exchanged a worried look.

"What?" I said. "What? Is she okay?"

Luisa shook her head. "This way." She led me to a hut set apart from the others.

"She's here?"

"The slobbers came to the river where she was working. She put up a good fight, but she's been human too long. They brought her here." Luisa stopped outside the door. "Be warned, October. She's not doing well. Jed and I are trying to take care of her, but she's a troll. We don't know what she needs."

Luisa knocked softly and opened the door. The hut was dark with a rock floor, rough splintered wood walls, a small table and a single rickety chair. In the far corner was a cot. It looked empty to me. I looked again. My mother was under the tattered quilt. She had shrunk to almost nothing, her feet and her head made the only bumps in the bed. I ran to her side.

"Mom," I whispered. Her eyes opened. "It's me. I'm here."

Tears slid from the corners of her eyes. She was too weak to lift a hand to wipe them away. I took a corner of the quilt and dried her face. She tried to smile at me.

"Go home," she said. "This place is The Pits."

As sick as she was, she had tried to make a joke. "Ha ha ha. Madame Gold's sense of humor sucks," I said.

"Don't say her name. She'll hear you."

"Down here in jail?"

Luisa spoke up. "For fairies this is hell. They're given all the alcohol they want and no sunshine. Not so bad for me." She smiled and took Jed's hand. "I have Jed."

"He's not a fairy?"

"He's human. He's decided to live here with me. Or he decided to live in the Fairy Canopy. Neither of us counted on this place."

"Doesn't matter where you are, Babe—that's where I am."

He was so devoted to her I almost cried. He was human and had decided to leave our world—his world—behind. I didn't know that could happen. I turned back to my mom. "Why didn't she kill you? I'm glad she didn't, but I thought that was the plan."

Mom spoke with effort. "She must be part fairy or part troll. We can't kill. We are physically and mentally incapable. A part of our brain shuts down and we just can't. But we can hurt each other—badly—so badly that sometimes the victim dies. Like me."

"I have to get you out of here." From outside I could hear the rumble of the inebriated fairies' anger, the occasional shout as they argued—most likely about me.

"Where's the dude? Walker?" Jed asked.

Hearing his name made me feel better. He'd be looking for me. He would help me save my mom. "He couldn't come through the portal."

Luisa nodded. "Her." She said it like a curse.

"I'm sorry," I said. "Sorry, sorry, sorry. About everything."

She looked from my mother to me. "You saved my life. It was the one thing she promised that she did—I think just to prove she could. She made me well." Jeb put his arm around her. "Then she sent us here."

"And making you a panther?"

"I don't know how she did that."

"That Amazon is way, way strong," Jed said. "All kinds of wicked powers."

We couldn't stay there. "How do we get out of here?" I asked.

Luisa sat down heavily on the only chair. "There is no escape.

Jed and I have tried everything, traveled in every direction. It goes on forever. No way out. None. And now you're stuck here too."

My mother made an odd scratchy rasping noise. She had begun to cry. I was used to her helping me, taking care of me, not the other way around.

"There has to be a way."

"This is all my fault," Mom said. Her voice was like an old woman's.

"Are you crazy?" I was the one who had done everything wrong.

Mom whispered. "I knew that on your eighteenth birthday you would change, your powers would develop." She shook her head. "I knew that. But you got into college. You were excited like any human. I hoped whatever fairy or troll traits developed would be tiny, unnoticeable, so I never said anything. I waited. I waited too long and when I finally went for help, it was at the worst possible time."

"What help?"

"That's why I wasn't there for your birthday or to help your father. No good. I should have stayed home."

I kissed her cheek and smoothed back her hair, shaggy now like a troll's and mostly gray. I didn't know what to say.

A chant began outside. "Give us the girl. Give us the girl."

I looked around the dilapidated hut and knew the rotten boards wouldn't keep the drunks out for long. I wasn't safe, but neither were my mom or Luisa or Jed as long as they were with me.

"I'll go," I said. "I'm fast. They won't be able to catch me. I'll hide somewhere."

"No," Mom said. "No."

"Absolutely not." Luisa and Jed were just as adamant.

I looked down at the vine and flowers marking my leg. I touched my thick hair, now sopping wet and heavy on my shoulders. "I can turn off lights with my mind," I said. "I can communicate long distance. But I just keep hurting everyone I love."

The chant grew louder. "Give Us The Girl. Give Us The Girl."

"Don't you dare feel sorry for yourself," Luisa said to me. She bent close to my mom. "Ruth, you said you went looking for help. Did you find it?"

"Maybe." Mom pulled something wrapped in a handkerchief out from under the quilt and handed it to me. "Maybe."

I opened it carefully. Inside were two mushrooms unlike any I'd ever seen. They glowed as if lit by batteries, one green, and the other red. In the gloom they turned my mother's face half red and half green.

"Mycena luxaeterna Duo," Mom said.

"Luxaeterna," I repeated. "Eternal Light."

They were awesome. Each 'shroom had spikes all over its cap and gills underneath in a bright, electric pulsing blue. They had long fragile stems and as I bent over them the red one smelled like... like...

"Roasted marshmallows!" I said. I sniffed the green one and grinned. "Chocolate." I turned to Luisa and Jed. "You should smell these. Fantastic. They're like spore s'mores. All I need is a graham cracker."

Luisa recoiled, covering her nose, totally disgusted.

"Not fairy fare," Jed said.

That was obvious. Luisa gagged and stumbled away. I remembered seeing another fairy gagging like that—even throwing up—but I couldn't remember where.

"So this thing, this Glo-stick mushroom," Jed said. "How's it going to help?"

Mom gestured at Luisa. "Bad for fairies."

She was right. I held the mushrooms out on my palm and I watched her break out in red, raised welts. The same kind I got when I was around Madame Gold. I looked at my hands. I had the rash too, but not as bad as usually. Luisa began to cough and I thought she was going to be sick. I wrapped the mushrooms up in the handkerchief and stuffed them under my sweater in the waistband of my skirt. Luisa stopped coughing almost immediately and I remembered where it was I'd seen the fairy being sick. She had been digging in the dirt under the fairy tree. And the answer came to me.

"These are what Madame Gold is looking for. She's forcing the fairies to dig for them. This is why she's killing the trees. But why? What for?"

"Power," Mom managed to say. "Very powerful for trolls."

All this time the chant from the drunks outside had been growing louder. They began to pound on the door and the walls. They chanted and pounded and the boards were loosening, nails popping out towards us. The hut wouldn't hold up for long.

Luisa picked up one of Mom's tin dinner plates and spun it on one finger. She handed Jed a dented saucepan. They faced the door. I picked up the only possible weapon left, a wooden spoon, and stood between Mom and the door.

Jed opened the door.

At least a hundred dirty and intoxicated fairies went silent when they saw us. Their eyes were red and bloodshot. Some were having trouble staying upright.

Luisa began, "This is not October's fault—"

They heard my name and shouted as one, "GIVE US THE GIRL."

Before Luisa could say another word the crowd surged toward her. They had no weapons, only their bare hands, but they were terrifying just the same. Luisa sailed her dinner plate like a Frisbee across the front of the crowd pushing them back. Jed used his saucepan as a club and began whacking fairies on the head. One larger, fatter male fairy got past Luisa, lunged at me and lifted me in his arms. I kicked him and stomped on his toes, but it just made him angrier. There was no point in calling for help. Jed and Luisa were surrounded and doing the best they could. The big guy threw me into the crowd as if I had jumped off the stage into a mosh pit. Hand over hand, multi-colored fairies propelled me to the back of the crowd, to where and what I wasn't sure, but I knew it couldn't be good.

I tried to use my thoughts and tell them to stop and that we needed to fight together against Madame Gold, but their rage made it impossible to reason with them— even from inside their own minds. I struggled, I fought, but three larger fairies had me and were carrying me toward a lone hut.

I was desperate. I needed more power than I had. I opened the package of mushrooms and put them both in my mouth.

22.

I chewed and swallowed. The taste was delicious and then the taste was disgusting. I choked as a rush of heat coursed through my body. Sweat broke out on my forehead, my temples, my upper lip. I had never been so hot. I was burning up, my fingertips worst of all. I looked at my hand. I gasped. It really was on fire, each finger like a crazy birthday candle. One of the fairies carrying me screamed and all three dropped me hard. The fairies stopped fighting. They stared at me. I stood with my arms outstretched as the flames moved down my arms, circled my chest and belly, and licked down my legs. I was ablaze and I was as shocked as everybody else.

Luisa ran to me. "October!"

"I'm okay." It was true. I was hot and uncomfortable, but I knew how strong I was becoming. Now I could hear all the fairies' thoughts—all of them at once, a cacophony of exclamations and alarm. I breathed deeply. Count to ten, I told myself. I concentrated on calming down. The flames emanating from me slowed and quit, but the heat and surge of strength continued. I turned in a slow circle. The piles of rocks were wavering before me. The endless gray sky was streaked with a brilliant blue. I took Luisa's hand. She winced at my burning touch, but held on.

"Look," I said. "Look!"

I pointed at a pile of rocks that were dissolving. I could see right through them. We were in a field somewhere under a blue sky. It wasn't even raining. Rock after rock turned into bushes or nothing. The wet ground became grass. The Pits weren't real. They were an illusion.

"Do you see?" I asked Luisa.

I sent what I was seeing into her mind and she gasped. "It's all a trick."

I sent the same picture to Jed and all the fairies. There was a collective murmur of awe and then joy. The sun was shining through clouds. The sky and grass were a balm to the poor deprived fairies. They dropped their bottles. They lay down in the grass and let the sunshine and fresh air soothe them.

"That's how she made me a panther," Luisa said. "She made us all see me as a panther. Even myself. It was just an illusion. That's why I couldn't fight Oberon. The real me can't fight those teeth."

"She created The Pits," Jed said. "What else has she invented?"

I searched for Madame Gold and in my mind's eye saw her plainly in an industrial-type storehouse with Enoki. Madame Gold was furious with her for letting me drive away with Walker. Enoki was looking at the ground, shaking her head, letting Madame Gold yell at her. Ha ha ha. Most interestingly, as I looked at her in my mind's eye she seemed to waver and become transparent like the rocks did before they disappeared. Then Madame Gold's thoughts found mine. I felt her realize how strong I had become and for the first time I could sense a touch of fear. I didn't want her to know where I was. Ice cream! Ice cream. I ran back to my mother's hut.

Mom was lying motionless in the bed with her breathing rattling in her chest. She didn't have long. She was going. I had to save her.

"I took them, Mom. I took the mushrooms and I got us out of The Pits." Even her hut looked better than it had. "How long will they last?" I asked.

"I don't know."

"Then I have to go. Now."

Jed and Luisa were right behind me. "I'm afraid to leave her alone," I said. "Luisa, if you stay with her, I think you can call me just by thinking of me." I tried to smile. "Better than a cellphone. Mushroom texting."

"I'll keep her safe," Luisa said. "I have my tin Frisbee."

Jed said he'd go with me even though I told him to stay. I told him it would be dangerous.

"Tons o' fun," Jed said.

I kissed my mom, he kissed Luisa, and we ran out. Jed carried his saucepan. I let my mind go to Madame Gold and I knew exactly where to find her. It was as if she was a beacon I was following. She was like a lighthouse, I thought, but inviting me in to crash and die instead of warning me away from the rocks. Fat chance, I thought. I was strong. I felt unbeatable. We left the fairies behind. They didn't care about me anymore and I hoped they'd find their way to what was left of their homes. I sent my thoughts to Walker and happily, wonderfully, I could reach him. He and Oberon were struggling through a jungle of roots and plants to get to this world. I knew he would find a way. I was so strong and powerful that I felt confident and sure that Walker really did love me. All my doubt and insecurities had vanished. I was going to wring Madame Gold's scrawny neck and save my mother, my father, the fairies, and even the trolls. I was.

I smelled sulfur. We were close. The clouds rolled in and the sky was gray and heavy. We came over a muddy rise and saw spread out in front of us the industrial wasteland, the mud, the damaged and dying trees with their roots exposed, and the desperate fairies sniffing and vomiting as they dug in the once beautiful ground. Jed grimaced. Luisa must have told Jed, as

Walker had told me, that this was a paradise, the true fairy glen, lush and flowered and beautiful. Instead it was all dying trees and rusted gray buildings and giant trucks and cracked pavement. I heard the backhoe revving up to dig deeper. With my added powers, I knew it was not an illusion. Madame Gold had made this happen. I knew how the mushrooms made me feel. No wonder Madame Gold wanted more of them. And more and more. She was addicted. Maybe it had something to do with whatever secret she was hiding—maybe it was just about power. I saw her in my mind and again she seemed to waver, become almost transparent. Something else was behind her or under her or inside her. She glanced up as if she heard me.

"Vanilla." I turned to Jed and pointed at my head. "She's using our thoughts to search for us. Imagine ice cream cones."

We walked slowly down the hill toward the warehouse. She knew we were coming, but I didn't want her to know how soon. What if my mother died? What if my father couldn't return to normal? I stretched out my hands, concentrated, and tiny flames, like birthday candles, flashed from each of my fingers. Ha, I thought. She can't stop me.

I worked on throwing an illusion over us, blending us into the background. If Madame Gold could do it, so could I. I listened to the plants and the birds and animals trying to survive in the damaged forest. I felt their pain and struggle and it made me angry and the anger made me stronger. I combined that anger with the heat and fire I already had inside. I pictured myself bigger and I was. I could feel myself growing in my veins, in my muscles, in my bones. I motioned to Jed to go around the back and I strode right through the front door into the storehouse fully ready to confront my nemesis.

No one was inside. It was cold and there was a low hum from the refrigeration units. The cavernous room was badly lit, the sun almost invisible through a high bank of narrow filthy windows. And it wasn't a warehouse; it was a laboratory. All around me were shelves of mushrooms in various states of decay. In rows down the center of the room was table after table filled with laboratory equipment and trays of mushrooms. They sat under grow lights beside test tubes and beakers filled with clear and colored liquids. The mushrooms didn't look good. They were misshapen and had blotches from some kind of blight. None of them were glowing green or red. Most in the stacks on the shelves were dead or dying. I could hear the mushrooms moaning. I knew Madame Gold could too. Wherever she was, I knew she was angry. She needed these mushrooms to survive and they were no good to her dead. Maybe she was powerless without them. Maybe she wanted them all so she would be all powerful. I shuddered. The mushrooms I had eaten had smelled sweet and delicious like chocolate and marshmallows. This place smelled only of fertilizer, mold, and rot. I felt Madame Gold's worry. Worse than that, I felt her desperation.

I heard voices outside. Madame Gold and a lower pitched, obsequious, apologetic voice. Enoki. I ducked behind a stack of empty boxes as the door opened. Four people were silhouetted against the light from outside. The middle one, the tallest in the billowing, diaphanous dress was Madame Gold. Her thoughts were like tentacles spreading, searching for me. All she would find was ice cream. Vanilla. Vanilla. Vanilla. On her right, tall and surprisingly slim, was my father. Beside him, short and muscular, was Enoki. Who was it on Madame Gold's other side? A fairy. Tall and thin with curly hair that caught the only bit of sun and glittered gold as he stepped further into the room.

Walker? Walker! My vanilla ice cream cone splatted on the floor.

My skin went cold. I shivered. I tried to conjure up the heat and strength I had felt before, but all I could think about was Walker.

Another person walked in the door. She flipped her long hair back over her shoulder and stopped beside Enoki.

Luisa! Madame Gold did not seem surprised to see her. She barely glanced at her. She was busy peering into the shadows trying to find me. She waved her flapping sleeves and the room wavered and faltered. I saw different boxes stacked up replacing the clear Plexiglas trays filled with mushrooms. I saw cage on top of cage of fairy prisoners. Like chickens in a truck on the freeway on their way to market. Some of them were obviously dead. I looked at the center tables. Instead of mushrooms and dirt under the grow lights, they held fairies, stretched out as if they'd been operated on, with tubes running into their veins and medical equipment surrounding them. The walls vacillated between prison and laboratory. Prison and laboratory. Which was true? Which was illusion? I put my hand on the box of mushrooms closest to me. It felt real. But I had climbed on the rock piles in The Pits and they weren't real at all. There was a terrible pain in my hand and I almost cried out, sure some awful bug had bitten me. I watched big red welts emerge all over my hands and arms, my Madame Gold disease.

No. The fairies weren't real. She wasn't experimenting on fairies. This was another of her tricks.

"Walker. Darling," Madame Gold said loudly. "My right hand man. Thank you for bringing her here." She turned to Luisa. "Luisa. Head of my disciplinary forces."

I had been betrayed by everyone I knew.

23.

My heart stopped beating. I was a block of ice, unable to move, to speak, to think. He had told me he loved me. He had stared right into my eyes and said, "I love you." Those astonishing blue eyes looking into my plain, ordinary, brown ones. Faintly I thought I heard Walker calling to me, saying he was on his way, but I saw him standing just across the room, looking at Madame Gold with a little smile on his face.

Enoki said, "Now you want Walker? He's your darling? First her dad, then Trevor, now her boyfriend? Fine with me." She started for the door. "I'm going to find my brother and tell him you made your choice."

Madame Gold roared. "Don't you dare."

"You can't have everything," Enoki said.

"I can and I will. Do not move!"

Enoki's shoulders slumped and she stayed where she was. It was odd that neither Walker nor Luisa had moved or spoken. Where was Oberon? Where was Jed? Luisa was here, so that meant my mother was alone... or worse. I tried to find my mother with my mind. Nothing. I was afraid to think what that might mean. Walker. Luisa. Walker. My heart was broken, smashed, shattered into a million pieces. I heard Madame Gold in my head. "Love you?" She snickered. "How could he love you?" Despite the mushrooms, I felt my confidence draining. Impossible to concentrate on ice cream.

Someone new bounded in so quickly, leaping and turning

somersaults, I knew it was a troll. Some kind of old man troll in a long robe. "Wedding?" he exclaimed. "Are we having a wedding?" He smiled at Madame Gold. "As you humans say, let's get this show on the road."

Wedding? Madame Gold turned to my father and put out her hand. He took it without looking at her. No! Madame Gold was marrying my father.

"How does it begin?" asked the troll Reverend. "Dearly beloved or is it Beloved dearests? "

"Get on with it." Madame Gold snarled like an animal.

I tried to find my dad with my thoughts. Wake up. Don't do it. Wake up! He didn't respond.

I couldn't allow this to happen. "Stop!" I leapt from my hiding place. "Stop!"

Madame Gold smiled and turned to me.

Enoki's eyes narrowed. "I thought I smelled a half-breed," she said.

Walker and Luisa didn't move. Walker, I screamed with my mind, but he was frozen with that strange little smile on his face. Under some kind of Madame Gold control. My father didn't react. Luisa did nothing. I felt Madame Gold inside my head. Vanilla, I thought. With sprinkles. I filled my mind with the cool creamy goodness of my favorite ice cream. Ice cream. Ice cream. Ice cream. I needed more of those special mushrooms. The heat was less, my power wearing off. I looked at the center tables. Would any of those experiments help me? I salivated thinking of the mushrooms' taste and aroma and the power they gave me. Enough of those and I could stop Madame Gold for sure. Then, faintly, like a very bad cell phone connection, I heard Luisa telling me my mother was asking for me. I looked at Luisa standing next to Enoki and not moving. I sent her a thank you, but she didn't even look at me, even though she had told me my mother was still alive.

"You can't marry my dad," I said. "My mother is still alive."

Madame Gold shrugged. "Details, details. She'll be gone soon."

She and I both heard Luisa tell us, "She's getting better."

Luisa was still at my mother's bedside. I saw her as plain as day. I looked again and the Luisa standing beside Madame Gold wavered. She was just an illusion and when I realized that, she dissolved. Madame Gold hissed at me through her teeth. My mushroom power was wearing off, but I could still feel her mind seeking Luisa and not finding her. I heard her calling to me, but I pushed her out by chanting all the flavors I could think of. Strawberry. Chocolate. Coffee Almond Fudge. Her dress floated around her. She was frustrated. Perplexed. Annoyed. With her every frown, my strength returned. As I studied her, Madame Gold became insubstantial, almost see-through. I tried to see what she was underneath.

Suddenly she solidified. Her mind was too strong. I had to look away. "Enoki," she said. "Your turn."

"With pleasure."

In a flash Enoki took off toward me. The Reverend hid his face. I braced myself for her attack. I knew I couldn't fight her. I was no match for her years of practice. I held my breath, I tried to deflect her with my mind, but she barreled forward. Just before she got to me, Green jumped out in front of her. Enoki yelped in surprise. She grabbed his arm, pulled him off his feet into the air and threw him hard against the closest wall. His head made a sickening smack and he slid to the ground, stunned or dead, I wasn't sure which.

"Oops," Enoki said with a smile at me. "I've been working out."

"Chris!" I ran to his side. Once again little Green had shown up when I needed him most. Luisa, Green, how did I deserve such friends? Maybe Walker had betrayed me, but they were still on my side. But Walker still wasn't moving. That I couldn't believe. No reaction, nothing, still staring up at Madame Gold with that simpering smile. That's when I knew it wasn't really Walker, just like it hadn't been the real Luisa. I concentrated and the Walker standing beside Madame Gold faded. My stomach calmed and in the midst of all it I felt the tiniest joyful warmth. He hadn't betrayed me. I could see right through him. So that's where that expression comes from.

Madame Gold turned to the Reverend. "Do it," she cried. "Marry us right now!"

"But his wife isn't dead," the Reverend squeaked.

"Close enough!" Madame Gold grabbed the Reverend's arm. The Reverend began reading the marriage vows. They were different than human vows, but I admit I wasn't really listening.

"Stop!" I shouted again.

"Keep going," Madame Gold hissed.

Enoki laughed. Green wasn't moving. Walker, I screamed his name in my mind. Half a second later he and a beautiful black and yellow bird—Oberon in his true form as a Western Tanager, Piranga ludoviciana—literally flew into the room. In his arms he carried my mother. Still alive.

"Reverend," Walker said touching down. "This marriage is illegal. This woman is far from dead."

My mother lifted her head slightly to look at the troll Reverend. He knew her and he dropped to one knee. "Your Lowness," he said.

Madame Gold stamped her feet. "Get up. Get up! Forget this woman." She whispered in my mother's ear and my mother writhed in pain, then fainted. "She's as good as dead."

I ran forward and grabbed her arm. "You will pay for this."

I shook her hard. "I am stronger than you!"

And it was true. The anger, the frustration, the indignation, and the fear of this terrible conniving manipulating woman had made me invincible. I grew taller, but I wasn't slim like a fairy, I was muscled and fit like a troll. I shook Madame Gold and she wobbled in my hand back and forth like a rag doll.

"Enoki!" Madame Gold commanded.

Walker gently set my mother down to one side and leapt in front of Enoki before she could touch me. "Dirt eater!"

"What did you call me?"

"You know what you are."

"For once and for all," she said. "I hate fairies."

Enoki had her legs around his neck so quickly I didn't see her move. She squeezed. Her legs were very strong, but before I could even begin to worry, Walker seemed to elongate, become taller and even skinnier, and slipped right out of her hold. She tumbled to the ground, rolled and and jumped to her feet.

Madame Gold tried to wiggle out of my grasp. I held on tighter. Her arm was odd, almost pipe cleaner skinny inside her big sleeve. I squeezed and her arm seemed to disintegrate and she was free. She pushed Walker toward Enoki, throwing him off balance. Enoki took the advantage and kicked him hard. He flew and hit one of the center tables shattering trays and beakers. When he got to his feet his sky blue eyes had turned a shiny, dark cobalt and his face was all hard angles. A tougher, scarier version of himself. I would not have wanted to cross him.

They circled each other. Enoki laughed. From my spot clear across the room I could smell her slightly muddy sweat and feel the adrenalin zipping through her veins. She wanted him to die. If she wasn't able to actually kill him, she wanted to hurt him so badly he would not survive. Her mind was an easy one to visit. She had only that one thought. She didn't care if her brother got married. She didn't care who was King or Queen. All she cared about was her hate. Hating fairies. It made her a very simple target for me. Madame Gold could feel what I was doing, but in my enhanced state it was amazingly easy to shut her mind out of Enoki's.

I showed Enoki one of my memories of my dad taking six-year-old me out to the woods to show me the birds and the flowers. Mom was along and she pointed out weeds and fungus and beautiful, tiny bugs in the earth. We were all three holding hands. My dad was grinning and he was fun and he looked at my mother with so much love. A fairy and a troll together and happy. Another time when I was eight. And another out in the woods when I was eleven. All good times. All times when a fairy and a troll got along.

Enoki faltered. She shook her head as if to clear it. She looked at Walker and in her mind I saw her begin to see him in a new way. As if he was smiling at her. I sent her pictures of Walker helping Trevor plant a tree, Trevor and Walker playing ball in a field of flowers, driving in a fast car. I had no idea what they might do together, so I had to make it up, but it wasn't hard to imagine. Two guys doing things. I sent the same scene to Walker—and to Trevor wherever he was.

As I concentrated the walls of the warehouse disappeared and a forest materialized all around us. The sun was shining. An image of Walker, Trevor, and Enoki laughing together at a picnic flashed in the center of the room. I was kind of amazed and very proud. I had created this illusion, just as Madame Gold had created The Pits and then the dead fairies in cages. It wasn't easy and I couldn't hold it for long, not like Madame Gold, but it was long enough. Walker and Enoki stopped, straightened, blinked at the picture they were seeing of themselves. They weren't so interested in fighting anymore.

Before I could stop her, Madame Gold dug in her dress and pulled out a glowing red and green vial. Mushrooms! I tried to grab them, but she downed them before I could. She shook her head and laughed her screeching witchlike laugh.

"Garbage! Lies! Trolls hate fairies and fairies hate trolls." Madame Gold roared and my illusion popped and disappeared. "They always will." New pictures appeared of Enoki fighting fairies and leaving them to die. Fairies in cages. Fairies fighting back, running through the underground and destroying troll homes. "Fairies hate trolls," Madame Gold said again.

I tried to keep Enoki seeing good things, but hate was easier to foment than love. Much as I didn't want to admit it, it seemed hate was the much, much stronger emotion.

"Enoki," I said. "It doesn't have to be like that."

"It doesn't," Walker agreed and I loved him for it. "We both want the same thing for our worlds."

Enoki frowned. She blinked a few times. It wasn't easy to give up a lifetime of warring. I heard a high-pitched zing. Luisa—the real Luisa—had snuck in the back and launched her tin plate Frisbee. "No!" I sent my thought to Luisa. But it was too late. The plate whipped across the warehouse in a blur and sliced into the back of Enoki's head. She didn't even yell, just crumpled.

"That's for Chris," Luisa said quietly.

Madame Gold swirled to face Luisa. "Good shot." She sounded friendly and impressed. "Come over here. Seems I have an opening for someone like you. Since my General has been… incapacitated, I could use a good soldier."

She continued calling her by name and Luisa began to walk toward her.

"That was wonderful," Madame Gold said. "Wonderful. You are very talented with that old plate. Imagine what you could do with a weapon specially made."

"Luisa. Snap out of it. Listen to who's talking to you." Walker urged, but Luisa kept walking toward her.

"I have a special, very special job for you," Madame Gold continued. "A very important job that only you can do."

Walker ran to Luisa and grabbed her arm to stop her, but she pushed him away.

I had to do something. I recognized Madame Gold's gently persuading voice and the way her sleeves waved back and forth in front of Luisa's eyes. It was what she had done to my dad. Not again, I thought. Not Luisa. Luckily Luisa was not as susceptible as my dad had been. Madame Gold had to use a lot of mind power to reach and control Luisa, leaving me free to concentrate on her. There had to be something she was afraid of, something she was hiding, and once I found it, I could use it to stop her.

I searched down deep inside Madame Gold. There were swirling memories, things that didn't make much sense to me. I saw the Fairy Canopy beautiful and lush. Smelled the fresh, rich dirt the trolls love so much. I saw a cluster of the luminescent Luxaeterna Duo mushrooms glowing red and green in the swamp and I felt the strength and power they gave her. I also saw a crib in some kind of hospital and parents, human parents, looking into the crib and crying, but I couldn't see the baby. I saw children taunting and teasing and pointing at something on the ground, but I couldn't see what. I saw a TV screen and the clock above it spinning hour after hour through show after show. It was all part of her, but I didn't know why. I saw that Madame Gold's worst fear was that her secret would be revealed. I couldn't see the secret; she kept it hidden even from herself. It had something to do with the mushrooms. She was afraid there wouldn't be enough and she wouldn't be able to grow more. I saw her screaming at the troll scientists to try again to make a synthetic version of the luminescent mushrooms. It didn't matter. I focused on her fear. I made her believe I knew her secret and that I could expose it. I would show everyone. Everyone would see it.

And, yes, I made her tremble. Luisa stopped in her tracks. I felt Madame Gold go sick with dread. The deeper I went, the more frightened she became, and strangely the more I empathized. Her sickness became mine. Her fear became my fear. She was afraid I would reveal her secret and she would be alone forever. I knew how it felt to be lonely, to feel as if you don't belong. She was absolutely terrified that she would have to live her life without a companion, a lover, or a friend. She had no friends. That was the picture of her night after night at home alone in front of the TV watching the hours tick by. I'd been lonely, but I had never felt Madame Gold's utter desolation and despair. Why? Why didn't she have anybody in her life?

I couldn't bother with the why. Not yet. Not until Luisa and my father and all of us were free. Instead I showed Madame Gold pictures of Luisa working for her, but not liking her and talking to the other soldiers behind her back. I showed Luisa not having dinner with her and not inviting her to parties. I didn't know what Madame Gold expected from a friend, so I thought about the things I wanted. I had always wanted a friend who would go to the mall with me to hang out and then spend the night at my house and dance on my bed to bad music and be unembarrassed and silly. Luisa had never done those things with me, but she would definitely never do them with Madame Gold. I didn't need to put thoughts in anybody's mind—that was just the truth. Luisa was not going to be Madame Gold's BFF. At least I had college ahead of me. There I would meet fellow oddballs, animal lovers, like-minded people who wanted to be my friends. I was sure of it. Where could Madame Gold go to make friends? A supernatural Queen convention?

Madame Gold groaned, a ghastly, grating sound. Again her form faltered and her face and hands became translucent, only her dress hid whatever was underneath. Luisa shook her head and came out of her trance. Walker put his arm around her and pulled her back next to my mom. Still breathing, I could see it. My mom was still breathing.

I wiped the tears from my eyes. Going down into that loneliness, that dark, that cold, was devastating. I had to think of something else. Enoki was lying on the floor in a puddle of blood. Luisa had hit her hard. A tin plate was not a plastic Frisbee. Enoki was smaller and paler than a troll should ever be.

Madame Gold stamped her foot, shook me out of her head, relieved that I had ultimately not revealed her secret. She grinned at me wickedly—understanding that I still didn't know what her secret was. "Trevor," she said out loud and in her mind as well. "Your sister needs you."

I had seen Trevor bend the bars on his window and escape. I hoped he was very far away.

"Come to me." Madame Gold smiled at me as she said it. "Trevor. Come immediately. Enoki is almost gone."

Trevor bounded into the room moving so quickly he was a blur. He fell on his knees beside his crumpled sister. "Enoki," he said. He looked up with his hands and his knees covered in blood. "Who did this?"

"It doesn't matter," I said. "Just take her to the hospital or wherever trolls go."

He seemed to notice I was there for the first time. Then he saw Walker, and Luisa, and my mother lying in the corner. His face was angry when he turned to Madame Gold. "You did this."

"Hardly. It was your—" She stumbled over the word. "Half-breed girlfriend."

"Go, Trevor." I pleaded with him. "She needs a doctor."

Trevor picked Enoki up in his arms.

Madame Gold shrugged. "Just leave her. No one can save her. She's practically dead already. Trevor, really, don't bother, it's her own dumb fault."

Silence. We were all stunned.

Madame Gold waved her arms as if trying to wave her atrocious words away. "I mean." She smiled grotesquely at Trevor, a beautiful woman made ugly by her desperation. "I mean there is nothing you can do for poor Enoki. She fought hard. I'm sad too. Of course I am, Trevor. Darling. It's too late for her, but if October gets away, everything we want, everything we've worked for will disappear." She almost begged him. "Trevor. Don't you want to be King?"

Trevor hung his head over his prone sister. I knew Madame Gold would never really have Trevor. And she knew it too. That was an easy picture to put in her mind. He would do what he had to do to be King, but there was no love in him or even friendship for Madame Gold. The warehouse faded away again and I created the troll palace, and Madame Gold sitting all alone at the head of a long and lavishly appointed table. It was set for two, but she was the only one sitting there. Alone, alone. Madame Gold knew it and it was like a knife in her heart, the terrible realization that this was her future. She groaned again and her gauzy dress shimmered and I thought I saw a child underneath. Then the gossamer dress was back and I had to have imagined it. It was painful to create this much hurt, and exhausting and I could feel my strength slipping away, dripping out of my fingers. I couldn't conjure up flames anymore. I wondered how Madame Gold kept her illusions going for so long, how many mushrooms she had to eat and how frequently.

"Fine. Good." Madame Gold pulled herself together.

"Where is that Luisa?" She strode across the floor. "Come to me. Right now."

Obediently, Luisa stood. No, I thought. And then I remembered Jed. Where was he? Where had he been? Jed, I called to him with my mind. Hurry. I saw him sleeping somewhere nearby, lying on the cracked cement roadway, under the tire of a truck. He opened his eyes groggily. Madame Gold had put him to sleep. His human mind was a piece of cake to manipulate. That meant it was easy for me too. Wake up! Luisa needs you!

Madame Gold crooked her finger at Luisa. "On second thought, Luisa. Stay where you are and destroy October's mother. That's a good thing for you to do. It shouldn't take much. Make sure there's nothing she can do but die."

Walker jumped in front of Luisa and with seemingly super-fairy strength she tossed him out of her way. Her powers, diminished when she was in the human world, had come back with a vengeance.

"Stop, Luisa!" I thought it as hard as I could. "Run away. Don't do this. Run, run."

Luisa stood over my mother. Walker tried again and again she threw him across the room. But she was conflicted. I could feel her uncertainty. She heard Madame Gold and then me, back and forth. She was pulled in both directions.

"Luisa! Run!" It was Jed. She looked up and over at him. He didn't have any special powers except the power of love. He loved her and she heard him. She came out of her trance.

"Run!" I said to both of them. Madame Gold was too strong and I couldn't keep her away from them for long.

Luisa ran, but instead of out of the building, she ran to the far wall. Madame Gold could still stop her. What was she doing?

"Babe. This way," Jed said.

Go out! I hollered in my mind. Then I saw her pick up

Green in her arms. She was rescuing him. Oh! I felt my heart expand; she was a good, kind person. She really was.

But carrying Green was slowing her down.

Madame Gold tried to step in her path. Jed barreled into her and knocked her aside. He and Luisa, with Green, ran out the door and out of sight. Madame Gold spun in a circle and came up none the worse. Jed's attack didn't seem to have hurt her. How strong was she?

Trevor began to carry his sister out the door.

"Stay with me!"

Enoki flopped in his arms as if all her muscles and even her bones had turned to mush.

"It's too late, Darling." Madame Gold used her most soothing voice. "Stay with me."

"Save her," I said.

"Now's the time," Walker said. "Go."

Madame Gold roared. "Put her down. You will stay by my side!"

The effort was costing Trevor a lot. His nose began to bleed as he stood with his sister in his arms. His feet wanted to walk away, but his mind kept him leaning toward Madame Gold. Her hold on him was intense. But there was love again. The real love Trevor felt for his sister. I didn't like her, but he loved her.

I sent the love into his mind, the memories of growing up together.

"Do not even think of leaving me."

Trevor looked once at Madame Gold. And I had just enough strength left to make him see her in the worst possible way. Her red hair stuck out in all directions. Her hands with the long sharp fingernails looked like claws. He took one halting step away.

"No!" The witch wailed.

"Yes!" Walker said.

And I kept thinking, go. Go. Go.

Slowly, as if he was walking through cement, Trevor headed for the door. Madame Gold ran over and walked beside him. She called him darling and cupcake and sweetheart and precious. She reminded him how fun it would be for them to rule together. He was strong, but it was hard, awful, wrenching both physically and psychically for him to leave her. Finally, he did. He walked out the door and once outside I felt his mind and his heart open.

I slumped. I knew I didn't have much more fight in me.

Madame Gold shook herself all over and she grew even taller. She just got stronger. I wondered if she had another vial of mushrooms in that crazy dress of hers.

"If you want something done," she said, "you have to do it yourself." She strode over to my mother. "Reverend! Get ready." She pointed her finger at my mom and closed her eyes and Mom began to moan. Bruises appeared on her skin and cuts opened up down both her arms.

I ran between them, but I was too late. Mom was too weak. She gave a final, rattling gasp, and then was still. "No!" I screamed. "No!"

Walker hurried to me, but even his touch didn't help. I fell to the ground.

"You promised," I said to Madame Gold through my tears. "You promised."

"So did you."

"When you're Queen everybody will hate you."

Madame Gold growled at me in frustration. "If that's what it takes."

"My mother could have helped you grow those mushrooms you like so much."

"I see you like them too."

"She could have helped you."

"I have hundreds of trolls to do my bidding. I needed your mother to die." She turned to the waiting Reverend who was hiding behind a stack of empty trays. I could see he was terrified. "Neal?" Madame Gold snapped her fingers and called my father over to her like a dog.

"Remember," Walker said to me. "Everything she does and says is an illusion."

Madame Gold turned her creepy smile on Walker. "Not everything. Not everything. I really did destroy your trees. The Fairy Canopy is gone."

Walker cried out as if he'd been punched. "But we made a deal."

"Are you that naive? Or just that stupid?" Madame Gold laughed. "I told you, deliver her to me and your people can go free. I didn't say anything about the trees. I had to find those mushrooms and I did it the easiest, quickest way possible. The only deal I remember is October in exchange for your beloved fairies."

I spun to look at him.

"Oh yes," Madame Gold said. "Walker gave you up."

I tried to search his mind, but it was a jumble of images and regrets and anger and oddly human emotions. He did love me, but he had betrayed me to save his kind. He had some idea that he could save me at the end. It all made a dreadful kind of sense. He loved the fairy world so much. He loved being a fairy. He loved all the fairies. Way more than he loved me. Of course he would sacrifice me to save all of his family and friends and the fairy world. Sacrifice the one for the good of the many. I really had been such a fool.

"And here she is," Madame Gold said. "Thank you." She

smiled. "Now your precious fairies will go free. Once she's dead, I mean."

"Just send her back," Walker said. "Make her stay in the human world."

"You know that won't work." She turned to me. "It's true I can't kill you. You're strong and I probably can't even hurt you as badly as I hurt your mother. So I'm just going to offer you something to drink. Something delicious. It's completely up to you, but I think you'll find it irresistible." She took a small vial out of one of her huge sleeves. It had a liquid inside that glowed like the mushrooms, but purple. She unscrewed the cap and stepped toward me, holding it out.

"October," Walker said. "It's poison. Poison to fairies."

"You can't make me drink it," I said to Madame Gold. "That's the same as killing me."

"I don't have to make you do anything," she said. "You're going to want this. It's the best. It's all I can do not to drink it myself."

She was right. It smelled incredible. So, so good, better than the alcohol in the troll club, better than Chinese food, better than birthday cake, better than anything. One sip would make me immortal—that's the thought that came into my mind. One sip would change my life.

"Wait." Walker stood in front of me. I tried to push him out of the way. He wouldn't budge. "No. No." He implored Madame Gold. "You said you'd keep her in The Pits. You didn't say anything about killing her." He turned to me. "October, stop. It's not good. It's poison. You can't drink it."

"It's immortality," I said. "It's the answer to everything." Finally, I thought, I won't be worried or afraid or feel stupid or inadequate. Finally, I'll be perfect.

"It's a trick," Walker said.

Madame Gold held the vial out to me. She blew its scent in my direction. I was crazy to get my hands on that vial. Walker grabbed me, held me. I fought him.

"You!" I said. "You betrayed me. You don't love me. I hate you. I hate you."

Madame Gold laughed. Pictures flew through my mind of me falling down at school, of Jacob making fun of me, of walking alone through the hallways and home after school day after day after day. I spent night after night on the couch in front of the TV. Those were my days and my nights going by all alone. My cell phone never rang. I heard about Saturday night parties on Monday morning when everybody was talking about the crazy things that had happened. But that drink she held in her hand would make me beautiful and popular and take all the pain away.

"October Fetterhoff," Madame Gold said to me, "your power is useless. Without this drink, you are useless."

"Don't listen to her," Walker said. "Be strong. Don't listen!"

Madame Gold laughed her horrible screeching laugh. It ran down my throat and burned in my stomach. "He betrayed you," she whispered, but I heard her clearly. And I saw the pictures she was sending, of Walker in the park with the crows, of Walker studying me in that odd way he had, of Walker giving Madame Gold that little bow, of Walker and Oberon laughing as I disappeared into the tunnel by myself.

Madame Gold continued, "Every step along the way, he let you down. He wasn't there, was he? Every time you needed him, he disappeared. He was always working for me."

"October! That's not true. What I said in the car—all of it—I meant it."

But I couldn't even look at him.

Madame Gold sighed. "He doesn't love you. Frankly, October, who could? You are so ordinary in every way."

I was frantic to get to that vial. With my mind I pushed over a stack of trays and they crashed and broke on the hard cement floor. The light bulbs hanging from the ceiling flashed on and off, on and off, until finally they shattered. I had power. I did.

She laughed again. "That's not ability, that's a party trick. We all wondered what you would be like. Child of a troll princess and a fairy prince. Such powerful stock. Such potential. We expected great things from you." She gestured at the mess I'd made, the pool of blood left by Enoki and then at my mother's body. My mother. "Turns out you're nothing special."

I wanted the roof to cave in on her. I wanted her to fly into the air and come smashing down. But first I wanted that drink and she wasn't going to give it to me. She was going to keep it for herself. Because I wasn't good enough to have it. Walker's arms tightened around me as I began to cry. Despair fell like a curtain.

"Shut up," he said to Madame Gold. "Stop."

She just kept speaking in my head. Walker couldn't hear her and for that I thanked her. I didn't want him to hear the truth about me. She went on and on until it was practically a chant: "You're not very good in school. You're not very pretty. You've never had a boyfriend. And you know why? Because you're so ordinary. Completely dull. Dull as dishwater."

I hunched against her words. Her truth seeped into me, through the defenses I had put up, through the pretending that I was a princess, that I had power, that I wanted only the best for everyone. The things I had accomplished, the memories of happy moments rushed away like over a waterfall. I could not think of one good thing about me.

"October," Walker said into my ear. "Please don't listen to her."

He had never really liked me. He wasn't really a bad guy; he was just doing whatever was necessary to save his world. The fairies would probably give him a medal for making this deal. I was just part of a scheme to achieve his goal. Of course. I was so damn ordinary. The more Madame Gold's words dripped into my head, the more I became convinced she was right. I was less than average, less than everyday, not even humdrum or commonplace. I was nothing. Nothing. Ordinary October had become October Nothing. I couldn't have the drink she offered. I wasn't even good enough for poison.

Madame Gold went on and on. "What a waste! Your mom and dad were so disappointed in you. Forget any fairy skills, like flying or stretching or talking to animals. Forget the troll abilities like strength, agility, or speed. You can't even play the piano or tennis or checkers. Your mom is a scientist and you barely passed Algebra I. You're not really good at anything, are you? Little October Nothing."

By the time she finished I had dragged Walker down to the ground with me, sobbing, agreeing with every word she said. I had said it all and more to myself countless times. Those times when I woke up at three in the morning and lay in the dark remembering every stupid thing I had ever done, every opportunity I missed, every time I fell or flunked or messed up somehow. And there were plenty of them.

I was ready to surrender to her. There was no point in going on.

I took a deep breath. "If I die," I whispered, "Let my father go back to his normal self. Marry him if you must, but let him live out in the human world with his birdhouses. Let Walker and all the fairies be free. Leave Luisa alone. And be nice to Trevor. Let him be King and you Queen and then leave him alone." It was everything I could ask for. I had asked for it before, but this time I would die to make her do it. I turned to Walker. "If you ever loved me at all, even a little bit, will you make sure she does this?"

Madame Gold frowned. "What kind of trick are you pulling?"

"No trick." I was so unhappy it was hard to stand up. "Promise me and let me have that drink." It still smelled incredibly good, only it smelled too good for me. I didn't deserve it, but I would drink it—and I knew it would kill me.

Madame Gold looked at me with her head tilted to one side. She didn't believe me.

"You're right," I told her. "I'm nothing. I'm not important. But they are. Walker is smart and brave and wants to do good things for his world. My dad is the nicest man in the world and his birds need him. Luisa and Jed love each other and should live in peace. Trevor is cute and funny and deserves to be happy. Green is a pain in the ass, but he's just a kid. Even Enoki—you should fix her, if you can."

Madame Gold was astonished. "They all left you here to fight me alone. Even your father didn't love you enough. He never complained, never tried to stop me—not once."

I looked over at my dad. I walked up to him and hugged him, the new skinny him. He didn't hug me back. He was trapped. He had always been trapped, from the very first day Madame Gold arrived at our house. She was right, but I was numb. She couldn't hurt me anymore because she had already destroyed my heart. I nodded. I agreed with her. Wasn't that enough?

"Will the poison hurt?" I asked.

"Don't, October." Walker seemed to be talking from a very great distance.

"You would really do this?" Madame Gold held out the vial of liquid death. Her voice was almost gentle; she seemed truly dumbfounded. "You would drink this?"

"Say you'll do as I ask, then hand it over," I said. "Quick, before I change my mind."

"This is historic!" she said. "In all the reading I've done, all the battles I've waged to get where I am, I have never seen or heard of any troll, fairy, goblin, or anyone giving themselves up. Plenty have sacrificed others, even loved ones—" She looked at Walker. "Of course many have tried to make deals. But no one has ever offered up her own life. In that small way, you are remarkably unusual."

I heard that. I heard the tiny lilt of admiration in her voice. And that was enough to start a little fire in my heart. She was wrong. I knew plenty of stories of humans sacrificing their own lives to save others—in shipwrecks, plane crashes, fires. In my world, the human world, people did amazing things in adversity. The guy that went back into the burning building time after time to get every last person was completely ordinary—he couldn't fly or talk to birds or anything—until that one moment when he risked himself for another. He was just a regular guy, but out of love he did something extraordinary. That woman in the train wreck who let everyone else get out first—who helped people through the window she could have gone through right away even though she knew if she stayed she'd probably die— she didn't have super troll strength, she just did what she had to do to save another human. That's what she was: a human. And so was I.

But first, before I did anything else, there was something I had to know. "One thing," I asked, "What is your secret?"

"What?"

"I know you're not all fairy." That was an understatement. "I want to know what you really are. That's what your secret is, right? You're not who you appear to be. Show me. Then you can give me the drink." I nodded at the poison.

Walker touched my arm. He put a finger under my chin and turned my face up to his. "We can fight her," he said.

"No, we can't. We can't do anything. Not anymore."

"You don't understand," he began.

I ignored him. "Show me," I demanded Madame Gold. "Give me my last request. I want to see my enemy as she really is."

"No one sees me like that."

"It doesn't matter. I'm not fighting you anymore."

Madame Gold considered it. Finally, she nodded to me. "It won't take long. You're going to be dead for eternity. What're a few minutes more?" She waved her arms at Walker. "Go. I mean it, go!"

Walker looked at me. I turned away. I didn't want to see him leave. I didn't think I could stand it. I heard the warehouse door shut and I turned back to Madame Gold. She put the lid on the vial of poison and put it in a pocket somewhere. She took off her dress, and as it passed up and over her head she suddenly disappeared. Or I thought she did. I heard a small voice. "Here I am."

Sitting on the floor was a tiny misshapen young woman, with strange black and silver hair, both straight and curly. She had a bizarre, ugly face. One eye was blue, and one was brown. One was big and one was small. Her nose was hooked, but her mouth tiny. She had enormous hairy feet, troll feet, but totally out of proportion and one long leg, one short. She was only three feet tall. Her arms were too long for her body. She was skinny on the bottom and barrel-chested on top. Her skin was blotchy and she put her hands on her uneven hips and scowled at me. Her expression was angry and superior and cruel, but when I looked at her I saw myself.

"You're a half-breed," I said. "Like me."

"You think you're so special. You think you're the first. I was the first," she exclaimed proudly. "My parents weren't royalty, my father and mother had a one night stand and when I arrived, my mother gave me away to a human family—who couldn't stand to look at me." She did a quick spin. "You think you had trouble in high school? How do you think it was for me? Then four years ago, when I turned eighteen—all alone, without parents or fairy guides to help me—I discovered that I too had a power, the power of thought and mind control. Just like you but better, bigger, more. Plus I'm smart. I'm quick. I read about those mushrooms your mother discovered and I knew they would make me stronger. I've spent the last four years working on my power, developing it, discovering the right combination of red and green fungus. I can make people see whatever I want them to see."

"You can be beautiful."

She laughed, but it was the titter of a sad child. "It's been payback time ever since. Ha! So you got the pretty parts of fairy and troll. I got the ugly. But I will be Queen!"

She wore little girl rumba underpants with a zillion ruffles on the back and a white sleeveless undershirt with a pink rose in the center. She wasn't a child, far from it, but I guessed that was all that fit. She waited, her one big eye staring at me, the small one squeezed shut. She was challenging me to say something rude. I wanted to, at first. But no wonder she was lonely. No wonder she was afraid that if people knew this about her, she would never find love. We were both weirdoes. Maybe my oddities were on the inside, but we weren't so different. Neither of us really belonged anywhere. And I knew how bad it felt not to belong anywhere. At least I'd had my parents. Her mother had given her away.

So I just said, "What cute underpants. They're adorable."

Her little mouth fell open. "Really?"

She turned to look at the ruffles across her baby-sized ass and I jumped her. It was easy. I may not be strong or agile or anything special, but she was tiny. I pinned her down. She wiggled and tried to slide out of my grip. With my last bit of strength I bored into her mind. I showed her a picture of life as it could be. People who accepted her as she really was. Friends walking down the street with her. Someone who looked at her with love.

"You can't!" Her little voice was filled with tears. "That'll never happen."

"It could!" I knew it was true. "I could be your friend. I would be if you weren't such a bitch."

She didn't believe me, she didn't want to hear it, and she still wanted to be Queen. She managed to grab a corner of her dress, to reach into a sleeve and pull out another mushroom. She popped it into her mouth before I could stop her. Instantly, she grew, changed, one body part at a time, back into her beautiful illusory self. She tossed me easily to the ground.

"As long as I eat these mushrooms, I can look like this. I can have this much power. There is no way I will ever give that up."

I scrambled back away from her. She was searching for the poison somewhere in her voluminous dress. If the vial was closed, I could resist it. Plus I knew her secret. Could I use it?

"Walker!" I shouted.

He ran into the warehouse. Had he seen? Or stayed away?

"Her eyes," he shouted to me. "Don't let her look into your eyes."

She was walking toward me with the vial in her hand.

"Don't look in her eyes," he said again. "Trust me!"

I would never trust him again. I got to my feet. I was strong. Maybe I was more human than troll or fairy, but I could be as strong as she was. I stared right at her and she stared back at me. I defied her, thinking I could deflect whatever she did, but I was overcome by the oddest feeling, as if me, whatever made me, was draining down the back of my throat and slipping away. She waved her sleeves in my face. The top of my head was no longer mine. Then my forehead. Then my nose. I knew when she reached my chin, my thoughts would be gone and she would have me completely under her power. Like Luisa. Like my father.

"Think!" cried Walker. "Think your thoughts! Your human thoughts."

It wasn't easy, but I thought about school, and I thought about being hungry, which surprisingly I was, and I thought about college in the fall. I was sorry my skirt and sweater were ruined. I worried that my hair looked awful. It worked. Mostly. I stopped her from going further, but I couldn't free myself completely. I kept thinking typical teenage girl musings like the look on Jacob's face when he saw me that morning and what I would wear to graduation. It worked only because I was so ordinary, so human. And I remembered that humans don't believe in witches and ghosts and goblins. I hadn't believed in fairies since kindergarten. She tried, her eyes drilled into mine, and I couldn't step away, but she couldn't take over completely.

I felt her frustration. We really were sisters in a way, the only two of our kind. She had gained full power and it wasn't working. She found the vial of poison. In my peripheral vision I saw her begin to take the top off. If she opened it, I was doomed. I wanted that drink. Already, just seeing it, made me desperate for it.

Walker ran to her, tried to knock the vial from her hand. She pushed him back—throwing him clear across the room. He staggered to his feet. He was going to come at her again. Far away, beyond my mind, I heard chirping and flapping and the high voices of little birds.

"Stop her!"

"Get her!"

"October! We're here."

The air was filled with birds, hundreds of lovely yellow and black Tanagers, led by Oberon. And with them came all kinds of flying bugs. Bees, wasps, flies, mosquitoes. I heard their clamoring little voices yelling to each other to get her, to stop her. The birds and the bugs swooped around Madame Gold, landed on her head and shoulders, flew up inside her sleeves. She swatted at them, turned around and around, got tangled in her big dress. The birds plucked at the fabric, pulled it this way and that. They pecked at her hands. The wasps stung her. The mosquitoes bit her. Through it all I could smell the poison. I could smell it and I wanted it. I watched it in her hand, open now. It tipped as she slapped at the birds and a few drops spilled. I tried to catch them, but Walker was there first. He pulled me back and we watched the drops hit the floor. They sizzled and smoked. Even as I watched the liquid burn holes in the cement, I craved it. But I could tear myself away. If I concentrated on Madame Gold, I could forget about my drink.

I watched her smack a bird, smash it into the ground, and laugh.

"I am ordinary," I said. "But you are just plain nasty."

"You said you'd drink it! You said. You said." It was her childlike voice. I concentrated on that voice, on the true self I had seen. "You said you wanted to do it!"

I was absolutely sure that no matter what I did, she wouldn't keep her word. I couldn't save anybody by killing myself.

She popped the lid all the way off the bottle and I had to concentrate harder not to reach for it. More of it splashed onto the floor. The birds continued to surround her.

"Watch out!" I told them. "Don't let the poison touch you."

She lunged at me. Walker sprinted around behind her and stepped on the bottom of her dress. She stumbled, almost fell, then whirled and tried to tip the poison onto him, but it got tangled up in her enormous sleeve and she only succeeded in spilling more of it.

With luck, I thought, she'd spill it all.

"Run, October," Walker said. "Get out the door. I'll stop her."

A look passed between us, just for an instant, and in that look I knew everything he was thinking: I'm sorry; I thought I could save you too; I really do love you. All true. But I couldn't think about him. I had to concentrate on her, her secret, what she really was and what she didn't want anyone to know. Like peeling an onion, I took off layer after layer. First I made her dress disappear until it seemed she was fighting in her under-wear—her little girl underwear. Then I made her hair, that glori-ous, luxurious red hair, go away revealing her misshapen head with the awful hair. Walker took a step away from her. I saw that Trevor had returned. And Luisa had come back too, with Jed still carrying his saucepan. They were all there to help me fight, to help me beat her, and I was glad, but I didn't need their help. They stood behind me and watched. I showed them Madame Gold's big troll feet covered in hair. And her legs, one long and skinny like a fairy, one muscular and squat like a troll. The birds pulled back. She was twisted, almost naked, and lopsided. Only her beautiful face remained, incredibly beautiful, magically beautiful, hard to resist beautiful. I was sweating I was working so hard, but I just had to do it. I closed my eyes and I took away her fake face and showed everyone the real Madame Gold.

There was silence. She spun from one of us to the other. "No. This isn't me. This isn't really me."

Luisa stepped forward. "I think it is. I think the human say-ing is true, 'Pretty is as pretty does.'"

"How could you?" Madame Gold beseeched me.

"I had to stop you. This was the only way. It doesn't matter. Maybe now we can talk."

"Talk? To you?" She whirled in a circle until she was back to the beautiful, tall, imposing figure she hid behind. She held the open vial in her hand and I didn't care anymore. I didn't want it. She looked at Walker, then at Luisa, finally at Trevor, and they each turned away from her. She was defeated, crushed, and silent tears coursed down her perfect cheeks. It hurt me. I was the same freak. I was every bit as deformed as she was, and I wasn't anywhere near as powerful.

"Let's figure this out," I said. "There's a job for you, I'm sure of it. Advisor. Head wizard. It'll be fun." I finished lamely.

She shook her head. "Why you?" she asked. "Why you and not me?"

"Really, you don't look that bad. If you would just stop being so mean to everybody."

"If I can't be Queen—"

She brought the vial up toward her mouth.

I dashed forward, tried to pull her arm away. She was too strong and in a single gulp she drank it all down. She screamed, a painful, sad, truly bloodcurdling scream. She fell onto the ground, writhed and squealed, shrank and disappeared under her dress. We heard sizzling and smelled something like plastic burning.

Walker and I stared at the pile of fabric. Gingerly, I pulled it up. She was dead, her odd face surprisingly peaceful in death. Eyes closed. A little smile. She was almost pretty. I really was sorry. She was the only other creature like me in the whole world. Not that we would have started a club or anything.

24.

My father fell to the ground when Madame Gold died. He didn't move and I was scared he was so connected to her that her death had killed him.

"Dad?" I put my hand on his chest. I tried to feel him breathing. I tried to will him to breathe.

His eyes fluttered and opened. "Pumpkin?" He was disoriented and sore all over, but I could see him in his eyes, my real Dad. He was himself again.

Luisa yelled from the other side of the room. "October. Over here."

My mother was moving, waking as if truly from a sleep like death. It was all an illusion. Madame Gold couldn't kill my mother, but she could make her look dead. My father staggered to her side and they embraced. Their love was real.

Mom, Dad, Walker, Trevor, Luisa, Jed, and I emerged from the storehouse onto the cracked blacktop of the industrial park. Through the dirty windows in the other building we saw fairy workers wearing gray coveralls delivering sacks of mushrooms to the troll scientists. All of them unhappily doing Madame Gold's bidding.

Luisa ran to them and through them. "She's gone. She's dead." She told each one. They looked at her without understanding. "Madame Gold." They cringed at her name. "She's dead. October saved you."

I shook my head. I had tried to save Madame Gold.

"My daughter is the one true Queen! She is Queen of the Canopy and of Trolldom!"

"Dad, please." I wanted to hush him up. Dads can be so embarrassing.

"It's another one of her tests," a troll called. "Don't believe her!"

"Can't you feel it?" my mother asked them. Her voice was still weak, but clear. "Look!"

She pointed up. A strip of blue was widening between the grey clouds in the sky. Long fingers of sunshine were spreading across the sky. Workers began to shake their heads, rub their eyes, and stretch as if coming out of a long, deep sleep.

"Help me," Luisa said. Together we went around emptying the fairies' pockets of the stones that had been holding them down. Immediately a girl floated two feet off the ground. She beamed with pleasure.

"I have to check on Luisa and Green," Walker said.

"And Enoki."

His eyes narrowed. "She tried to—"

"We all did things we shouldn't have," I said. "All of us."

He dropped his head, chagrined. "They're at the hospital, I guess. This way." He started to lead me, but I shook my head.

"I'm taking my folks home."

"But this is your home."

He gestured to the industrial park. It was changing as if color was slowly fading up on a black and white TV. I saw a flower bloom and others begin to sprout. The roadway turned back into grass. The buildings shone with new paint in bright colors. The muddy mushroom fields and the damaged trees would take time to recover, but I knew the fairies were up to the task. I had to go home.

"Remember? I'm ordinary." It hurt like hell to say it, especially looking at his amazing face, but I had to. I didn't belong in his world. I didn't really fit in mine, but I was going to try.

He pushed my hair off my face and I felt the familiar tingle from his touch.

"I wanted to protect you," he began. "I thought you'd be safe in The Pits. I thought I could release the fairies and then I could get you and your mom out. I tried to tell you in the car. If you had told me to take you back to school, I would have."

"You knew I'd never do that."

He hung his head. "I just wanted to keep you safe. I thought I could save the fairies and save you and have it all."

"I know." I had figured that was the case. What upset me the most was that he didn't think I was strong enough to fight my own battles. I didn't want a boyfriend who just wanted to 'keep me safe.' I wanted to stand on my own two feet. "It's okay, Walker. I understand now."

He was good and smart and if he could get over his fairy superiority complex, he would be a great guy. I smiled at him.

"You're the Queen," he whispered. "They need you."

I looked over at my folks. They were greeting people they knew and hugging old friends hello. My dad was six inches off the ground. Flying. My mom had a grin on her face bigger than I'd ever seen. It was obvious they had missed their friends and family and home for all these years.

I had an idea. I ran over and climbed up a stack of wooden crates. I looked out at what had been the parking lot and was now turning into a lush, green meadow. The fairies and trolls were smiling as they peeled off their coveralls and returned to their multi-colors. I clapped my hands. No one paid any attention. I shouted hello, but they were too busy talking to each other. Finally I thought as hard as I could, Hey! Up here! Every face turned to me.

"Hi," I said. "Hello." I wasn't sure where to begin, so I just launched right in. "I am October Fetterhoff, daughter of Princess Russula the Troll and Prince Neomarica the Fairy. I am the rightful heir to both the troll and fairy thrones." There was applause, even a little cheering. They were cheering me. I have to admit that was kind of cool and for a moment I was tempted not to go on. But just for a moment. I took a deep breath. "I have lived my entire life in the human world and frankly, that's my home." Boos and groans. "No, seriously. If I belong anywhere, it's there. But you need a ruler. All of you, trolls and fairies both. So." I paused dramatically. "I think it's time you guys got over this rivalry, this competition, this war between trolls and fairies. From where I sit, it's ridiculous. You're dying out. You need each other. Solidarity! Unite!" I was trying hard for another cheer—it always worked in the movies—but my audience was grumbling. They'd been adversaries for years; one speech from me wasn't going to change their minds, but it was way past time something did. I looked over at my parents and continued, "Therefore, I, as your rightful Queen of both lands, do hereby pass the crown to this fairy, Neomarica, and this troll, Russula, as King and Queen in my place. They shall rule both kingdoms together as one."

My parents looked up at me in shock. They started to protest, as I knew they would, but I held up my hand. It was the perfect solution; they were trained for this.

"Long live the Queen and King," I shouted, "Of Trolldom and the Fairy Canopy. One from each land. Working together for the good of all."

Silence. It was a tough crowd. Fairies looked at trolls suspiciously and vice versa. "Come on," I said. "Try something new."

I got a smattering of grudging applause. My parents weren't going to have an easy time of it. I was really glad it was their problem, not mine. I jumped down from my perch and my parents pushed through the crowd to hug me.

"Why did you do this?" my mother asked.

"Tell me it's not a good idea."

My dad kissed my cheek. "It'll be your turn one day," he said.

I shook my head. "This is not my thing. I don't know what my thing is, but ruling a couple of kingdoms of the wee folk is definitely not it." The trolls were beginning to chant "Russula" and the fairies "Neomarica," each group trying to out shout the other. "They're calling for you," I told my folks. "Go on."

My mom and dad climbed up on the pile of crates and waved. Very refined, very regal, with their hands cupped like a debutante's in the Rose Bowl parade. Then my dad shouted, "Trolls are the best," and kissed my mom while his feet left the ground. Everybody laughed and it broke the tension. I knew they'd do a good job.

Walker was at my side. He took my hand and I felt the energy flow between us. He made me feel peaceful and he made me feel so good. He led me to a quiet spot out of the madness.

"Look," he said. "Look what you've done."

All around us the industrial park was flowering. I saw fairies flying overhead. I saw trolls scampering through the underbrush. There were birds and rabbits. A breeze blew carrying the scent of fresh mown grass and flowers and fertile, clean dirt. It was like a child's picture book about fairyland.

"It's back," Walker said. "Thanks to you."

I smiled. "It even smells good."

"October, I'm sorry."

"You didn't mean to hurt me."

"When I said to you—"

I cut him off. "Don't." I didn't want him to say it was all just part of his plan. I wanted to remember the things he had said and the kisses we shared as the most romantic moment of my life. So far.

He gave me a sad, little smile. "Please, please don't go. I don't care if you're a queen. Just stay with me."

He was so unbelievably handsome. He opened his arms and I wanted to curl up against his chest and let him take care of everything. It would be so easy. I'd never have to think or worry about anything ever again. My whole body leaned toward him, but I knew I didn't want to be taken care of. I wanted to live my life the way I wanted, mistakes and all. I wasn't done being a normal, boring human.

"I guess I'll be here for holidays," I said. "With my folks. And if you need me—you know, to save your ass again—you can text me."

He reached in his pocket and pulled out the original necklace. "Take it," he said. "So I'll always know where you are." He dropped it into my palm. It was warm and smooth, just like him.

"We have a connection," I said. "Remember? I don't need a necklace to know where you are." He leaned forward to kiss me and I pushed him away. "If we start with that, I know I'll never leave."

I walked away from him and I didn't look back. The sun was shining and the sky was a brilliant, wonderful blue—exactly the color of his eyes.

Epilogue

Colorado is the prettiest place I've ever been. Snow-capped mountains, crisp cool air, and the golden aspen trees. I love it. And school is okay too.

I miss my parents, but they're both fine and healthy and so, so happy to be home—their real home. They stayed in our house with me until I left for college, zipping back and forth to the other world to rule. The last couple months of high school were uneventful, except I went to the senior prom with Jacob. He isn't such a jerk after all, at least not all the time. He sends me some pretty funny texts from his college in Boston.

My dad has managed to keep the weight off—now that he's flying again—and he is back to cracking his terrible jokes. He and Mom are crazy busy doing human government-type things like setting up joint committees and building new troll and fairy schools and solving problems. My mom has quit growing Mycena luxaeterna Duo. My dad says he can smell them when she comes home from work and they stink. But I know she has a stash in case I need them to save the day or something.

I may have given up the throne, but I still have my "tattoo," I'm still a couple inches taller, and my hair is curlier, thicker and a shiny, deep red. I still use my mind to send messages to my folks, and so far I've resisted using it to convince a professor to give me a better grade. I can still understand the birds and animals and the bugs. No one understands why I'm not bothered by mosquitoes or flies or those ticks that carry Rocky Mountain Spotted Fever.

And sometimes, maybe more than just sometimes, when I smell Chinese food or see a fluffy black dog or watch a Porsche go by, I think about Walker, and sometimes I know he's thinking about me too.

"Get your head out of the clouds, Fetterhoff!" Mr. Powers, the intramural track and field coach, yells at me. "Starting line, please!"

I'm still klutzy and mostly average in every way except one: I can run really fast. Really fast. As I run and leave all the other competitors behind, I touch my silver necklace and send a thought to the other world.

I'm still here. Plain old ordinary October.

ACKNOWLEDGMENTS

This story was my daughter's idea and I could not have written it without her. All through elementary school she was ridiculed for believing in things we cannot see. She never capitulated just to make the teasing stop and she never stopped believing. Her courage and conviction are an inspiration to me.

I want to thank my early readers: Norah Lunsford at 13 came up with a great title and helped me with details. Jen Hunter was enthusiastic and positive and pointed out some places that needed work. Ellen Slezak encouraged me to continue when I was ready to give up. And I thank my late readers: Denise Hamilton for an afternoon of tea and plotting and Heather Dundas who found the special mushrooms the story needed.